ELISA GREB

Actually Invisible

For Dad
1960-2012

- 1 -

Thursday, March 28, 2019

The cold tile under my bare feet is proof that I am awake and standing in our bathroom before dawn. I am not having one of those dreams about standing in the same location, squinting at yet another white plastic stick.

The particular vulnerability brought on by peeing on a pregnancy test can't exactly be put into words—especially if you have peed on about a hundred of them with various degrees of hope or lack thereof. If I put all of those sticks into a pile and set a match to them, I could have myself a stinky, terrible-for-the-ozone bonfire.

Tempting.

Here I am, staring at the white window of another plastic stick, searching too early for a line. I set it down, wash my hands, and check my phone for the time before shining its light on the pink box that I had prematurely tossed into the garbage basket. *How many minutes do I have to wait this time?*

Three minutes.

I'll check again in two.

On the wall above the mirror, the painting of a robin watches over me from above the medicine cabinet, and I can't avoid it this time. I close the lid of the toilet and sit down, my flannel pajama pants not much of a barrier between my skin and the cold plastic, and silently ask the robin a list of questions: *Do I deserve to be pregnant? Am I a good enough mother to my existing child to have earned a second—but first biological— one? Could I face the world with a pregnant belly—maybe able to embrace my large belly for the first time in my life—maybe feeling like an impostor because I have never been with a man? Would that pregnant belly make me feel unusually feminine? Am I too old at 36 to carry a healthy baby and then—in some ways more importantly—parent that child with the enthusiasm they deserve?*

The robin doesn't have any answers for me today. And the truth is that not even a pregnancy test can distract me from the fact that today marks three years since my dad died and thirteen days since an innocent gesture in my classroom led to a series of events that have irrevocably changed my life.

\- 2 -

Friday, March 15, 2019

In the waiting room of the fertility clinic, Jennifer Aniston was smiling at me from the cover of *People* magazine with just a hint of amusement in her blue eyes. I winked quickly and subtly at the image—a secret gesture I had learned in middle school that would sometimes fill me with a strange, quiet, sexual satisfaction as if I were flirting with the girl in the Calgon commercial. I can still remember the off-putting tingle I felt in the seventh grade when I saw Ross and Rachel kiss for the first time, and I realized I was imagining myself in his place and not hers.

I picked up the magazine and tried tilting it under the light to make out the name and address hidden under black Sharpie lines. Was it a doctor's? Do doctors read *People* magazine? I tried to picture my favorite fertility doctor, Dr. Kenneth—a sixty-something-year-old sophisticated woman—lounging on a couch in sweatpants and a hoodie, flipping through a *People* magazine. *Nope.*

"Josephine ... Rain?"

I stood obediently and smiled, choosing to ignore the mispronunciation of my last name. My name has been mispro-nounced for my entire life. I usually tell people that Rein rhymes with "sign" when I first meet them, but that doesn't always work for them to remember to say it correctly the next time, which I have used as a litmus test for potential friends. I know people who have continued to say Rain for years, and at this point, it would be too awkward to correct them again. How do you tell your boss he's been saying your name wrong for thirteen years?

The nurse stepped aside to let me through the door and into the narrow hallway of examination rooms. I always find myself unsettled by the framed photos of babies hanging in that hallway. *What about the people who are there because they can't have a baby? Way to rub it in, assholes.*

What if I'm one of those people?

We arrived at one of the last rooms, and the nurse pushed open the already-ajar door, triggering the light.

"You'll be in room six today. Go ahead and get a gown on, and the doctor will be in to see you soon."

I entered the room and set my wallet, keys, and phone on a brown vinyl chair, hearing what my grandmother would say disapprovingly if she were looking at the haphazard pile and scolding me for not using a purse. *"Grandma, purses are so girly. That's just not me. I'm fine to carry stuff in my pockets. No, I also don't want to wear makeup. No, I do not wish to be a man."* I shook my head to force away the negativity. I'm supposed to relax as much as possible for these procedures, so I tried to remember what exam room I was in and did the familiar mental math while I got undressed:

Six. Exam room six.

Dad died on March 28th, so that's 3/28.

Three plus two is five plus eight is thirteen.
One plus three is four.
Wait, it was 2016.
Thirteen plus two is fifteen plus one is sixteen plus six is twenty-two.
Two plus two is four.
Four is half of eight.
Wait, did I forget a number?
Shit. Start over.

There was a quiet knock on the door as I awkwardly settled onto the exam table, trying not to rip the clean white paper. The nurse peeked her head in.

"Sorry. The doctor is running late, but I wanted to let you know your husband's sperm count looks great today. I saw in your chart that this is your eighth procedure, so I thought you might want to know."

I inwardly rolled my eyes and felt a familiar prickly sensation. "Donor. The donor's sperm. I have a wife, but she doesn't have any sperm."

What they don't tell you about coming out is that you have to do it over and over and over again in your life, in places you haven't even been yet, and it never stops making you feel like a bit of a freak or, at the very least, like you're the only one in the room who seems to be oversharing.

The nurse stepped fully into the room and grinned. "Oh, how wonderful! That is so cool! You know, I have a friend from high school who is a lesbian, and they've been talking about having a baby. That is just so cool."

Suddenly aware of the fact that there was only a too-small hospital gown between this over-enthusiastic nurse and my drooping, bra-less breasts, I smiled quickly and nodded with the hope that she would take a hint and *go away*, especially because I could tell by her dramatic, loud response that she is most likely (air quotes) "opposed to same-sex marriage."

Another quiet knock on the door sent both of our eyes in its direction, and Dr. Kenneth stepped in—confident and sleek as always. At the sight of her short, salt-and-pepper hair and small-framed glasses, I breathed an audible sigh of relief. Dr. Kenneth has been the only person who has been able to get me pregnant at all in this process, even if the other pregnancy ended in an early—very early—miscarriage. The other fertility doctors and assistants are apparently not my uterus's type. I smiled gratefully at Dr. Kenneth, completely forgetting the nurse's existence.

"Dr. Kenneth," I started, "I am so glad it's you. This is our eighth try, and it's the last vial from our daughter's donor, and we were really hoping to give her a half-biological sibling." I could feel my voice starting to break.

Dr. Kenneth replied, "Well, Josie, I will do my best. I think the timing is right."

The nurse smiled politely at me. "I'll leave you to it."

A familiar numbness crept into my limbs as I leaned back and put my feet into the stirrups, mildly embarrassed by my green argyle socks in honor of upcoming St. Patrick's Day. I'm not even Irish. I scolded myself for not shaving my legs that morning but then tried again to push away any negativity and relax. Closing my eyes, I pictured Dr. Thomas's calm, attentive face when he delivered our daughter almost three years ago. Dr. Kenneth's energy always reminds me of his. *Oh, I hope Dr. Thomas will deliver this—*

I winced as Dr. Kenneth silently slid in the speculum, irritated that it never gets easier. *Maybe it will feel less like it's manually creating the Grand Canyon after I've actually given birth to a baby? If I ever give birth to a baby. When. If.*

The long, thin tube tickled my insides quickly and was pulled out just as fast. *Wham, bam, thank you, ma'am.* That's all it takes for plenty of women to get pregnant. One shot of sperm, and there you have it—whether you like it or not. Whether you want it or not.

Squeezing my already-shut eyes, I silently chanted: *please, please, please, please.* Then, I opened my eyes to watch Dr. Kenneth wordlessly clean up. She patted my knee, gave me a distant, motherly smile, and left.

That's the part when I'm always supposed to lie still for a while to increase the chances of a single sperm finding a single egg. I briefly listed the reasons why I haven't been getting pregnant: *too fat, too selfish, too unlovable, too clumsy, too fat, too old.*

Stop. No negativity.

I fixed my eyes on the dream catcher above me and noted that each exam room there—and I've been in all of them at this point—is decorated slightly differently, with things that are supposed to make you feel … inspired? Calm? This particular room had framed pictures of oceans and a dream catcher made of beads and feathers. The feathers were a beautiful, probably-unnatural robin's egg blue.

Shit—robins. I tried to fight the lump in my throat but was overwhelmed by the physical need to cry. So I let it happen and allowed myself to murmur quietly, "Please let this be the time it works. Daddy, why aren't you here to hold my hand? Why am I completely alone in this room? Why has no one cared enough to offer to come with me to any of these eight fucking procedures?"

I had to stop myself from wailing those last few words. Tears slipped past my eyes onto the white paper beneath me, into my ears, onto my neck, and into my smooshed, unruly ponytail. I wept without a sound.

- 3 -

Saturday, October 10, 1998

I leaned forward to turn up the volume of the Tori Amos CD playing in my dad's car and then leaned back to belt out the song I had been listening to over and over again in my bedroom.

He smiled at me from behind the steering wheel, the sun bringing out subtle red tones in his short dark hair. "You're too young to actually appreciate this song. She's, like, looking back on her childhood and adolescence, and you're all singing along like you're not still an adolescent."

"Shut up, Dad, and just let me sing." It was my favorite part, so I closed my eyes and mimicked the singer's voice as well as I could before opening my eyes and musing aloud, "You know, that really is sad. She's singing about someone calling her ugly. She's not even ugly, but once that guy said that to her, she probably couldn't unhear that word ever again." Briefly, I pictured my high school cafeteria with its sea of unfriendly faces, and the word *rhinoceros* echoed in my mind. I forced out a breath through my nose to push the memory away.

He laughed, shaking his head. "You're just a little bit in love with her, so you're biased."

"Maybe," I gnawed at the skin under my cuticles, awaiting the sweet release that floods me every time a piece of one rips off into my mouth—a bad habit I still possess. Dad was the first person I came out to when I was fourteen years old, and he had barely blinked when I told him. When I asked him about a year later why he hadn't really reacted, he reminded me that I had had an imaginary wife when I was in preschool, so it was no surprise.

"But seriously," Dad continued, "this song is so angsty. It reminds me of being a teenager but also reminds me that I may not have outgrown that angst at all."

He was forty years old, and he and my mom had been separated for a couple of years at that point, ever since he had accidentally fallen in love with someone else. He still loved my mom, but he wasn't (air quotes) "in love with her."

"What, and you think I'm angst-less? Give me a break!" I tilted my head back and placed the back of my hand on my forehead dramatically.

"Oh, I know you're plenty angsty." He smirked. "You're just not old enough yet for any hindsight."

He kept his smirk while turning the volume down a little (never much of a Tori fan but allowing me—always—to listen to whatever I wanted in the car) and rolled the window down before lighting a cigarette. I was too amped on the music to bother reminding him like I normally did that he was going to earn himself lung cancer.

"Hey, how's that new song coming? The one about Emily?" He brought the cigarette to his lips and glanced at me.

I blushed. Even though I hadn't told Emily to her face—and never would, in fact—I constantly wrote songs about my love for her. It was unquestionably unrequited, but I held onto tiny moments each day when she would smile at me or talk to me at all. We were barely more than acquaintances, but I plotted my every move at school in order to run into her as much as possible.

"Okay," I said. "I was working on it last night but couldn't quite get the chord progressions to flow. Plus Mom kept yelling down to the basement to tell me random stuff, so I couldn't actually get through the whole thing to record it." The basement was my sanctuary. The floor was concrete, and it was always cold down there, but I had my fold-out chair, my Casio keyboard, and my cassette recorder.

"Ahhh, yes, the Mother Interrupter. I remember it well." I couldn't tell if he meant my mother or his, but I didn't ask. "Are you talking about at the end—that part after the last refrain when you sing 'I look on'?" He turned the radio all the way down. "Why don't you repeat that line a few times and play with the notes within that last chord?" He hummed the melody a few times to demonstrate and raised his eyebrows to see if we were on the same page. "Can we go to your mom's house tomorrow and work it out? She's going away for the weekend with Sam, isn't she?"

I rolled my eyes. "Yeah, like every chance she gets."

"Excellent!" He flicked some ashes out the window. "You think your sister will be able to tear herself away from her boyfriend long enough to have lunch or something?"

Covering my eyes with my hands, I groaned. "Ugh, I swear she hasn't been home longer than five minutes to grab some clothes and then leave again. She absolutely forgets she's still in high school, and I don't even think Mom notices."

He nodded pensively for a few seconds. "I feel like I haven't talked to her in a month. She's never home when I call the house. Is she okay?"

"How should I know?" I shrugged. "She barely talks to me anymore. Last time she did, she said some cheesy stuff about how she's nineteen and spreading her wings or something when I called her on never being home."

He drew his eyebrows together and then, unexpectedly, chuckled.

"Did I ever tell you," he inhaled smoke, "about the time a robin chased me," he exhaled, "all the way down my street when I was a kid? I must have been six years old, and I found a bird's nest in a bush about a block away. The eggs were so pretty that I wanted to take one home and give it to Grandma Louise. So I picked one up and turned to go home, and I don't think I made it two feet before a bird started chasing me and pecking at the back of my neck. I ran as fast as my chubby little legs could take me! I was all AHHHHHH," he screamed and waved his arms around, bringing his knees to the steering wheel to keep the car from swerving. He flicked some more ashes out the window and shook his head at the memory. I knew he was steering the subject away from Amanda on purpose, but I went with it.

"What happened to the egg? Did you just, like, set it down and run away? Did you apologize? Did the mama bird forgive you?" I was grinning at him, interested to hear a story about little Tommy who was always getting himself into mischief.

"You know, I think I dropped it. I started fearing for my life and just wanted to get out of there. I have literally been afraid of birds ever since." His hair was flip-flopping in the breeze.

"So, all that, and Grandma Louise didn't even get to see the egg?" Grandma Louise—though one of my favorite people in the entire world—was never easy to please, so I imagined my dad being so proud of that egg and so hopeful that it would put him in her favor for a little while. It broke my heart a little bit for a second.

"Nope." He took a long drag on his cigarette and then abruptly tossed it out the window. "She probably would have smacked me for bringing it into the house, anyway."

- 4 -

The parking lot of my school was nearly full, and someone had taken my usual spot: number 13, which is one of my favorites because it's my birth date. The exam room number reappeared in my mind: six. Dad was born on the sixth. How had I forgotten that? Maybe that room was lucky after all.

Putting my car in park, I grabbed the evidence of my drive-thru lunch: two cheeseburger wrappers, an empty french fry carton, an empty chicken nugget carton, and an empty milkshake cup. I had done that thing where I pretended I was ordering for two people, as if the workers actually cared that I was eating an extra-large of everything. *Um, yes, I'll take one cheeseburger and a large fry, and ... let me think ... I think she said she wanted a cheeseburger, an order of nuggets, and a large vanilla milkshake.* Cringe.

I tried unsuccessfully to shove it all into the paper bag, but the cup wouldn't fit. Taking a deep, grease-filled breath, I picked up my brown-leather work bag from the passenger side floor and gathered the garbage into my hands to be tossed into a garbage can outside of the entrance. It occurred to me that that old, trusty garbage can had been there for me through thick and thin—but mostly through thick.

Laughing sardonically at my own joke, I swiped my ID card to get into the school. I always feel especially vulnerable arriving for a half-day of teaching after I've been to the fertility clinic, but I can't afford to take the entire day off if I'm saving for a supposed maternity leave. I always wonder if my students can sense my desperation. Do they know where I've been?

Hardly. I have always spoken very little about my personal life to my tenth graders; unless one of them has asked me privately, I don't even acknowledge my own relationship status, other than to refer to "us" and "we" when talking about taking our daughter places on the weekends. (Some of us gay people are very good at The Pronoun Game.) Liesel is a bit of a sacred subject to me, so I mention her rarely and cautiously, for fear that someone will call me out. How do you have an almost-three-year-old when nobody ever saw you pregnant? Why do you go by Mrs. Rein-Thompson and never talk about Mr. Rein-Thompson? How tall is he? Where does he work? Does your daughter look like him or you?

I passed my classroom to go and sit in the empty faculty room. I had fourteen minutes to obsess over every detail of that morning's insemination and think about whether Cam and I should start talking about which donor we are going to try next if this round doesn't work. I thought about how it's okay if our two kids don't have a blood relation. They will be siblings no matter what. They will grow up together and call us both Mommy and Mama and—

"Hey, Jo," Dana interrupted, startling me briefly because I hadn't seen her come in. "I thought I saw you come in. How did it go?"

I took a breath and shrugged. "Okay, I guess."

She sat down next to me. "I know it sucks. And I know that, deep down, you want to scream and punch someone. It's okay to talk about it."

"It's not all that 'deep down.'" I bit at the skin on my left thumb. "I feel like I'm on the brink of madness and could fall apart any minute."

A loud roar of laughter traveled down the hallway from my classroom. My fourth-period class is a rowdy bunch for me and always even rowdier for a substitute teacher.

"I could go save that poor soul, but I won't. I still have six more minutes of peace."

Dana smirked. "You absolutely deserve those six minutes."

The truth is that I am a good teacher. I care about my students and try to connect with them as much as I can while still keeping my distance. I'm an English teacher, so much of that connection is done through various types of writing. I have always loved writing, and I love teaching it even more. Seeing the look on a kid's face when a feeling is finally put into words ... well, that keeps me coming back every day.

Dana is my closest friend at school. She teaches tenth-grade biology, so we share many of the same students and, therefore, many of the same joys and concerns. The school district where we teach is not where either one of us could afford to live. It's an affluent, suburban district where many of our students are children of doctors, professional athletes, or lawyers. Cam and I are both teachers, and neither one of us has chosen the career in order to become a millionaire.

"Well," Dana changed the subject, "your day should be a little better knowing Brandon won't be in your eighth-period class. He's suspended for what he said to you yesterday.

Although I hear he's less concerned about having to miss school and more concerned about being benched for the basketball game today."

I nodded uncertainly. "Well, I'm less worried about him not being there and more worried about how the rest of the class feels about my outburst. If only I could tell them I've been on fertility medication for months, and my emotions are all over the place." I gave a short laugh.

"What were his actual words? I didn't get a chance to call you last night to ask. Weston had soccer practice, and then he had, like, two hours of homework. Seriously, I hate homework. If we weren't required to give it here, I would never give it. Wait until you see how much Liesel's homework will take up your time."

Assuming Dana had forgotten the question she asked, I stood up to go to class. The bell rang to let out from fourth period.

"Wait," Dana said. "Tell me what Brandon said to you."

Quickly, I summarized, "I tried to sit next to him to help him with his essay, and he told me his mom told him that he shouldn't get too close to me because he might turn out gay. It took me off guard, so I stepped back and pretty loudly told him that maybe I shouldn't get too close to him because I might turn out lazy."

Dana threw her head back and guffawed. "That's hilarious. Well, he *is* lazy. And he's entitled."

"Yeah, and his dad is also on the school board. Plus, I feel like an asshole because the rest of the kids in that class are super sweet, and I have never so much as even raised my voice at them—and now they've seen me turn into a monster at the drop of a hat." I glanced at the clock and noticed that the late bell would be ringing in one minute. "I have to go. Talk later."

I entered the busy hallway and put on my teacher smile, high-fiving the basketball players for winning yet another game the previous night and saying "excuse me" to the kids who were walking too slowly and the kids who were walking too quickly. I told one girl to take out her earbuds and one boy to take the hood off of his head. Finally, I gave myself my usual half-day-after-insemination mental pep talk, "This is what you're good at. This is what you can control."

My substitute—a sweet, elderly man who should be retired and living in Florida—walked out of my classroom, looking tired and eager to leave. "Hey, Mr. Hanson," I said. "I bet my fourth period gave you a run for your money, but I'm hoping the rest of your morning was okay?"

He chuckled, "You could say that. That Savannah girl sure has a lot to say."

"Say no more. I was trying to teach them about gerunds the other day, and she came out and asked if I had ever seen a peacock before, followed by announcing that she would enjoy being a peacock." I shook my head, mildly amused.

"I don't know how you do it every day. I think I'll take a senior class tomorrow. All they want to do is sleep or text or whatever kids do on their phones these days."

"I wouldn't blame you one bit."

The late bell rang, and I stepped into my classroom to greet my fifth-period class.

"Good morning! Take out your journals. Today, we're going to write about luck. Emily Dickinson once wrote," I began to write on the interactive whiteboard:

"Luck is not chance—

It's Toil—

Fortune's expensive smile

Is earned—"

Then, I spun around on my heel to face my class. "Since St. Patrick's Day is this weekend, write about whether or not you believe that luck is earned. Try to think of an example to support what you're saying."

Most of the kids began writing. Two boys started smacking each other in the front of the class, so I opened both of their binders for them and took out their journals. "Hi, guys. What do you think about luck? Do you think random people are lucky, or can people bring their own luck upon themselves?"

They both looked up at me, and one responded, "I don't know. I mean, Jaiden never gets lucky, so maybe you should ask him."

He elbowed the kid sitting beside him (Jaiden), and the class erupted with laughter.

"Okay, okay. Your minds are always in the gutter. Should we define 'luck' as a class for some people who aren't quite sure what to write about yet?" I looked out into the class. "How would you define luck?"

A few hands went up, and I called on a girl in the back—Kate—who doesn't normally say much.

"Luck isn't even real. If you want good things to happen to you, you have to make them happen."

Jaiden, recovered from his embarrassment, spoke up, "But, like, what about people who don't have money to make good things happen?"

I interjected, "Do we always need money to make good things happen? Aren't some of the best things in life free?"

Kate nodded. "Yeah, but sometimes even the free stuff doesn't happen unless you make it happen."

"I see what you're saying." I agreed, returning her nod.

"Can you give an example?"

Kate thought for a few seconds. "So, like, some kids are just born into families who love them, and some kids aren't. The kids who aren't can't just sit around waiting for someone to love them. They have to find good friends and make their own families."

"That's a great example, Kate." I looked from Kate to the rest of the class, careful to make eye contact with multiple students as I spoke, always wanting to engage as many kids as possible. "Hopefully, you all have some ideas now. Take about five minutes to free-write about the topic, and then we will share."

I walked around the classroom as they wrote, reading over their shoulders. I love that part of class—getting to watch all of their different hands writing about all of their different thoughts and opinions. When I got to Kate, I was surprised (read: understatement) to see the words she had written on the page:

I know what Brandon said to you yesterday and I am so sorry that happened to you. You are a kind-hearted person who doesn't deserve to be judged just because you happen to be married to a woman. Don't let the douchebags get to you.

I hesitated, unsure of how much I should acknowledge it but knowing it would be callous and ungrateful to not acknowledge it at all. I was, in fact, so grateful that I felt tears start to form in my eyes, but I quickly reminded myself of where I was and simply patted Kate's shoulder.

"Thank you for that. I really appreciate it."

Kate nodded with her eyes still on her journal. I continued walking around the room, finding it harder to concentrate on the words on the pages. My mind was racing with questions about how many students had been talking about me since the afternoon before and how many of them had potentially mentioned it to their parents. Putting one loafer deliberately in front of the other, I returned to the front of the room to ask for volunteers to share their writing with the class.

To my terror, Kate raised her hand. This was not something I was ready to publicly speak about—not what Brandon had said, not my relationship with Cam, not any of it.

But Kate's hand was the only one raised.

"Kate?" I feigned nonchalance. We made eye contact, and I quickly widened my eyes, hoping to indicate that I wasn't interested in revealing the situation to all twenty-five kids in the class. I could feel my ears getting red—something that has happened ever since I was a kid when I feel embarrassed or excited.

Kate said, "Like I said before, I think life is what we make of it. If someone is mean to us, it's not because we are unlucky and deserve it. It's because they're mean and probably have their own issues. Our job is to remember that there are plenty of people in this world—the majority of them, actually—who are perfectly nice and understanding and accepting, and they are the ones who deserve our attention."

Several students nodded in agreement. I nodded along, trying to be supportive and casual and not just immensely relieved. "Does anyone else want to share today?"

When no one else raised their hands, I said, "Okay then. Many of you were writing some interesting stuff in your journals, so I hope you had some time to reflect on the topic today. Go ahead and put your journal away, and take out your grammar book. Today, we're focusing on everyone's favorite grammatical enigma: the participle!"

- 5 -

I pulled my silver hatchback into our driveway, noting that Cam's car wasn't there yet and figuring that she and Liesel must be still on their way from Cam's parents' house. Her mom and dad watch Liesel on weekdays while we are both working. It's a lifesaver, really, considering how much daycare would cost. Since I work at a high school, and Cam teaches kindergarten in a district nearer to her childhood home, our hours are slightly different, but we tend to get home at around the same time.

Walking through the front door, I had to step over several of Liesel's toys. She is currently interested in *My Little Pony* and has several small, plastic, sparkly animals she plays with (and leaves) all over the house. She and Cam had clearly been playing together that morning and had to rush out of the house without the time to clean up. This is not an unusual occurrence, by the way; I often tease Cam that I think she loves teaching kindergarten because she thinks like a small child—easily entertained and entertaining yet carefree and oblivious. They are qualities that drew me to her all those years ago, but they don't lend themselves very well to housework.

A car door closed outside, and I bent down to clear some toys out of the way before someone tripped. Cam and Liesel were singing "Mary Had a Little Lamb" and giggling as Cam took our daughter out of her car seat. I moved the door curtain to the side to watch them. They looked like carbon copies of each other with their straight blonde hair and slender bodies. We had chosen an anonymous sperm donor with blond hair and blue eyes because both Cam and I share those traits (and are often confused for sisters). We wanted our children to look like us, and Liesel certainly fits the bill. Sometimes, when I have Liesel out somewhere and it's just the two of us, people assume I am her biological mother. I love that.

I opened the door to let them in. "How are my girls?" I asked with a grin, opening my arms wide.

Liesel ran to me and jumped up to be caught. I squeezed her and gave her a kiss on the cheek. "Hey, baby! How was your day with Pop and Grandma? Who took you to preschool today?"

I set Liesel back on the floor as she rattled off a story about helping Pop in his garden and then getting to eat a doughnut on the way to school. I uttered an appreciative "wow" or "cool" at intervals.

Cam walked in and kissed my cheek. "Hey, you," she said. "You got home before us? Did you get all of your grading done?"

"Most of it," I replied with a sigh. "I had to get out of there. My eighth period was tense, and I just didn't have the energy to sit and read any more essays today. I brought some home—"

"I doubt you'll have the time to look at them tonight after Liesel's concert, and I want to enforce a strict no-working policy this weekend for both of us. You already look exhausted." She tucked a piece of my hair behind my ear.

A smile crept onto my face as I remembered that night was Liesel's first stage performance. She and her preschool classmates would be singing nursery rhymes accompanied by adorable hand motions, and I couldn't help but think back fondly on the many days and nights I myself had spent on stage in musical theatre productions. I thought about how I hoped that at least one of our kids falls in love with it, too, so I can live vicariously and be a stage mom.

Then, I remembered we only have one kid and might never have any more, and I felt the smile leave my face. Cam noticed and asked, "So how bad was your eighth period? Did that kid say anything else to you today?"

"Actually, they suspended him. I was really surprised because his dad is on the school board, you know? And he's like the star of the basketball team that's undefeated, so I thought he'd at least be allowed to play in the game today, but nope. The rest of the kids just seemed afraid to speak at all, like I'm a fragile glass vase. Anyway, Dana told me Brandon was suspended when I got to school at the end of fourth period."

Cam gasped. "Oh, I'm so sorry, Josie. I forgot you were going to the clinic today. I should have texted you or something."

"It's fine. Same old, same old."

"Well, how do you think it went?"

I rubbed the back of my neck. "It is literally the same thing every time, so I have no idea. Now it's the same two weeks of excruciating wait time when I will obsess over my every twinge or cramp."

Liesel ran up and put her arms around both of our legs. "Mommy and Mama! Mommy and Mama!"

I tried to push down the irritation that was rising in my chest. Cam hasn't come to the clinic with me even once. She says she doesn't want to take the days off because she is still rebuilding her balance of sick days after taking time off when we had Liesel nearly three years ago. I haven't told her that going to that clinic and lying on that table has been the loneliest thing I have ever done. I haven't said that to anyone, in fact, because no one I know would understand—least of all Cam, who got pregnant on our first try with me by her side.

"Liesel," I started, looking down at the top of her blonde head, "I think you need to pick up some of these toys. We have to get ready to go to your special concert today, and we don't want to come home to a messy house."

"We can do it after dinner," Cam added. "Let's make some spaghetti!" Sweeping a smiling Liesel into her arms, they headed toward the kitchen.

- 6 -

Tuesday, November 7, 2000

"I can't believe you're not voting," I said to Amanda. "It's, like, your civic duty as an American." It was presidential Election Day, and I was finally old enough to vote and couldn't understand why she didn't share my enthusiasm.

"I quite literally do not give a shit," Amanda replied, tossing her wavy dark-brown hair behind her shoulders. "Mom is gone for this entire week, and I promised myself and my friends I would have a party every single night. I have to clean up from last night before they come over tonight."

I scoffed. "Do you actually think that your slimy friends care if there are still beer bottles laying around?"

"It's embarrassing enough that I still live with my mother at the age of twenty-two. I don't also want to be a slob." Amanda bent down and began collecting beer bottles by their necks, the glass clinking rhythmically.

"Whatever, Mands." I considered helping but decided against it. "Can you still give me a ride to the polling place? It's freezing outside. I'll walk to Dad's afterwards if you just take me to the church first."

She tossed the bottles into an empty garbage bag, and we both jumped slightly at the noise. "As long as you promise not to show your face at home any night this week. Dad is still okay with you staying with him, right?"

I shrugged. "He gave me a key. He's been working every night at the bar, and I've been asleep when he gets home, and he's been asleep when I get up for school. I'm kind of worried about him, actually, because there has been an excessive amount of beer bottles in his garbage can. You might as well invite him to your party, so you can drink together!"

"Please," she tied the garbage bag closed, "the only thing worse than living with my mom would be drinking with my dad. Why does he think you're staying with him this week?"

I shrugged again. "Honestly, he didn't ask. You're still taking me to rehearsal tomorrow and Thursday night, right? That was the deal. I can't ask Emily again. I'll seem desperate to be in a car with her."

"You *are* desperate to be in a car with her." She narrowed her eyes at me and smirked.

"Shut up." I shoved her not-so-playfully forward as we ascended the basement stairs to the kitchen. When we reached the top, Amanda dropped the garbage bag next to a few others near the back door. "You know what I mean. I'll bum a ride home from someone, but I just feel weird asking anyone to come get me beforehand."

"You are weird. Weird and desperate." Amanda grabbed her car keys, and I followed her out back to where the car we shared—a 1987 wooden-paneled station wagon named Woody—was waiting in the alley.

I stomped my foot. "Amanda! Will you give me a ride or not?"

"A deal is a deal. Now get in the car to go fulfill your civic duty. I don't have all night."

We drove in silence to the church that was serving as the polling location.

"Remember when we used to come here every Sunday as a family?" Amanda asked quietly as she pulled up to the front entrance of the banquet hall. "Then we would go out to brunch at that place with the buffet?"

"Of course I remember. Those hash browns were the bomb."

"I don't mean the food, fatso." Amanda rolled her eyes, and I pictured myself asking for her leftover hash browns. She always left food on her plate, which probably explained why she could pull off bikinis and crop tops. She sometimes enjoyed pointing this out to me since she had started hanging out with her party friends. Before Dad left, she never would have said anything like that to me, but callousness was her new normal. "I mean, like, being a family. Before Dad left."

"You think I don't remember being a family before Dad left?" I unbuckled my seatbelt, aware that Amanda's didn't have to stretch as far as mine did across my middle. "Do people forget that kind of thing?" I still hate when Amanda asks me questions like I'm a toddler.

"I don't know. I think Dad has." Her voice was still quiet.

I felt myself get defensive. "He has not. He just didn't want to be with Mom anymore. Mom seems to be surviving just fine without him, so I guess it worked out."

Amanda stared straight ahead at the setting sun. "Yeah. I guess. See you tomorrow."

"Don't be a dumbass tonight," I said as I closed the car door.

Looking up at the stained glass window above the banquet hall, I remembered the stiff church shoes that Mom made me wear every Sunday. The memory flooded me like a familiar, long-ago scent.

Stepping into the banquet hall felt surreal, like stepping back in time. Not one thing had changed in the four years since I had last been there. The coat racks lined the entryway, and the gray marble floor shone like someone had just waxed it that morning. I took a deep breath and smelled distant incense and old lady perfume. Yep, that was the right place.

Suddenly, I felt nervous I was going to do something wrong. I had my driver's license and the key to Dad's apartment, but I felt like I was forgetting something. "Probably my childhood," I thought as I rolled my eyes, remembering my sister's dumb questions. I spotted the line of people waiting to vote and joined the end of it, reminding myself to breathe and that it was okay to do something for the first time. It was even okay to ask questions if I didn't know how to do something.

The line went quickly. I took note of how everyone checked in first by signing a paper before going over to a voting booth. My palms felt clammy as I approached the girl sitting behind the table who looked like she wasn't much older than I was.

"Name and license please," she said cheerfully.

I took my license out of my pocket, not making eye contact with her. "Josephine Michelle Rein," I told her, eyes on the hand taking my license.

She chuckled and said, "You don't need to say your middle name."

I looked up, feeling my ears turning red, and started to say, "Sorry—"

"You're new to this. I can tell. I can spot a newbie from a mile away." She raised her eyebrows with amusement.

I smiled sheepishly as I signed my name—first and last only.

She handed me my license and told me to step to the last voting booth on the right. "Have fun!" she beamed.

As I approached the voting booth, I felt her eyes follow me before she asked for the name and license of the next person in line. The voting process itself was easier than I expected. When I finished and looked up victoriously, the girl who had signed me in was giving me a half-smile. I watched her lean over to the man next to her and whisper something to him. Then, as I was walking toward the front door, she caught my eye again, grabbed her coat, and motioned with her hand for me to follow her out the back exit.

We both stepped out into the back parking lot where she lit a cigarette, offering one to me. I shook my head and watched her squint as she inhaled slowly, exhaled at the same pace, and then said, "I've been here all day. It may not look like hard work, but it's hard to smile at people who are about to vote for someone you wish they wouldn't."

That took me off-guard, and I smiled. "What makes you assume anyone is voting for a certain person?"

The sun had fully set by that point, and we were standing under a lamppost in an empty lot reserved for church services. Under the bright light, I could see her striking blue eyes. I wondered how I hadn't noticed them inside of the banquet hall but then remembered that I had felt too awkward to look at her much.

"I can tell." She looked around conspiratorially. "Some people just have that look—like their noses are turned up. Your nose isn't turned up at all, Josephine, so I know we are on the same team."

I don't like being reminded of my larger-than-average nose, which I absent-mindedly covered with my hand just then. She laughed. "I didn't mean that there's anything wrong with your nose. It suits your face perfectly."

The red ears returned. I wanted to cover them at that moment, too, but I didn't have enough hands. I just laughed quietly and didn't know what to say.

"I'm Cameron, by the way," she stuck her right hand out to gesture for a handshake, cigarette in her other hand. I took it tentatively, always worried my handshakes are too damp or weak.

"I'm—oh, you already know my name. But not many people call me Josephine, aside from my grandma who died last year. Most people call me Josie."

"Nice to meet you, Josie," Cameron smiled. She looked like she was going to say something else when a white pickup truck pulled into the parking lot and right up to us.

"Hey, Cam." The driver was a male who looked to be about the same age as Cameron. His eyes were disconcertingly intense, but I couldn't make out much else about him from that lighting.

"Hey, Brad." She stepped on her cigarette. "I told you I'm not done until eight o'clock." She looked down at her watch, a few strands of straight blonde hair falling into her face, so she pushed them back and looked back up at him. "It's only 7:20."

"I know, babe, but I couldn't wait to see you." He flashed her a smile so intimate that I slowly stepped back into the shadow of the brick wall, embarrassed to be the third wheel.

"I'll call you when I'm done. I told you I was driving myself here, anyway."

"I know, but I thought you might want to leave your car here and go grab a drink with me." He looked at her expectantly.

"I'll probably end up cleaning up here after we're done. I

promised John I would help."

He pouted. "Fine. I'll be expecting your call by 8:30, and you can meet me wherever I am."

"I'll do my best!" she smiled sweetly at him. He blew her a kiss and pulled away.

Still in the shadows, I started to quietly make my way toward the corner of the building, in the direction of my dad's apartment complex. It was about three blocks from there, so I put my hands in my coat pockets to brace against the cold wind I knew would hit me when I lost the protection from the church building.

"Hey," Cameron called. "Where are you running off to?"

I stopped and looked back at her apologetically. "Oh, sorry. I didn't mean to stick around for so long. You clearly have to get back to work. I bet the line is out the door by now."

"Oh no, my shift is done. Do you need a ride?"

"But you told—"

She snorted. "Yeah, I know what I told him. That was Brad, my ex-boyfriend. He hasn't exactly come to terms with the fact that we aren't together anymore, so he still kind of acts like we are."

"Um, okay. You could have fooled me."

"Eh," she shrugged, "it's just easier to play along sometimes. If I would have called him out in front of you, he would have flipped. Not worth it."

I half-turned to face her, uncommitted to staying. "I don't even think he noticed I was there."

"Trust me—he noticed." She looked certain.

"But I didn't say a word."

"I'm standing alone in the dark with a beautiful girl. He noticed."

My voice caught in my throat. The only person who had ever called me beautiful was my dad. I wasn't sure if I had heard the words correctly.

"So," Cameron asked again, "do you need a ride?"

I wasn't sure what to say. It would be nice to get out of the cold, but I was always worried that I was inconveniencing people. "If you don't mind," I replied shyly.

"Not even one little bit." She reached for and grabbed my hand to lead me in the opposite direction. I tried to will my palms to not start sweating. Who was this girl? A fresh, sweet scent floated from her hair, and I was dizzy with anticipation.

We arrived at a beat-up old red sedan parked near where Amanda had dropped me off.

"This," Cameron gestured to the car, "is the Red Rocket. Rocket, meet Josie."

I laughed. "Nice to meet you, Rocket."

"Hold on." She got into the driver's seat and leaned over to open the passenger-side door. "It only opens from the inside." She shrugged, and I laughed again.

Once we had both settled into our seat-belts, she asked, "So where are you headed? You must live pretty close if this is your polling place."

"My dad does. He lives about three blocks that way," I pointed, "on Highland Avenue."

"Cool. That's not too far from my folks. It's barely even out of the way. I was going to ask you to get out if your destination was going to be more than a mild inconvenience." She gave me a side-eye and started the car. The radio immediately began blaring a Dave Matthews Band song, and she reached quickly to turn down the volume. "Sorry about that. I guess I was jamming."

I smiled. "I do the same thing in my car, except it's more likely to be someone like Tori Amos or Jann Arden."

"Who?"

"Which one?"

"I kind of know who the first one is, but I have no idea who the second one is."

"Yeah," I chuckled, "a lot of people say that. She's Canadian and not exactly famous here, but you would probably know one of her songs."

"Sing it for me."

I felt my blood start pumping. Singing was my thing. I did it on stage several nights per week and did it for fun by myself. I did it in my car and in the shower and while cleaning my room. But, for some reason, I froze.

"I don't want to." I felt the urge to bite my finger but resisted it.

"Why? Can't you carry a tune? I mean, I really can't carry a tune, and I don't even pretend to be able to, so I respect it if you can't, either."

I winced at the idea of myself not being musical. "No, I can. I'm just not emotionally prepared to give you a concert right now."

Cameron snorted. "A concert? I'm asking for a few lines from a song, not an entire album! Wow, you are *dramatic*."

"You're not the only person who has told me that." I grinned.

Dave Matthews serenaded us quietly as I considered what to do next. This gorgeous girl—who had called me *beautiful*—had asked me to sing for her. It would be epically stupid to say no. I leaned forward and turned the volume all the way down and sang the chorus to the most famous Jann Arden song, which just so happens to reference driving someone home. I stopped and said, "It's funny to sing that to someone who is actually driving me home."

Cameron blinked a few times and said, "Damn, you're beautiful, and you can sing. Now what am I supposed to do with that?" She stopped at a stop sign and looked over at me. I felt my entire body start to tingle, and my mouth became incapable of forming any words. I had no idea how to react in such a situation. I had never been hit on by a girl before, and I was pretty sure that was what she was doing—hitting on me. I had come out of the closet when I was fourteen years old and still had yet to meet one other lesbian in my small town—let alone a sexy one who was looking right at me with intrigue in her stunning blue eyes.

"Well, what do you want to do with me?" I realized how brazen that sounded after it left my mouth. Cameron laughed loudly again and continued driving.

"How old are you, Josie? I don't feel like I've seen you around, and I'm pretty sure I would have noticed."

Eighteen suddenly felt like eight, but I was honest. "I turned eighteen last month. How old are you?"

"I'm twenty-two. Are you still in high school?"

"I'm a senior."

She nodded. "So am I ... in college. I'm doing my student teaching in a second-grade classroom about fifteen minutes from here."

"Oh, you're going to be a teacher? That's awesome! I'm going to go into education, too. Not for little kids, though. I want to teach high school English. Writing and grammar are my second and third loves after music."

"So why don't you go into music then?"

"It's not that easy. I would love to record my music in a studio—"

"Wait," she glanced at me, "you actually write your own music?"

I suddenly felt shy again. My music was emotional and private and so not professional enough to even be talking about it. "Yes. It's not great, but it's my favorite thing to do. To write it. So I figure I can write music for my entire life in my free time when I'm not teaching writing."

"Well, I'm here to tell you that teachers don't actually get much free time, contrary to popular belief!" Cameron sighed. "I have, like, three lessons to plan for tomorrow, so I know I won't get to bed until close to midnight."

"Yikes. Well, I hope you get some sleep. This is my dad's apartment complex." I pointed to a gray brick building coming up on the right, and she pulled into the parking lot. "Thank you so much for driving me here. My sister has kidnapped the car for the week because she insists that driving her loser friends around is more important than—well—anything in the world."

"Wait a minute," Cameron parked the car. "You're Amanda Rein's sister? I don't know why that didn't occur to me when I saw your last name."

"The one and only," I shrugged. I didn't know what she was going to say about Amanda next; in fact, I almost didn't want to know. Ever since Dad had left Mom a few years before then, Amanda had gone haywire. She used to be a straight-A student and a great basketball player, but she suddenly barely got C's and spent all of her time either with a boyfriend (not always the same one) or with her stoner friends. I missed her. I missed everyone in my family in different ways, but Amanda was the one who hurt the most because weren't siblings supposed to stick together in the face of a divorce?

"Huh," Cameron said in a well-what-do-you-know revelation. "Where did you get that blonde hair? Your sister's hair is practically black."

"Everyone always asks us that, and I have no idea. Both of our parents have dark hair."

"Ahhh, so you're the milk man's daughter," she teased.

"Yep, that's me," I smiled at the joke I had heard many times before, certain that I am both my mother's and father's daughter. "How do you know Amanda?"

"I don't actually." She shrugged. "I just used to see her around school sometimes. She wears really short skirts, so it's hard to miss her."

I felt defensive of both my sister and myself; people were always noticing Amanda before they noticed me. That's just the way it was.

"Well, thanks again for driving me." I put my hand on the door handle, ready to resign myself to being swallowed whole by my sister's reputation yet again.

"Wait, I didn't mean that in any way. I just meant that I know who she is by how she dresses." Nobody ever meant to unsee me, but they did it as soon as they knew I was Amanda's younger sister. I became less me and more Amanda's opposite. *Oh, you're Amanda's sister? But you're so innocent/nice/blonde!*

"It's fine." My hand lingered on the door handle, and I studied a tiny piece of skin hanging beside my thumb nail.

"Aren't you at least going to ask for my phone number?" She asked matter-of-factly.

Startled, I quickly turned to face her to find her leaning over the armrest with her eyebrows raised.

"You could ask for mine," I retorted. "It's a two-way street." I silently admonished myself for the cliché.

"You're right. But first … " Cameron leaned forward and kissed me gently on my lips and then backed away slowly with her eyes still closed. "Yep. Compatible."

I was stunned. My legs felt weak, and I wasn't sure I would be able to get out of the car. I didn't know where to look, where to put my hands, what to say.

Cameron took one finger and tilted my face toward hers. "I don't need your number. I'll pick you up right here tomorrow night at about eight o'clock."

"I can't," I said quietly, my lips still tasting like her cigarette and minty chapstick. "I have rehearsal for the show I'm in."

She brought her hand to her heart. "Oh, God, you mean I'm going to be able to watch your pretty self sing that pretty voice up on a stage? I might die."

I shifted in my seat and smiled apologetically, not exactly sure what I felt the need to apologize for.

"Okay," she continued, "what time will you be home?"

"Well, if you want, you can pick me up from rehearsal. We will be at the high school, and I'll be done by nine."

She considered it for a second. "Sure. That should be fine. I'll see you then." She looked at me and smiled. "Good night."

I opened the door and stepped out of the car and then leaned back in to say, "Good night, Cameron."

$$- 7 -$$

Friday, March 15, 2019

While washing my hands after dinner, I stared with ambivalence at my reflection. My face looked swollen from a combination of hormonal bloating due to the fertility medication combined with the increased frequency of my drive thru trips. I was considering changing my shirt before going to Liesel's preschool concert. I couldn't decide if the one I was wearing was too tight or too loose; either way, it seemed to accentuate all of the wrong places.

"Mama!" Liesel called from the dining room table about ten feet away.

"What?" I responded with more irritation in my voice than I expected.

"Want to color with me? I making a picture of a spaceship." I loved how she said "pitcher," and I felt my mood soften.

"Not now, baby. We have to start getting ready for your concert." I checked my watch and then looked back at my reflection, staring into my own eyes and trying to decide what it was that I was feeling. My irritation wasn't just about the shirt. Was I tired? Worried about that morning's insemination? Dreading seeing Brandon during eighth period on Monday?

"We need to stop and get gas on the way," Cam yelled down from the upstairs bathroom. "We should leave soon."

Liesel gasped. "My tutu!" She jumped up and ran up the stairs to her bedroom.

When Cam and I had found out that our first child was going to be a girl, we had known immediately what we were going to name her because Liesel was the name of one of our favorite characters in one of our favorite books—*The Book Thief* by Markus Zusak. We had daydreamed and chatted about her being just like a combination of the two of us: athletic and friendly like Cam, musical and determined like me. We weren't prepared for the actual parenting of a human who is more feminine than either of us put together, so it has been a constant adventure in pink sparkles.

I listened to their feet above me as they finished getting ready, and I moved my attention to the painting of a robin on the bathroom wall. Cam knows how much robins mean to me, so she never protests when I add birds or blue eggs to the decor anywhere in the house. I often find myself staring at this particular painting, and while I brush my teeth in the morning, I sometimes silently send my dad a message through the bird's small dark eye.

Cam came running down the stairs in form-fitting jeans, a sweater, and tall brown boots. She looked attractive and confident as usual, and that only served as another reminder of how I don't quite match up, with my extra thirty-or-so pounds. I frequently wonder if Cam looks at me and wishes she had chosen to be with someone else—someone who had the sense to take care of her appearance more.

"Last one in the car is a rotten egg!" Cam shouted, and Liesel ran down the stairs and straight out the front door, her pink sparkly tutu flapping around her. I followed them outside, envious of their giggles and forcing a smile that I hoped looked genuine as I helped Liesel climb into her car seat.

On the way to the school, we pulled into a gas station. I offered to pump the gas in order to take advantage of some extra oxygen. I watched as the price ticked upward until it clicked and landed on $35.35. *Three plus five is eight. That's two eights.* I considered that maybe this was a sign that I am pregnant on our eighth try, and I felt my mood brighten—confirmation that my irritability had been residual from that morning. I reminded myself that it wasn't like it was my first two-week wait or like I didn't know what to expect if I wasn't expecting. I just needed to get over myself and move on with life as usual. Rolling my eyes to myself, I got back into the passenger seat.

The school auditorium was a whirlwind of parents brushing their kids' hair and giving hugs and kisses before coaxing them onto the stage. Liesel had no trouble at all walking up and taking her place. Cam and I found two seats next to each other and spent the remaining five minutes before the show making snide comments about some of the snobbier moms who hadn't given us—or Liesel—the time of day. When the lights dimmed, we looked at each other and grinned and then both gave the stage our full attention.

The set list included rousing renditions of several nursery rhymes, including Liesel's favorite, "Mary Had a Little Lamb," and classics like "Twinkle Twinkle" and "Old McDonald." Liesel was really hamming it up—smiling, singing, and doing the hand motions that were being modeled by her teachers at the front of the stage. She spotted me smiling at her and waved happily, saying, "Hi, Mama!" and then looked at Cam and said, "Hi, Mommy!" We both waved enthusiastically back.

At the end of the show, which lasted about ten minutes tops, the kids bowed and started filing off the stage in a semi-orderly fashion. I stood to go and greet Liesel when I noticed a cookie table tucked into a corner. I immediately began to salivate at the sight of sugar cookies covered in colorful sprinkles and admonished myself with a reminder that I hadn't fit into the pants I had planned to wear that morning. Just then, Liesel came rushing up to me and hugged my legs.

"Hey, baby girl! That was some excellent singing up there! I am so proud!" I grabbed her face, bent down, and kissed her forehead.

Cam found us and squatted down to meet Liesel's eyes. "You are an absolute rock star, my love. Like, you were totally the best performer up there."

Liesel giggled and threw her arms around Cam's neck.

"You want a cookie, honey?" I asked her. Liesel wouldn't have even noticed the cookies otherwise, but I couldn't help myself. If I got one for Liesel, it wouldn't seem so odd that I was eating one myself. No other adults were eating cookies, but I thought I might just have to be the first one. Without waiting for a response, I headed to the cookie table and chose one pink cookie for Liesel and one blue cookie for myself.

On my way to deliver the cookie, I saw Cam was talking to one of the moms that we had been joking about—the one who always has on workout clothes no matter where she's going, like she could break into a jog at any moment.

"I recognize you from the gym," I heard the woman saying to Cam. "I didn't know our kids are in the same preschool class! My son is Jackson." She pointed to a little dark-haired boy running around the seats, pretending to shoot people with an imaginary gun.

I stopped short of standing next to Cam and listened to the two of them share quips about how funny and exhausting it is to parent a preschooler. Putting the cookies in my coat pocket, I tried in vain to avoid letting the sprinkles fall off. Cam turned to look at me and then looked at Exercise Snob mom and told her we'd better get going because it was getting late, adding, "It was very nice to finally meet you, Sharon."

A familiar cloak of invisibility enveloped me, bringing with it both comfort and shame. I felt my ears turning red and quickly pulled my hands out of my pockets to reposition my hair to cover them. A few stray sprinkles flew into the air and onto the floor at Liesel's feet, and she said, "Hey, I want a cookie!" So I took her to the cookie table to pick one out and saved the ones in my pocket for myself.

"What's with you?" Cam asked me, glancing sideways at me from the driver's seat as we pulled out of Liesel's school's parking lot.

"Me? Nothing." I looked straight ahead at the headlit road.

"Then why are you biting your fingers?" I hadn't actually realized that I was. Cam tried to take my left hand into hers, but I quickly pulled it away and put both hands into my coat pockets.

"You seemed real friendly with Sharon in there," I said flatly.

She laughed. "Oh, please. She approached me because she recognized me from the gym. What was I supposed to do—run away from her?"

"No," I lowered my voice, so Liesel—who was slowly falling asleep in the back seat—couldn't hear me, "but you could have at least introduced me."

"You literally had just said, like, fifteen minutes beforehand that she was the one you couldn't stand the most," she half-whispered.

"Yes, and you agreed with me."

"That was all in fun! I was just joking with you."

"What makes you think I wasn't also joking?"

"Josie, you don't like anyone. You never like anyone."

"That is absolutely not true. I don't dislike many people at all. I just don't *like* that many people, either." I fingered the crumbling cookies in my right-hand coat pocket.

"Same thing."

"No, it's really not. I have never wished harm on any person in my life—except for one."

She knew I was talking about Brad, but when I glared at her hard and waited for a response, I didn't get one. After about a minute of nothing, she looked to the back seat and spoke in a full whisper, discovering Liesel's closed eyes and sagging head.

"Can you believe she remembered all of those words? I think maybe you gave birth to her without us noticing." Without apologizing, this was her way of admitting she was wrong and hoping we could change the subject. I only allude to Brad when I am feeling especially wounded, and I don't misuse the privilege. Because I was tired and didn't feel like fighting, I gave in.

"Yeah, if she was your kid, she would have started taking off her clothes and leaving them all around the stage for other people to pick up," I mumbled.

Cam snickered and tousled my hair, and we rode in silence the rest of the way home.

- 9 -

Wednesday, June 13, 2001

It was nearly midnight when my cell phone—a purple face-plated Nokia that was a graduation gift from my dad—began ringing. I reached toward my nightstand to see who it was, even though I already knew.

"Hey, you," I said quietly to Cam, so I didn't wake up my mom who was sleeping in the bedroom next to mine.

"Come outside. I need to see you."

I looked down at my old heather-grey t-shirt and bare legs. "Give me a minute to get dressed." I slipped on a pair of shorts, a bra, and a clean shirt before grabbing a pair of flip flops and tip-toeing down the stairs to the front door, turning the knob slowly to prevent any loud clicking or creaking and stepped onto the front porch.

Cam was sitting in the Rocket with the windows down and the engine idling. She grinned when she saw me approaching the passenger side and told me, "Get in. We have somewhere to go."

I looked behind me and up to my mom's bedroom window. The light was off, so she was almost-definitely asleep. If I only stayed out for a little while, she would never know. And if she did find out, I could tell her I was eighteen years old and could do what I pleased, just like Amanda had done at my age. It wasn't like she was always around to check on me, anyway.

I got in the car, and Cam pulled slowly away. "You were incredible on that stage tonight. I wanted to rip your clothes off right then and there." She reached to put her hand on my thigh.

That night had been my high school graduation. My best friend Andrew and I had written and performed a song together about growing up. When I had finished singing, and just as Andrew was playing the last notes on the piano, I had noticed Cam standing in the back of the auditorium. She was too far away for me to see her face, but I saw her put her hand to her heart before she turned around and walked out.

"Easy, tiger. Watch the road." I smiled. "And thank you. I saw you standing in the back at the end."

"I was there for the whole thing." She squeezed my thigh, and I grabbed her hand. "Tonight, I want to celebrate you finally graduating from high school, so I no longer have to feel like I'm robbing the cradle."

"Ha! You're the one who is always insisting that I'm legal because I'm eighteen."

"Yeah, well, I still sometimes feel icky dating a high schooler, so this just makes me feel better." She leaned toward me, keeping her eyes on the road, and I gave her a quick kiss.

"So what are we doing to celebrate?" I asked.

"My cousin Ashley called me today and asked if I would dog-sit for her while she and David go to the beach for a long weekend. They have a sweet golden retriever. Anyway, as soon as they asked me, I thought of spending four days in their house with you and immediately said yes."

Ashley and David had no idea who I was. In fact, no one in Cam's family knew I existed. My mom was fine with Cam, but when she was home and not at Sam's, we were always having to find secret spots to meet up and have some privacy—somewhere where Cam's parents wouldn't accidentally happen upon us. She is the only child of two conservative parents of whom both she and I were terrified.

"Okay then," I said tentatively. "Are you sure it's okay if I'm there?"

"No one will ever know." Cam wiggled her eyebrows suggestively.

I nodded and looked out the window at the quickly-passing trees and street lights. It took about ten minutes to get to the house, and as soon as we parked the car out front, we were greeted by excited barking from inside the front door.

"Her name is Patsy. She's sweet but also ... uhhh ... energetic." On cue, Patsy jumped on us as we opened the door. We laughed and pet her, allowing her to sniff and lick our faces. Cam closed and locked the door behind us, and I looked around at the clean, modern decor.

"Hmmm, not my style but nice," I commented as Patsy took off down a hallway.

"What *is* your style?" Cam wrapped her arms around my waist from behind me, and I felt my usual butterflies.

"I don't know yet. Antiques? More colorful? More—"

Cam spun me around and started to kiss me feverishly. I immediately followed suit, and we headed toward a black leather couch, panting and giggling. After a few minutes engrossed in each other and removing clothing items one by one, we heard a man's voice coming from directly outside of the sliding glass patio door about five feet away from us.

"Cam, let me in." We both froze.

There was a curtain covering the door, but we knew exactly who it was.

"Cam," Brad continued, "let me the fuck in. I know you're in there because your car is parked out front. I'm holding a cinder block, and I swear to God I will throw it through this fucking door."

Cam shoved my shirt at me and told me to get down on the floor. She quickly put her own shirt and shorts back on and smoothed her hair.

"Brad, it's late," she called. "I'm going to bed. I'll call you tomorrow."

"No," he said firmly. "I know she's in there with you. I'm going to kill her, I swear."

I was lying face-down on the carpet, too much bare skin touching the rough, beige wool. I wished I were still at home in my bed, drifting off to sleep.

"No one is in here with me, Brad. Now go home." I could hear her breath quiver as she feigned nonchalance.

He heaved a sigh of frustration. "I watched you both walk in the door. I followed your car from her house to here. You don't want me to tell everyone that you're a dyke, do you?" His voice started to rise at the end of the sentence. My adrenaline was pumping as I remained frozen and shirtless on the floor, thinking that I should just get up, put my shirt on, and tell him to go away. He wasn't going to kill me. He might have been desperate and angry, but he wasn't stupid.

I started to sit up at the same moment that the glass shattered. Jumping up, I ran to the nearest bathroom and closed the door, fumbling for a lock. Patsy was barking excitedly at

Brad as he bypassed Cam and came straight to the bathroom door, pounding on it with both of his fists.

"I'm going to kill you! I'm going to kill you!" He roared over and over again. I covered my ears in a vain attempt to not hear his bellowing voice or Patsy's frightened barking.

Cam shouted, "Stop it, Brad! Stop it! Go home! I can smell an entire twelve-pack of beer on your breath. You're acting like a lunatic, and look what you did to Ashley's door! How the hell am I going to explain that to them? Patsy, it's okay, girl. Shhh, come on. Go ahead down to the basement for a little while." Patsy must have obeyed because I heard the basement door close, and her barking became more distant though just as persistent.

Brad's fists hesitated, and he said almost in a whisper to Cam, "Why are you doing this? You don't have to do this."

For the next several minutes, I couldn't make out what they were saying to each other in soft voices. I could only tell Cam was trying to soothe him while he cried. I took deep, conscious breaths in and out. As I put my shirt back on, I caught sight of my reflection in the mirror and reminded myself that I was okay and that he wouldn't dare hurt Cam. I reminded myself that she loved me. I reminded myself that she never, ever claimed me.

After what felt like an hour of trying to listen, I gave up and slid to the bathroom floor. I was seriously considering lying down on the softest bathroom rug when I heard the front door open and close. Soon after, there was a knock on the bathroom door.

"It's me," Cam said.

I sat up straight and couldn't find any words to say.

"Come out. I'll take you home."

Still silent, I stood, unlocked the door, and opened it. Cam's eyes were bloodshot, and they didn't meet mine. She was holding a broom and a dustpan, and I could feel the cooling summer air drifting in through the broken door.

"He's drunk. It won't happen again." She bent down to sweep up the last of the broken glass.

"How do you know that?" My voice was louder and angrier than I expected. I couldn't stop myself from continuing, looking down at her as she swept up the sparkling shards, "He threatened my life. Look, you two have some issues to work through. For six months, I've been suffocating inside a closet that isn't even mine, and—"

"I know." She finally stood and looked at me. "I explained everything to him the best way I could. He obviously already knows, but he doesn't want to accept it. We dated for a lot of years, Josie." She held my gaze.

I looked away. "Honestly, at this point, I don't care if you were with him for fifty years. This isn't fair to me, and you know it." I pushed past her toward the front door, and she grabbed my arm.

"It's not fair. You're right. It won't happen again." She tried to pull me closer to her, but I wouldn't let her.

"Just take me home. I don't want to be here anymore."

- 10 -

That weekend I had taken Cam's suggestion and not done any school work. It was wonderful, really, because we had the time to catch up on some Netflix, play lots of *My Little Pony*, and just enjoy each other's company.

I arrived at school about an hour early to grade the essays I had ignored all weekend. As I sat at my desk to check my email, I was not exactly happy to see a message from Brandon's mother with the subject line: "Suspension."

My heart sped up as I considered whether I should open the email now or wait until my third period prep time. Before I could consider it further, my finger made a decision of its own and clicked.

Dear Miss Rein Thompson,

Brandon was suspended yesterday for what he said to you in your English class, and I want you to know that while we do not condone him disrespecting his teachers, we fully support his First Amendment right to hold his views and not be forced to deny them.

52

His father and I have advised him to not bring it up again unless provoked. His chance at a basketball scholarship cannot be further hindered by additional suspensions.

Mrs. Marjorie Stoneman

First Amendment right? I guessed it had been a while since I had read the Constitution, but I didn't remember it allowing people to just be assholes to each other. I sighed and reread the words—not apologetic but not technically rude. Not warm but not accusatory. I was going to have to accept it. I began typing.

Dear Mrs. Stoneman,

I appreciate your message. But you can go to hell.

I smirked and then hit the backspace button a few times.

I appreciate your message. In my class, I encourage students to use words to speak the truth, but they must do so in a respectful way. Thank you for your support in this matter.

Mrs. Rein-Thompson

There. Now no one could accuse me of forcing my "lifestyle" down anyone's throats or violating anyone's Constitutional rights.

My classroom door opened, and I expected to see Dana standing on the other side of it; instead, I saw Kate holding a piece of paper. She was wearing a red and blue Benson High hoodie that practically swallowed her whole.

"Oh," Kate said, startled, "I thought I would just put my essay on your desk. I didn't expect you to be here this early."

"It's okay, Kate. Good morning." I gave her a small, closed-mouth smile. "I was actually just getting ready to grade some essays, so yours can be first." I reached out my hand for the paper.

Kate shifted her weight from one foot to the other, keeping her eyes on her essay. "Sorry mine is a day late. Remember when I had the flu last week? I got a little behind."

"I know. I figured you needed some extra time."

She walked to my desk and handed me the essay without making eye contact.

"See you fifth period," Kate said quickly before darting out the door.

I sighed again, worried that Kate felt awkward after writing about me—*to* me—in her journal on Friday. I wondered if I should have said something encouraging to her just then but then considered whether that would have made it worse. Deciding to just move forward as if it hadn't happened—as if none of it had happened—I would forgive Brandon and pretend like Kate didn't know a thing.

I looked down at Kate's essay and reread the assignment prompt typed on top of her outline paper: "In honor of Women's History Month, write an essay about a woman who has had a positive impact on your life." I love doing this assignment and reading all about students' moms, grandmas, and older sisters, and there are usually a few about Beyoncé or a Kardashian or whatever female celebrities are currently popular. In tenth grade, I would probably have written about Grandma Louise or Madonna. I wondered how I would have chosen which one.

Resigning myself to do what I had come early to do, I settled into my chair to get more comfortable for an essay-grading shift and began reading Kate's opening paragraph:

There have been many positive females in my life. I am lucky to have two living grandmothers and a mother who loves me. I even have a few neighbors that I could have written about but I am choosing to write about Mrs. Rein-Thompson.

I stopped reading and looked up, surprised. I had been teaching for thirteen years and had used this prompt every March, and no student had ever written about me before. I felt honored but also undeniably nervous as I continued reading Kate's thesis statement:

She has had a positive impact on my life because she is kind, successful and true to herself.

I began to smile to myself and then froze when I realized what that last part might mean. Had Kate actually written about my sexuality in her essay? *This could get interesting.*

First, Mrs. Rein-Thompson is kind. No matter what kind of day she is having she always has a smile on her face and is willing to help any student in her classroom. She must be in a bad mood sometimes but she never shows it. I have seen her go out of her way to talk to kids in the hallway and have even seen her help other teachers when they need it. This has inspired me to be nicer to people too.

Next she is successful. She always talks about how writing is her favorite thing to do and she made a career out of it by being a writing teacher. I think that success is defined by doing something that makes you happy and also makes you money and that is exactly what she is doing. I want to be just like that when I get older.

The classroom phone rang, and I jumped. "Hello?" I answered, forgetting to identify myself.

"Good morning, Josie." It was my principal, Mr. Dunham. "Can you stop by my office during third period? I'd like to talk to you about something."

"Sure," I said uncertainly. "Is this about Brandon? He's back today, right?"

"Yes, he is." He hesitated. "And I guess you could say it's related. See you then."

I sat with the phone in my hand for a few seconds after he hung up, wondering what the issue could be now.

The bell rang for first period to begin, and my students started filing in. I blinked a few times to center myself and silently repeated my pep talk: "This is what you're good at. This is what you can control." As the late bell rang, I wished my students good morning and told them to take out their journals.

"Next week," I began, "we will begin reading excerpts from the novel titled *Red at the Bone* by Jacqueline Woodson. I won't give too much away, but much of the story deals with identity—that mixture of who we are, who we think we might be, and who we wish to be. In your journal today, write about one or more of those things." I wrote on the board:

Who do you think you might be? Who do you wish to be? Who are you really?

I would leave the prompt up for the rest of the day for all of the classes to write about. After I had finished writing it, I wondered how Brandon would respond in his journal. Would he admit to being a bigot? I thought that might be too harsh of a word for him. Plenty of kids at that age don't even have opinions of their own yet and are still regurgitating the ones that belong to their parents.

While my students wrote, I considered how I would answer the questions myself. I mentally recited, "I think I might be a good person. I wish to be creative and kind. I am actually invisible."

- 11 -

Monday, March 18, 2019

By the middle of second period, the suspense was killing me. The lesson I was teaching that day was all led by me, without much time for students to work on anything independently. I didn't exactly want to read the rest of Kate's essay with anyone else in the room, anyway, so I was just going to have to wait.

"On Friday, we began discussing participles. Anybody remember what they are?"

Crickets. I once saw a t-shirt that read "I'm like a participle. No one understands me." and almost bought it because it was so accurate.

"I get it. It's challenging. Okay, let's just focus on one of the participle's functions today: when a word looks like a verb but is acting like an adjective." I looked around to make sure that they were all at least mildly engaged. "Look back at what you wrote in your journal today about who you are. Underline any words in there that are acting as adjectives."

"You mean, like, funny?" a boy in the back right corner said.

"Yep, that's exactly what I mean."

"But, Kevin, you're not funny at all, so you must be writing about someone else," another boy yelled from across the room, and the class erupted with "oooooh" and "burn".

"Okay, okay. Good one, Perry, but I happen to think Kevin can be very funny." I was trying to save the moment for Kevin, but it didn't seem to help that the compliment was coming from who he viewed as some middle-aged woman. The class quieted down as I continued walking around the room watching them underline adjectives.

"So who thinks they've found a participle?" I returned to the front of the room.

Most of them looked unsure, but I saw a hand in the middle tentatively raise.

"Michaela?"

"Woke?"

I smiled. "Ha! Well, I definitely see what you mean because it can be a verb but also an adjective, especially in a slang sense, but the participles for the verb 'wake' would be 'waking' and 'woken'. I love your example, though! Keep them coming!" I said to the rest of the class.

Someone said, "I am so awoken!"

Before I could respond, someone retorted, "That's gay!"

And, suddenly, the class was silent. I looked out at a sea of faces whose eyes were either wide and searching my own or looking elsewhere so as not to have to look at me at all.

Well, then. This is happening. Think fast, Josie.

"That's gay? It's not very awoken of you to say that, Perry! Yes, I know it was you. It's fine. Moving on, so notice that we don't often use participles to describe our personalities but more like how we are acting in an actual moment. Something like: 'The screaming toddler stomped her feet.' We wouldn't use a word like 'screaming' to describe a personality, right? I mean, some of you *are* pretty loud, but ... " They laughed.

My specialty. I had taken the punch and rolled with it so quickly that it had disappeared. Perry looked relieved—after momentarily embarrassed that I had recognized his voice—and the dynamic had been restored. I was the happy, confident, closeted teacher they knew and loved.

I looked at the clock. Three minutes until the bell.

"All right, everyone, go ahead and clean up. We will pick up here tomorrow."

- 12 -

It was a cold, grey morning, and I was driving to my dad's apartment. He hadn't been answering my phone calls for a few days, so I knew he was drinking but wanted to see him to confirm it.

Besides, I needed something to keep me busy. Cam's baby shower was happening that day. I had not been invited because, according to her family, "it wouldn't be traditional to allow the dad to be present"—even though I could speak for days about the differences between being a "dad" and being "the other mother." Cam was nearly eight months pregnant with our daughter, who would be Liesel Beatrice Thompson, and I was not invited to the baby shower.

Since the month before, I had been driving around with a "Baby on Board" sign on the back window of my silver hatchback even though there was no baby in my car. I needed the world to know that I was having a baby—that the baby was my baby, too.

I used my key to open his front door. Mail was piled on a table in the entryway, and there was a crack in the mirror hanging on the wall.

"That's seven years of bad luck, Dad!" I called, squinting to find his figure in the dim light. He laughed gruffly from the recliner in the far corner of the living room. I leaned over and switched on a table lamp, noticing the pile of garbage that had accumulated next to it. "Let there be light!"

"You're full of originality today, Jo," he coughed. I was startled by how gray his hair was—including his unusually long and scruffy beard.

Forcing a smile, I walked toward him to kiss his cheek. "How are you feeling, Dad?"

"I've been better, but I've been worse." He shrugged.

I crossed my arms. "You look exhausted. Have you been sleeping?"

"Not so much. Too much on my mind." I could tell he didn't want to talk.

"I know you're stressed. Have you heard back about any job interviews?"

"Nothing."

Nodding sympathetically, I said, "Someone will call." Then, looking around the room, I continued, "I'm going to clean up a little bit for you."

"Don't bother," he grumbled and switched on the TV.

I walked into the kitchen and, on my way to the refrigerator, bypassed several full garbage bags on the floor and a mountain of dirty dishes in and around the sink. Inside the refrigerator, I found only three things: a nearly-empty case of beer, a nearly-empty pizza box, and a four-pack of chocolate pudding—with one missing. I shook my head.

"Dad," I said loudly enough for him to hear me, "have you had anything nutritious to eat since I was here last week?" I returned to the living room and stood where he could see me. "I'd offer to cook you something, but there's nothing to cook."

The football game announcer said something about a first down. He kept his eyes on the screen. "I had some pizza for lunch. I'm fine."

"There's beer in the fridge. Not much left of it, actually."

"So what?" He turned to look at me. "Can't a grown man have some beer in his refrigerator?"

"Not a grown man who spent two years sober and was doing great until about three months ago when he started drinking again." I moved closer to him and sat on the old navy-blue couch that we used to have in our house when I was little.

"I lost my job, Josie," he stated, half-obstinately and half-pleadingly.

"Dad, you lost your job because you were drinking. We've been over this. You can't manage a restaurant when you're drunk."

He turned his face to the window, and I followed his gaze. It had begun to snow lightly. I wondered what was happening right at that moment at Cam's shower. Were they opening gifts? Had anyone even said my name? He interrupted my thoughts by saying softly, "I should never have left your mother. She would take care of me."

I huffed, picturing my mom's closed bedroom door and hearing her long-ago, nightly stifled sobs. "Mom moved across the country to sunny southern California to start a new life with Sam. They're happy. You weren't happy with her." We had had the same conversation a hundred times over the course of the prior few months.

"Do I seem happy now?" He kept his eyes on the falling snow.

I paused. "No. But we're going to get you there."

"Tell me something, Josie." His voice sounded suddenly clear as he turned to face me again. "Did you two settle on a name for the baby?"

"We did. She will be Liesel Beatrice. Her middle name is for Cam's grandma, and her first—"

"I'm talking about her last name."

"Oh," I hesitated. "Well, to spare her a lifetime of mispronunciation, we are just going with Thompson."

His eyebrows furrowed. "No Rein at all? Not even a hyphen?"

"Hyphens are a pain in the ass. Trust me. I know from experience. It's just easier this way." I settled back into the couch cushions, searching quickly for a change of subject.

"Is that what you really want?" His eyes, suddenly clear and intent, locked on mine.

I wanted to say no. I wanted to tell him how invisible I had felt throughout the entire pregnancy and how I was terrified of feeling invisible as Liesel's mother, but I didn't. I didn't even pause.

"Yes." I wiped my palms on my pants and willed myself to maintain eye contact. "That baby is just as much yours and mine as it is Cam's and her parents'. Her due date is your birthday, for heaven's sake. You'll share that special bond with her, and she will love you forever for so many reasons. You'll see."

‐ 13 ‐

Monday, March 18, 2019

"Have a good day," I smiled as the last of my second‐period students left my classroom before closing the door and turning to face the empty room, soaking in the silence. Mr. Dunham was probably waiting for me, but I couldn't go down there without knowing what the rest of Kate's essay said. What if he had something to talk about that was going to take all period, and I didn't get to look at it until lunchtime? I would be wondering about it for hours, and that would be too distracting.

I returned to my desk and retrieved Kate's essay from the top of the pile, scanning it for the place where I had left off.

... I want to be just like that when I get older.

Finally, Mrs. Rein‐Thompson is true to herself. It can't be easy to be a gay teacher so I know that's why she doesn't really talk about herself in class but I admire her so much for just being married to a woman at all in the face of criticism from society. The truth is that I am also gay but I don't know how to tell anyone.

I reread that last sentence and slowly set the essay down on my desk. "Oh, boy," I said aloud, closing my eyes and shaking my head from side to side quickly, as if to magically arrange the feelings bouncing around inside of me. I picked the paper back up and continued reading:

… The truth is that I am also gay but I don't know how to tell anyone. My parents are what you might call closed-minded and they think homosexuality is a sin. I know they won't be okay with it.

In conclusion, Mrs. Rein-Thompson has had a positive effect on my life because she is kind, successful and true to herself and I aspire to be all three of those things.

My palms were sweating as I set the paper down again on my desk and told myself to breathe. I had had a few students privately come out to me before, but not one of them had ever done it in writing—let alone in an actual written assignment that I was supposed to comment on and grade. I whispered, "Calm down. Think before you do anything."

What kind of comments should I write on it? Should I thank her? Will her parents look in her writing portfolio for the graded assignment that I'll add to the grade book today?

I hadn't had any interactions with Kate's parents at all, aside from a quick hello at Open House at the beginning of the school year. I had never had a reason to contact home because of a low grade or a behavior issue—or even a note to mention that she had gone above and beyond in some way. Kate had always just been quiet and obedient in the back of my fifth-period class.

Should I let the school counselor know?

Yes. I should let the counselor know and try to be as hands-off with the situation as possible. Dom Madden will know what to do and will take it from here.

I wheeled my chair closer to my desk to compose an email to him but found myself daydreaming instead. Kate's epiphany against a backdrop of religion took me back to seventh-grade when I became friends with Layla who went to the same Catholic school that I did. It wouldn't be until the following summer that I would be conscious of it, but she was the first girl "in real life" who sparked something in me. Being around her made me sweat, but I also couldn't get enough of her, even when she talked about all of the boys she had crushes on. I just pretended to like the same boys, too, so I could allow myself to swoon over her while she swooned over them.

I was just beginning to wonder what Layla was doing all these years later when I noticed the time. Somehow, I only had fifteen minutes left in the period. "Shit," I muttered as I pushed back the chair and rushed out the door to Mr. Dunham's office.

Mr. Dunham looked at me over the top of his reading glasses as I knocked quietly on his open door. "Come in." He gestured to the chair on the other side of his desk. Behind him hung a floor-to-ceiling "Benson Bulldogs" that featured an angry bulldog wearing a red, white, and blue collar.

"Sorry I'm late. I started grading essays and lost track of time."

"It's fine. This won't take long." He paused, and I was struck by my sudden daughter-father need for his approval. I lowered myself slowly onto the chair—so as not to thump down on it like my mom has always accused me of doing—and waited for him to speak.

"Mr. and Mrs. Stoneman are very upset with Brandon for what he said to you in class the other day." He removed his glasses to be able to look at me directly. "I reassured them that teenagers make many mistakes, and this wouldn't be his last."

I forced a smile and nodded, waiting for him to continue.

"His mother's biggest concern is that it doesn't happen again because she's worried he will be kicked off of the basketball team with a second suspension. According to the handbook, she's right."

I continued nodding, wondering where he was going.

"The thing is," he placed his palms down on his desk and lowered his voice, "your private life is none of anyone's business. He had no right to say that to you."

I was beginning to feel like a bobble head. I hadn't told Mr. Dunham much about my personal life at all, but these things tend to travel through the grapevine. I didn't know if I should confirm or explain, so I just kept listening.

"However," he leaned back in his chair and put his hands on its arms, "to prevent any further problems, it is probably wise for you to not talk about your personal business in the classroom."

I stopped nodding. I had never once—ever—mentioned anything about being gay in my classroom. In fact, I went out of my way to rarely talk about myself at all, so it didn't accidentally come up. I heard myself say quietly, "I don't. I never have."

He stopped leaning back and sat up straighter. "Listen, I get it. It's not fair. Just do me a favor, and don't make any more waves. I already have parents calling and emailing me every day about Lord knows what."

I blinked. "Okay," I paused and then continued speaking, surprised by my confidence. "I told you I don't talk about my wife in front of my classes, and I don't. But I won't ever deny who I am to anyone who asks me. I won't lie. You don't ask any of the other teachers to keep quiet about their husbands or wives, do you?"

His lips formed a straight line as he considered my question. "I don't. And I imagine that must be hard for you."

I felt my brow furrow. "Okay," I stood up. "The bell is about to ring for third period. Can I go?" I was scolding myself for not thinking to bring union representation to the conversation, but I hadn't quite anticipated it going in that direction. I had thought maybe he would tell me to go easy on Brandon or maybe even give me some fatherly advice about not letting the words of an adolescent affect my self-esteem.

The bell rang before he could answer, and I turned and walked out. A flood of students flowed around me, laughing and talking with each other. One boy pushed another into a locker, and rather than tell them to knock it off and get to class, I sidestepped them and walked quickly away.

- 15 -

Wednesday, November 8, 2000

The Rocket was waiting outside the school when my friends and I left our musical rehearsal at 9:05. One of them asked if I needed a ride home, and I heard myself lie about my mom coming to pick me up. After I watched them all disappear into the dark parking lot, I smoothed my hair back into my ponytail and took a deep breath before approaching Cameron's car. I thought about the Jann Arden CD—*Living Under June*, the one that has the song on it that I had sung to her the night before— that I had put in my backpack that morning, hoping to give it to her as a gift.

She spotted me and pointed to the passenger side door and then leaned over to open it.

"Hi," I said casually as I got into the passenger seat. "Thanks for picking me up." She was looking at me with a half-smile, her blue eyes lingering on mine. The butterflies returned.

"Hi there," she replied. "It's no problem at all. Have you eaten yet?"

"Just some fries at lunch," I considered. "I could definitely eat."

"I know just the place." She made a right out of the parking lot, toward the highway. We drove in silence for a minute or two before she added, "How about that vote recount? They still don't know who won."

"It really is crazy. To think that a few people in Florida could make all the difference is even crazier."

"You got something against the people in Florida?" she asked.

I mentally kicked myself with the foot I was constantly putting in my mouth. "I didn't mean—"

"I'm just teasing you. I have never even been to Florida, and I don't know anyone who lives there." She grinned and looked at me briefly before returning her eyes to the road and getting on the ramp to the highway.

"Oh, good," I said. "I'm kind of famous for saying whatever is on my mind and offending people, and I thought I had struck again."

"Nope," Cameron kept smiling. "And I like a girl who speaks her mind."

I shifted in my seat, unable to accept that—once again—she was coming on to me. I looked at my knees and couldn't think of one single thing to say.

She glanced at me. "Relax," she said. "I'm not going to bite you."

I laughed nervously. "In the spirit of honesty, you should know I have never dated a girl before."

"So ... you're not gay?" She narrowed her eyes.

"Oh, I'm super gay. I've just never actually dated anyone before."

She laughed. "Yeah, I suppose there are slim pickin's around small towns like ours, huh? Well, then, are you calling this a date?"

I stumbled, "Uh, isn't ... I don't ... "

"I told you to relax!" she scolded me. "Okay, I'll do the talking for a little bit since you seem to be so nervous." She pinched my arm playfully. "Yes, this is a date. Last night, when I first saw you, I knew three things: 1) You were a new voter. 2) You were gay. 3) You were gorgeous."

I couldn't help but smile, thinking that I may have met my match in the candid speaking department.

"I mean," she continued, "look at those blue eyes and that delicious curly hair. Don't even get me started on those long legs." She bit her lower lip and looked at my legs which were currently covered by my favorite pair of boot-cut jeans. I self-consciously placed the palms of my hands on my thighs, and she took my left hand into her right and squeezed it gently. "Look, I can't explain why, but I felt an immediate connection to you. I had to pursue it, or I knew I would regret it."

I paused for a few seconds and then nodded. I had felt it, too. In fact, I hadn't stopped thinking about her since the night before but didn't want to wish too hard to see her again because what if she had changed her mind? Or what if it hadn't happened the way I had remembered it?

I forced myself to speak, "I felt it, too." I worried that my ears might catch fire, but I knew I would regret it if I stayed silent. "And I'm having a hard time accepting that a girl as hot as you is interested in me. I've spent the past four years of my life pining after straight girls, so reciprocation isn't exactly something I'm used to."

Cameron snorted. "Oh, honey, we have all been there. Have you really known for four years? What were you, like, fourteen?"

"Absolutely. I knew subconsciously for my entire life, but it didn't actually hit me until the middle of the night sometime during the summer before my eighth grade year."

"Oh yeah? What did it for you?" She squinted mischievously in anticipation of my response.

"Well, I had this friend named Layla, and she just always made me feel … well … hot. I never thought about why that was until that night, and I shot up in bed and actually said the words out loud: 'Whoa, I'm gay.' It was wild."

She laughed. "I was a bit of a late bloomer. I think I always knew, but I tried hard to move past it—like I could change it or something. Remember Brad from the other night?"

I nodded, remembering how familiar he had seemed with her.

"He and I dated for literally three years. He was my best friend, and I thought maybe it would turn into something more." She clicked on her turn signal to get off of the highway. "It never did."

Suddenly, she seemed more serious than I had seen her before. I didn't know if I should pry, but I was too curious not to ask some follow-up questions. "So when did you two break up?"

She calculated mentally. "About six months ago."

"What finally did it for you?" I turned to face her, trying to mimic the mischief she had shown me when asking the same question, but she looked more sad than playful.

"It was a mixture of things, really. There was a girl in one of my classes who had asked me out a few times, and I kept telling her I wasn't gay and that I was in a relationship with a guy." She paused. "But then I found myself picturing her when I was kissing Brad, and I knew something wasn't right."

A wave of jealousy overwhelmed me as I tried to picture her kissing Brad and—even worse—the girl who got to be in her thoughts.

I was afraid to ask but did, anyway, "So where is that girl now?"

"Oh," Cameron smiled and glanced at me as she pulled into the parking lot of what appeared to be a dive bar. "Josephine Rein, are you jealous? Oh, please tell me you're jealous." She parked the car and turned to face me.

"I think you might be changing the subject," I pointed out. "Look, Cameron, if you and this girl—"

"No," she interrupted, "I did go out with her a few times, but it didn't work out. Actually," she touched my red ear, "she turned out to be really boring. Like, there was just no spark at all. Do your ears always do this when you're nervous?"

I hunched my shoulders, feeling ticklish. "Yes, actually."

"It is unbelievably adorable." She leaned over the center console and gently rubbed her nose back and forth on my ear, making me shudder. "And please," she said quietly, "call me Cam."

"You," I felt breathless, "seem awfully brave for someone who has only been out for six months, Cam."

She sat back onto the driver's seat and laughed. "In hindsight, I've been imagining making out with girls for my entire life. So I think that counts."

We both unbuckled our seat-belts and got out of the car, and she said, "This place has the best chicken wings on the planet. Have you ever been here?"

I looked around and didn't recognize anything about where we were. "I have not."

"You're not, like, a vegetarian or anything, are you?" She

eyed me.

I laughed. "No. I love chicken wings. Can't you tell by this," I motioned to my curvy body, "that food is kind of my specialty?"

"I can think of some other things that might be your specialty," she whispered and then ran toward the entrance of the restaurant for me to follow her, but she stopped before we got inside.

"You should know," she turned around and looked seriously into my eyes, "that my family doesn't know yet." Her eyes left mine to dart around the parking lot, inspiring me to do the same. No one else was outside. When I looked back at her, her eyes had taken on an unexpected sadness again. "I'm an only child, and my parents are pretty conservative. They still think I'm with Brad, and I haven't worked up the nerve to tell them otherwise yet. It's why I brought you here, kind of far from home. I didn't want to run into anyone I might know."

I thought for a second, unable to imagine lying to my parents about anything—especially my dad. But I also couldn't imagine having parents who would judge me harshly for much of anything. I made a mental note to tell her to listen to a particular song on the Jann Arden CD—one about always feeling guilty about something—and said, "I guess I get it. My parents have known since about a week after I realized it because I can't keep my mouth shut about anything."

Her eyes were still serious. "Well, I'm sorry to have to ask this, but do you think you could keep us quiet for a while? Like not tell your family? I can just imagine your sister telling her friends, and then her friends telling Brad, and then Brad telling my—"

"Sure. Fine. I don't have to tell anyone." I had no idea she would expect me to keep us a secret for years to come. How could I have known? So I didn't find it to be that big of a deal.

I saw her visibly relax. "Thank you. It just makes everything easier. Now," her smile returned, "get ready for the chicken wing experience of a lifetime."

Monday, March 18, 2019

The bell rang for the end of fourth period, and I could feel myself start to clam up because I wasn't sure if I should mention anything to Kate about her essay when I saw her or if maybe I should just pretend like I hadn't read it yet, and that would buy me some time.

I walked into the hallway to supervise the class change and smiled at the students passing by, greeting the ones I knew by name and trying not to focus on who was walking through my door. The late bell rang, and I walked into my classroom, announcing a greeting to the class and beginning to explain the journal prompt about identity. Surveying the room, I noticed Kate was absent, even though I had seen her that morning. I made a mental note to remember to send that email to the counselor and to check the attendance list to see if Kate had gone home early.

"Mrs. R.," a girl from the center of the class called with her hand up.

"What's up, Madison?"

"Have you ever heard of slam poetry? My cousin was

watching slam poetry performances on YouTube last night, and I thought about how you would love it. Today's journal fits right in with one of the poems I just watched on TikTok this morning." She looked eager for my reaction.

"Yes, I have absolutely heard of slam poetry. Would you believe me if I told you that I've actually performed some of my own poetry before?" I thought back to the one night in college when I had done it, and the memory of the adrenaline rush got my blood pumping.

Some of the students "oohed," and some rolled their eyes. "I'm serious," I continued. "I don't just try to encourage you all to write because they pay me to. I truly believe in the written word because it has been transformative for me in my own life."

Madison was nodding. "Can we do slam poetry in class ever? I think a lot of us would really like it."

Many of her classmates groaned. "Oh, quit it," I said. "You guys don't ever want to do anything, and I bet most of you don't even know what it is! Yes, Maddie, I'm sure we can find some time for that at some point."

"Awesome!" she said. "We're talking about identity now, so we could write poems about that. It would be so easy."

I considered this. "Well," I began, "why don't we try it soon?"

Maddie looked at her friends, who looked just as excited as she did. "Can you play a video for us? Like Rudy Francisco's 'My Honest Poem'? It would be a perfect example."

"Let's get through this lesson first, and then we can watch it."

I continued introducing the novel we would be starting the next week. I spoke about the author's identity as a black woman and asked how those two factors—race and gender—can affect people's experiences. I asked the class to name other factors in our identities that contribute to our experiences, and they named some like education and money. I mentioned a quotation from the novel where the narrator talks about being too young for something to happen when she was a teenager when she "wasn't even anybody yet" and asked the class what they feel their age prevents them from doing, besides the obvious things like driving and graduating and drinking. They mentioned things about how adults don't take them seriously and how they wish they could travel the world. I did the participle activity with them and had them look back into their journal entries from that day. Nobody called anyone's examples gay that time.

Looking out into the class, knowing that we had a few extra minutes, I said, "So when we begin this novel next week, I want you to keep in mind how there are zillions of things that contribute to who we are and how we feel about ourselves—and who we want to and allow ourselves to be."

"Can we watch that video now?" a voice called from the back.

I checked the time again. "Sure. Let me find it online and put it on the board for you." I asked Maddie to remind me of the poet's name and poem title. "This isn't going to have, like, profanity in it, is it?" I asked Maddie.

"Not at all. You'll see."

I shut off the lights and pressed play. It's essentially a list poem about the poet's identity that twists and turns from humor to poignancy and back again. I couldn't remember the last time I had watched someone perform a poem, and I was transfixed. When he finished speaking, I looked at the kids' faces to find that almost all of them were feeling the same way.

"Wow," I said aloud. "That was awesome. Would you guys like to do something like that?"

Many of them looked uncertain, but quite a few of them nodded enthusiastically.

"Okay," I continued. "How about we make it extra credit? Nobody has to do it, but anyone who wants to can stay after school with me sometimes to write some performance poems."

"Can we have a poetry slam, like, on the stage?" It was Maddie again. She was looking directly at me with a mixture of hope and excitement.

"Why not?" I conceded, and several of them started talking to each other excitedly. The bell rang, and I wondered what I had just gotten myself into.

Brandon was uncharacteristically quiet during eighth period, but I was still exhausted by its end from being on constant alert to his every move. Once all of the kids left, I sat down at my desk and just put my head down for a few minutes, closing my eyes and willing myself to breathe evenly. The only other sounds were the air vent and the distant melody of the marching band practicing on the football field.

I knew I had to email Dom Madden that very day, in case Kate decided to mention something to her parents. If they found out about the essay, and I hadn't told anyone at all about it, I didn't think that would look great on my part. My role in the situation was to be the responsible adult who turned the matter over to a better-qualified responsible adult. As much as I sympathized with Kate and would be fine with her confiding in me off the record, I just didn't feel comfortable with what was becoming something of a paper trail.

Opening my inbox to no new messages was a pleasant surprise. Deciding to jump right to it, I clicked "compose" and typed "student concern" in the subject line before beginning the message:

Dom,

Hey! I hope you're doing well. We haven't chatted in a while. Liesel is almost finished with her first year of preschool, so your little one must be almost done with kindergarten. Time really does fly, doesn't it?

I'm writing because I got an interesting assignment from a student today that I'd like you to read. I'm not sure what to do about it, so I'll just drop a copy of it in your mailbox, okay?

Thanks, and happy Monday,
  Josie

I hit "send" and grabbed Kate's essay from the top of the pile to go make a quick copy of it. Thankfully, no one else was in the copy room, so it really was a quick job. Back in my classroom, I grabbed an envelope, folded the essay, and stuck it inside, writing "from Josie" on the outside. On my way out of the school, I stepped inside the office and slid the envelope into Dom's mailbox.

I felt myself breathe more easily as the essay was literally out of my hands, especially as I stepped outside into the recently-warming air. The sun was shining, and I knew I was going to roll the windows down on my way home and listen to music, probably shuffling the playlist that I've creatively named "Sing Loudly."

I took my phone out of my pocket to get the playlist ready. Sara Bareilles, Jewel, Celine Dion, Mariah Carey, Sarah McLachlan—oh yeah, I was going to crank that stuff up.

And then I saw her.

Kate was standing near the driver's side door of my car, wearing the same clothes I'd seen her in that morning. She was alternating between looking at me and looking everywhere but at me. I wondered if Dom had read the essay already and called her parents. But that wasn't possible when I had just put the essay in his mailbox ... what ... five minutes beforehand? Had I even mentioned her actual name in the email? I tried to remember.

"Hey, Kate," I tried to sound casual, putting my phone back into my pocket. "You okay? I didn't see you in class today."

She wasn't looking at me. "I know. I'm sorry." She glanced up and then back down. "I skipped English. You can, like, write me up or whatever."

Suddenly, I was keenly aware that she was about to start crying. "Hey. Hey, what's the matter?" I stepped closer to her, and she looked back up at me again—this time, her face collapsing into a sob.

My bag thudded to the ground as I fought the instinct to hug her. I looked around briefly and didn't see anyone watching, but I could still hear the marching band practicing, so we definitely weren't alone. Or maybe being alone would be even worse?

I ended up just awkwardly standing there, watching her cry and saying, "It's okay. I'm not going to write you up. You're not in trouble."

Shaking her head back and forth vigorously, she suddenly appeared resolute and said, "I don't care. I was afraid to face you after giving you that essay. Did you read it? Oh God, you didn't read it, did you?" She started crying again. "I almost didn't turn it in, but then after you put your hand on my shoulder the other day, I just felt ... " Her voice trailed off.

Put my hand on her shoulder?

My heart started racing. I pictured, in slow motion, how I had patted her shoulder after reading her words about Brandon.

And now she wanted to actually talk about the essay, which definitely did not mean it was out of my hands.

"Yes," I started, unsure how to continue other than to not acknowledge touching her in class, "I read it. I'm not upset about it, Kate. I'm ... flattered and ... proud of you."

Her eyes met mine. "Really? You're not mad?"

"How could I be mad? You didn't do anything wrong." I was suddenly positive that I had to make that clear to her. "Nothing you said was wrong, Kate. There is nothing wrong with you."

She sniffed and looked back down. "Tell that to my parents."

I hesitated again. "I can imagine that is really hard for you, but some people just take time getting used to when ... their kid isn't who they expected them to be."

We were both quiet for a minute before she said so quietly that I almost didn't hear her, "I meant what I said. All of it. I admire you."

I felt heat rise to my ears. "Thank you, Kate. That means a lot to me."

"And I meant what I said in class the other day about being born into a family who isn't accepting and having to make friends to fill those gaps."

I wasn't sure where she was going. We obviously couldn't be friends. "And I'm sure you have some great friends."

"No—I mean, I do—I mean ... " She was back to not looking at me. I watched her inhale sharply and then practically spit the words, "Will you sponsor a Gay Straight Alliance?"

I blinked—hard—a handful of times. *Sponsor a club—like, a literal gay club? Could there actually be anything more public than that? I might as well throw rainbow flags up around my classroom and wear a hat that says "DYKE" on it all day long.*

But fourteen-year-old Josie's voice was whispering underneath my doubts. She reminded me of the loneliness. She played a seconds-long highlights reel of all of the times in high school when I would have done anything just knowing that people there supported me and that I wasn't alone—that I didn't have to build up a wall and pretend to enjoy distancing myself from everyone.

Plenty of schools have a GSA, and Benson High School wasn't one of them, but I never thought of myself as someone who would be involved even if it did.

She continued, "There are lots of kids like me in school, and we just don't have anywhere to go to ... you know ... just be. And we thought you made the most sense as the sponsor. Well, you or Mr. Flemming, but I suggested you because you're always so interested in stuff like identity. Plus, Maddie told me about the slam poetry stuff, and I thought maybe we could, like, do that as a fundraiser for the new GSA or something." She was suddenly talking a mile a minute.

I put my hands up. "Whoa, whoa. Slow down. I hear everything you're saying, but I'm really going to have to think about it. A GSA would have to be approved by the school board. It would take some leg work."

"So you'll do it?" She looked giddy as she waited for my response.

I sighed, not wanting to disappoint her or the young Josie in my mind. "Honestly, I don't know. I want to, but I don't know. I hope you understand how ... vulnerable that would make me. I'm not sure I'm ready for that."

She bit her lip. "Yeah. Yeah, I get that. Okay ... you can think about it. And just because we don't have an official sponsor yet doesn't mean we can't start meeting, right?"

"Well, not on school property, unfortunately. And you can't

advertise or anything until it's approved."

"What about like on TikTok or something? Just to see who's interested?"

I laughed and shook my head. "Kate, I don't even know what TikTok is, but if it isn't school-related, then go for it."

Before I knew what was happening, she was hugging me. I instinctively raised my hands and stood there with them in the air and her arms wrapped around my waist. I looked around again to see if anyone was watching, saw no one again, and brought my hands down to awkwardly pat her back.

"Thank you," she whispered as she pulled away.

"I haven't done anything for you to thank me for. I'm just here, existing." I motioned at myself.

"No." She shook her head. "You do more than you know."

And, with that, she started trotting away, yelling behind her, "See you in class tomorrow!"

- 18 -

Sunday, May 13, 2018

Liesel and I sang "Old McDonald" for the entire ride to the grocery store that morning. We were both feeling tired because she had had a rough night—night terrors and a persistent runny nose—so I was trying to keep her awake by singing animatedly. Music has always both soothed and excited her. In the middle of the night, Cam and I had taken turns in her room. Cam calms her by cuddling, and I calm her by singing. Ever since she was a baby, she has pretty reliably calmed down by the end of my version of Eva Cassidy's rendition of "Songbird." Her bright blue baby eyes used to glaze over as she listened to the moving notes and forgot whatever it was that was upsetting her; it can still work that way most of the time.

Cam was training for a marathon and would be gone for hours at a time on her training runs, especially on the week-ends, so Liesel and I had fallen into a Sunday morning routine of grocery shopping together. I sang the animal sounds both enthusiastically and absent-mindedly as I drove and looked periodically in the rear-view mirror to be sure her eyes were open. Once, she caught me and smiled. We were singing about a cow, which I remember because she formed her mouth into a tight "o" with her mooing, and it made me laugh. I told her she was silly and adorable as we pulled into the busy grocery store parking lot.

We parked as close as we could to the entrance, and I picked her up out of her car seat. She wrapped her legs around my waist and her arms around my neck until we got inside, and I set her into a cart's seat, her chubby two-year-old legs dangling. Continuing our song as we entered the produce section, I put our usuals in the cart: apples, bananas, carrots, cucumbers, and some other things, and Liesel was singing about the fruits and vegetables like they were on Old McDonald's farm. We had a grand time thinking about what sounds they would make. (Apples would definitely crunch.)

Turning the corner to the cereal aisle, she spotted a box of Lucky Charms.

"Charms!" she yelled excitedly.

"I see them, baby," I said, "but we're not going to get any of those today. Let's grab some Cheerios." Amanda had introduced her to Lucky Charms at some point over summer vacation, which did not thrill Cam or me. We'd tried hard to keep her sugar consumption to a minimum for as long as we could control it, but not everyone in our families was on board with our efforts.

"Charms!" she yelled again, smacking her little hands on the cart's handle.

"Not today, honey," I said. "I'm sorry if that disappoints you."

I could see the tantrum in our near future, so I quickly tried to distract her by singing what Cheerios might say on the farm (obviously "oh oh" both here and there), but it was no use. Her face crumpled, and she started kicking her legs and pounding her hands on the cart harder.

"Mommy!" she screamed. "I want Mommy!"

"Baby, Mama's here," I tried to soothe her quietly.

"No! Mommy! Mommy!"

People were starting to look at us, and I could feel my ears turning red. Not many other situations can so accurately highlight the feeling of being "the other mother" as when your child is yelling for Mommy in a store, and other people start wondering if you've kidnapped her.

"Okay, baby," I said, wheeling quickly away from the cereal aisle—even past the Cheerios, which I knew she would miss. "Let's go see what kinds of yogurt we should get!"

"No! Mommy! Get away!" She was now hitting me instead of the cart. Her fists would sometimes catch my arms or my hands, and she was kicking her legs so hard that the cart was practically rocking.

And that was when I lost my composure. I bent forward and grabbed her arms to stop them from pumping, and I said through my teeth in her ear, "Stop it. You're making a scene, and people are going to think I'm not your mother."

"Mommy! Where's Mommy?" she was wailing at this point.

"Is everything all right?" a strange male voice asked and added, before I could even see where it was coming from, "Should we call her mother?"

I spun around to see one of the store workers holding an electronic price checker in one hand, staring at us. An elderly couple had stopped nearby, too, and were looking in our direction, the old woman shaking her head disapprovingly.

I stood up straight and said to the worker, loudly over

Liesel's screeches, "I am her mother." I hesitated. "I'm one of her mothers. Her other mom would be more likely to buy her Lucky Charms, so that's why she's upset." I tried to make light of the situation, but all three of them appeared at various levels of suspicion.

The worker nodded slowly, looking from me to the still-tantruming Liesel and back—probably assessing whether she looked like me enough to be my kid, as if that matters. He seemed satisfied and returned to his price checking, probably hoping we would leave soon. I fixated briefly on the tie of his red apron and didn't notice that the elderly couple had moved closer.

"Just get her the cereal," the woman said quietly, in an I-know-better-than-you voice. At the same second, Liesel began to sob as if she were devastated by the weight of the world on her shoulders, and she was reaching for me to hold her. I side-eyed the woman and picked Liesel up out of the cart and held her to me, rocking her a bit and telling her that it was okay. She whispered in my ear, exhausted: "Charms please, Mama."

I sighed. "Okay, baby. If they mean that much to you."

I held her with my right arm and pushed the cart with my left, guiding it back to the Lucky Charms. I let her pick a box off of the shelf and toss it into the cart while I made a mental note to murder my sister the next time I saw her.

- 19 -

Tuesday, March 19, 2019

The drive to work that morning was a blur. The night before was a constant struggle to not tell Cam about the whole situation with Kate because I didn't want to worry her about something that could actually turn out to be nothing. With Kate's parents not on board, she would probably lose steam on the GSA idea, and Dom Madden would take care of the issue with the essay.

... and yet I couldn't help calling myself a hypocritical coward for so quickly dismissing the idea of the GSA. I had become a teacher to positively impact the lives of my students, and I couldn't think of a downside when I framed it that way. Was it risky to put my own name on it? Depends on how you defined "risky." Could it piss off some students and their parents? Maybe, but it had the more likely potential to bring people together. Would it further highlight my own sexuality? Yes, but that seemed to already be circulating among the masses, anyway. What actual harm could it do?

So I diverted my attention from researching slam poems to researching local school districts' LGBTQ+-affirming extracurriculars. Benson High's neighbor to the south is significantly more liberal as it's closer to the city, so I started there.

Riverfront High School's website listed all of its clubs in alphabetical order, and it didn't take me long to skim from Art Club to the Gay Straight Alliance. I clicked on the link and was taken to a page that displayed a current calendar of events, a bright rainbow flag, and the following mission statement:

Join us each Wednesday afternoon in the RHS commons area for cookies and Harvey Milk! [wink emoji]

We are the Gay Straight Alliance, and we aim to be a safe space to bring together lesbian,
gay, bisexual, trans, and straight students in a positive environment where everyone can chat, learn, and express themselves.

Got questions? Ask Mr. Wise in Room 116!

I admired Mr. Wise's puns and simultaneously ached for my adolescent self. What I would have given to be supported like that at school—to know that I wasn't alone and that I was normal enough to have an actual school-sponsored activity just for kids like me?

While driving that morning, it occurred to me that I could look up Mr. Wise's email address and reach out to him to get some ideas. But, first, I had to decide if I was truly giving the sponsorship serious consideration.

Even if the answer was yes, I had to talk to Cam about it first.

Walking into the school, my mind turned to poetry. I had decided to have all of my kids write identity poems to coincide with the beginning of our new novel, and some of them might want to turn those poems into something performable.

Not many people were at school yet so early in the still-dark morning, so I took advantage of the quiet by closing my classroom door, turning on the table lamp on my desk, and settling in to research some more videos to show to my classes. There is a website called Button Poetry that frequently posts videos of performance poems, so I made my way to their "classroom friendly" section of YouTube and started considering which videos to show that day.

I was just getting to the end of an electrifying poem by Tova Charles called "Dark Skin" when a notification popped up in the corner of my screen that I had received an email from Mr. Dunham. I decided to finish the video first before reading it, and then, still smiling about the poet's metaphors and passionate delivery, I opened my inbox. The subject line of Mr. Dunham's email read "Fwd: Kate's essay."

My stomach flipped, and I had to steady myself by grabbing a hold of my desk as a wave of nausea swept over me. I considered calling Cam and telling her everything, so I didn't have to be alone when I read it, but I knew that would be selfish. She would still be getting Liesel ready to take to her parents' house. My pulse was racing as I picked up the phone and dialed Dana's classroom.

It rang twice before she picked up. "Wilson," she stated.

"Dana? Do you have a minute? I … "

"Josie? What's wrong?"

"I … I got an email from Dunham that I don't want to read alone. Can I read it to you?" My voice was shaking.

"No," I could hear her typing. "Let me finish up this email to a parent, and I'll be right over."

She hung up, and I set the phone down hard. I had done

exactly as I'd planned: I had emailed Dom Madden about Kate's essay. I had put her grade in the online grade book (a B+ with points missing for lack of detail and commas) and written a polite "Thanks, Kate!" at the bottom of the paper. I had briefly acknowledged the essay when she approached me in the parking lot, but I made sure not to make a big deal of it, and no one knew about that, anyway … did they? Did Kate tell someone that she had spoken to me in the parking lot?

Dana opened the door and closed it behind her. "What happened? Didn't you say he called you down to his office yesterday?"

"He did," I confirmed, "and he was weird about the whole thing, telling me to stop talking about my private life in the classroom."

"You don't do that."

"I know I don't. I kind of stormed out after telling him off a little bit and haven't spoken to him since. This email … I know what it's about, and I am genuinely afraid to open it." I couldn't look at Dana, a sudden shame overtaking me.

"What?" She came to stand beside me. "What's it about?" She leaned over my shoulder and read the subject line for herself. "Who's Kate?"

I breathed audibly. "She's a quiet girl in my fifth-period class who only very recently started speaking to me." I glanced up at her face.

She raised her eyebrows. "And?"

"And she wrote her Women's History Month essay about how I've had a positive impact on her." I leaned forward and put my face into my hands, and Dana put a hand on my shoulder.

"What am I missing? What's wrong with that?"

Shaking my head without taking my hands away from my face, I told her, "One of her reasons for idolizing me is because she and I are both gay."

"Oh, shit," Dana whispered.

"It gets worse." I looked up at her. "Her essay mentioned that her parents are homophobic. Oh my God, what am I going to do?" I felt a lump forming in my throat.

"Stop," Dana said firmly. "You don't even know what the email says yet. Here," she shooed me out of my chair. "Go sit at a student desk, and I'll read it to you, so you don't have to look at the words yet."

Not in the right frame of mind to argue, I obeyed and thumped down on a cold, metal student chair as she slid into my office chair. Her finger double-clicked, and her eyes began moving across the screen.

"Do you want me to read the whole thing before I read it to you or just read it aloud as I go?" She looked at me.

I groaned. "Just get it over with and read it to me."

"Okay," she looked back at the screen. "The top is from Dunham to you and says, 'What do you know about this?' The attached message is from someone named Brian Anderson. Is that Kate's dad?"

"I think so," I said quietly.

"Okay," she repeated. "That message says, 'Mr. Dunham, My daughter, Kate Anderson, came home from school today with a headache and mentioned something about turning in an essay late for English class. She seemed very stressed about it, so I checked online for her grade and saw she received a B on the assignment. Please ensure that she did not lose any points for turning in the assignment late. She had the flu last week and should have been granted extra time. Thanks, Brian

Anderson"

Dana smiled and looked at me as I breathed a sigh of relief. "See?" she asked. "The universe is smiling on you today."

"Yeah, okay," I slumped down in the chair and leaned my head back onto it. "This doesn't change the fact that the essay is now on everyone's radar when I had been hoping to ignore it for the rest of my life."

"I don't think this guy sounds like he actually cares what the essay says—just what the grade is on it." She raised one eyebrow.

Standing up, I nodded slightly. "I hope you're right. Thanks for coming so quickly. I thought I might have a heart attack."

She sang, "That's what friends are for!" as she walked out of the room.

I sat back down in my chair and hit the reply button, being sure to CC Mr. Anderson.

Good morning! Kate's essay was not marked late, but she did lose a few points based on the state writing rubric. Thanks for reaching out, and let me know if you have any other questions or concerns!

Have a great day,
  Mrs. Rein-Thompson

I hit send and was just about to close my inbox when an email from Dom Madden appeared. Blowing an enormous breath at my computer monitor, I reluctantly opened the message.

Re: student concern

Hey Josie! Yeah, time does fly. Our Dominic just turned six and is absolutely crushing kindergarten! Thanks for asking.

I read Kate's essay and see why you're concerned. I'm going to call her down to my office sometime in the next few days.

Happy almost spring!
  Dom

Before I had a second to think about his words, the bell for first period rang, and a group of basketball players came pouring in the doorway, horsing around and laughing.

"Whoa, guys!" I stood up and put out my hands to prevent them from literally wrestling into me. "Save that for practice. I'd rather not sustain any injuries today."

I lost my prep that day because I was asked to cover a class. It was a choir class, so I didn't mind. They were expecting to have the day off because their teacher was absent, but I made them sing the latest song they'd been working on—a lovely a cappella version of Mariah Carey's "Hero" that one of them called "an oldie" (Be still my 90s heart). For that short while, I let myself savor the warmth of the music and even sang with them once. One of them asked me why I wasn't a choir teacher, and I told her I loved writing and grammar too much to be anything but an English teacher ... but I did sometimes wonder the same thing myself.

All this to say that I didn't have much time to think about Dom's email or Kate or the GSA, so when Kate walked into my fifth period class wearing a literal rainbow on her shirt and another one pinned in her hair, I was ... taken aback. I tried really hard not to show it or to look at her too much at all while I took the class through the day's lesson on poetic devices, and I was managing okay until Jaiden interrupted me mid-sentence from the front row.

"Speaking of rhyming, have you seen Kate's latest TikTok, Mrs. R.?" Both challenge and amusement were in his eyes. I quickly considered my deflection.

"Honey, I don't even know what TikTok is. Let's raise our hands if we have something to contribute, okay? Now, many poems that rhyme have what is called a rhyme scheme—"

Jaiden raised his hand.

"Yes, Jaiden?"

"You should seriously watch it." He turned around to look at Kate in the back of the room and called, "When you rhymed 'gay' with 'castaway'," he showed her a chef's kiss, " … absolute bars."

Kate blushed as she looked at me and then back down to her desk.

"Come on, Mrs. R.," the student next to Kate—Alexis—added, "this is totally relevant. Kate did a TikTok about how we want to start a GSA here at Benson, and it's, like, a whole poem."

Kate's hand went to her forehead as more students agreed that I should at least watch Kate's TikTok. I raised my hands to calm them, for Kate's sake as much as for the sake of order, and they eventually quieted down but not without many of them looking at me expectantly.

"You guys, I'm serious. I wouldn't know the first thing about watching a TikTok video. Is that on Facebook? I don't use Facebook."

They erupted with laughter. Jaiden smiled and explained, "Just go home and download the TikTok app. We'll help you find the video tomorrow."

I glanced back at Kate who was now watching me shyly between fingers that covered her eyes. I shrugged. "Okay. You can show me tomorrow. Go ahead and clean up. The bell's going to ring any second."

While they chatted (mostly about TikTok) and got ready

to leave, I walked over to my desk to check my email. I was pleased to see that there weren't any other messages from Dom or Mr. Dunham, and everything else seemed uneventful enough—a reminder to submit calendar items to the office secretary, a bell schedule to include Friday's pep rally, a response to a group message about an upcoming potluck lunch, and a subject-less message from a person whose name I didn't recognize: I.C. You. I shook my head at what was probably a student's attempt at a creative alias and clicked on it.

Dear snowflake,

Sorry to pull you away from your career in virtue signaling, but I thought you might want to know that I saw you yesterday. See attached video.

I.C. You

The bell rang, and it didn't take long before my classroom was utterly silent. I read the words three or four more times before understanding them. My eyes traveled downward and landed on the attachment named IMG_1411.

One plus four is five.

Five plus one is six plus one is seven.

Click-click. And there I was, standing across from Kate, both of us within arm's reach of my car—and arm's reach of each other. As if in slow motion, she leaned forward and wrapped her arms around me. I hesitated with my arms in the air, looked around like a criminal, and brought my hands down to pat her on the back.

No. There wasn't anyone there. I looked around several times. The marching band was practicing on the field, but we weren't even close to the field. This angle is from ... behind the school van that was parked in the lot? Like someone was hiding behind it, waiting to see something? Waiting for me?

I closed the video file, the email, and my inbox in quick succession. What could someone do with a video like that? What would someone *want* with a video like that? I wished I had never agreed to talk with Kate when I saw her standing at my car. I should have told her that whatever it was could wait until school today. She could have waited to say whatever she needed to say in class, in front of over twenty witnesses. For some reason, she wanted to speak to me alone.

Except we weren't alone.

- 21 -

Monday, May 6, 1996

Mrs. Graham, our religion teacher, stood at the front of the classroom behind a worn wooden podium. The topic of the day, which had been written on the blackboard, was The Golden Rule. We were taking notes in preparation for our seventh-grade year-end final. I liked Mrs. Graham because she let us philosophize at a time in our lives when we were just learning how to do that. However, she was an incredibly boring speaker, so I found myself daydreaming frequently while she lectured us about this-or-that Bible verse.

The day before, Layla, Andrew, and I had stayed after school with Mrs. Graham to practice for the spelling bee, and Mrs. Graham had had a rough time keeping us from incessantly giggling. At one point, she had chided, "All right, you three, let's get focused. Layla, it's your turn. Miscalculations." And then Layla had wrinkled her nose and said, "Miss who?" Andrew and I then fell into an absolute fit of laughter, and Layla's brown eyes—usually wise beyond her thirteen years— had given away her embarrassment. I, through my tears, saw this and pulled Layla to me in an awkward side-hug.

While Mrs. Graham was reviewing for our religion final that day, I could not stop thinking about that hug and how soft her skin had felt—how warm my own body had felt after touching her. While I sat there in my itchy skirt, next to a boy named Raymond who was nice but smelled bad and had embarrassingly been my boyfriend for a few days the year before, I tried unsuccessfully to listen to Mrs. Graham but was expending much more energy stealing glances at Layla who was sitting three seats down the aisle from me.

After reminding our class what The Golden Rule was, Mrs. Graham asked for some examples. Layla raised her hand and said, "It's like when you see someone homeless on a sidewalk, and you give them money because that's how you would want someone to treat you."

"Great example, Layla. Class, write in your notebooks: 'Help the poor.' Who else wants to give an example?"

I was still looking at Layla, admiring her intellect and her brown eyes. She was a quick thinker and could always come up with an answer the teacher wanted. She must have felt me looking at her because she turned to look at me and smiled. I smiled shyly and looked down at my notebook to write the notes.

I missed the next student's response but heard Mrs. Graham tell the class to write down our next example: "Be kind to those who are sad." I wrote it down and then looked back in Layla's direction where I saw her quietly tearing off a piece of her notebook paper and folding it. She leaned over, handed it to Raymond while whispering something to him, and he handed the paper to me under my desk.

Looking down, I saw my name in Layla's loopy handwriting on the outside of the folded paper. I opened it and read the words inside, "Your hair looks pretty. Love, Miss Calculations. '' I stifled a giggle and looked over at her. She was smiling at me, and I mouthed the words "thank you" as I felt my body temperature rise.

Mrs. Graham spoke sternly, "Josephine, will you please repeat the last example that you were to write down?"

Widening my eyes, I looked not-so-subtly at Raymond's notebook, searching for the right answer, but he hadn't written it down, either. Mrs. Graham shook her head scoldingly and said, "Please pay attention. You will need these examples to write your final essay." She looked at the rest of the class. "Can someone please repeat the example for Josephine?"

Andrew raised his hand and half-smiled at me, "Love the sinner, but hate the sin, like if someone is a drug addict or a homosexual or something."

I copied down the first part of the sentence and wondered if I was supposed to write the rest, but I was too afraid to ask.

- 22 -

Tuesday, March 19, 2019

After the last bell of the day, I stayed in my classroom and leaned back against the closed door, listening to the familiar hallway chaos and feeling comforted by its predictability. I had taught my afternoon classes on autopilot, keeping any and all emotions at bay—even when Brandon entered the room for eighth period looking as smug as ever. He was easy to ignore because he rarely participated in class discussions, so I kept my attention on the students who wanted to engage. Now, with my eyes closed and the wood flat against my back, I reached for the door knob and locked it.

I kept my eyes closed and pictured my hands on Kate's back, tentative but undeniable, and felt the room start to spin. Sliding down to the floor, I pulled my knees in close, buried my face in my khaki pants, and forced myself to retrace every single one of my steps from the afternoon before in an attempt to remember who could have been in or near that parking lot.

On the way out of the building, I had passed Jim, a custodian, who was engrossed in scrubbing some graffiti off of a glass trophy case. Jim had no reason to want to take a video of me doing anything; in fact, he and I were on friendly terms and even chatted occasionally about the weather. Did he have some secret connection to someone who might want something bad to happen to me?

Brandon. I couldn't believe I hadn't thought about it before. Brandon was surely still pissed about the suspension. And he hadn't said a word to me since ... because he'd been planning his revenge?

I looked up and squinted at the afternoon sun pouring into the windows, deciding that I had to look at the email again to see if it looked like something Brandon could have written. I got up and went back over to my desk.

Looking more closely this time, I saw that the actual email address was i.see.you.snowflake@gmail.com. Whoever it was had called me "snowflake" in the message so had created the account just for me? A teenage boy could easily do that. Even Brandon, who really is very lazy except for on the basketball court, could do that.

A teenage boy could know the slang word "snowflake" that was meant to "own the libs," implying that my being a lesbian was somehow "a choice" in asserting my uniqueness and that being insulted about it was a symptom of my own pathetic emotional fragility ... right?

But what teenage boy would use the phrasing "See attached video"? Wouldn't a teenager say something more direct like "Look at this video I took"? "See attached video" sounded more like office-speak, so unless Brandon was being coached by a middle-aged office worker, I couldn't imagine that he had written those words.

Kate's parents. What if they had found out about the essay already, and they were following Kate to catch her with a girl or something ... and then they had caught her with *me*?

This knocked the wind out of me. I gasped at the sudden certainty that it had to be Kate's parents—at least one of them. It made complete sense. It was meant as a warning for me to stay away from their daughter, or else … what? Could they press charges against me for some sort of indecent advances on their daughter? Would that video be proof enough? Would Kate deny it, or would she be too afraid to stand up to the parents who had already made her feel unloved?

My dad's face appeared in my mind—how he used to look before those last few years when he stopped taking care of himself and was drunk most of the time. He had smiled so easily when I was a kid, and most people around him had done the same. *If I could talk to him now, he would say, "Well, Jojo, do you feel like you've done something wrong? Because if you do, you've probably done something wrong?"*

That's the problem, Dad. I'm not sure. I've spent my whole life as someone who some people feel is "wrong" simply by existing, and it's impossible not to sometimes believe them.

Against my better judgment, I clicked on the video again, imagining one of Kate's parents standing behind the device that took it.

I wondered what I was going to tell Cam. She didn't know anything about Kate at all, so how was I going to tell her the whole story from start to finish without completely freaking her out? It's true that we got married in 2014 and never pretended like we weren't together as we traveled through our family's life together, but Cam never supported the idea of me being out at work. She was too worried about me being harassed or somehow putting my job in jeopardy. She wasn't out to her students … but they were in kindergarten. It wasn't the same thing.

And if she was worried about me being harassed or losing my job, look what was already happening. I spent all of those years keeping my private life a secret, and for what? To be harassed and to maybe even lose my job.

I pressed the power button on the computer, grabbed my coat and bag, and walked out the door. By the time I was outside, I felt more angry than anything. *No, Dad, I didn't do anything wrong. What can I do about the people who think I did?*

In the distance, I could see a woman running on the track that loops around the football field. I hurried to my car, in case that woman was Kate's mom—who I was sure I wouldn't recognize, anyway. As I drove toward the exit and closer to the track, I was surprised that I actually did recognize the woman. It was Sharon, Cam's friend from the gym. She was jogging in a sports bra and bike shorts—a little risqué for the mother of a preschooler, if you ask me.

I bet Sharon never has to deal with this shit. She's a perfect, skinny, straight woman whose husband probably posts pictures of their family vacations on Facebook and brags about her to his co-workers while they play golf on a Tuesday.

My stomach growled. I hadn't been hungry for lunch after reading the email. I pulled out of the parking lot, and it didn't take long before McDonald's was in view. I decided to grab some fries and a milkshake and then head home to make dinner. No one would ever know.

- 23 -

Wednesday, March 20, 2019

I woke up that morning about twenty minutes before my alarm, disappointed that I had cheated myself out of that last precious sliver of sleep. I was just coming out of a dream in which the screen of a digital pregnancy test had read "NEVER" in big, bold letters, and it caused me to wake with a boulder of disappointment lodged in my stomach. Rolling over, I slipped my head under Cam's outstretched arm as she slept, and she pulled me closer, her long, warm hair falling onto my face.

No, I hadn't told her about Kate the night before. Instead, I had downloaded TikTok, and after we put Liesel to bed, we laughed and laughed at about a hundred videos of strangers doing ridiculous things. It would have felt blasphemous to break the spell.

Burrowing into her that morning, I took a mental inventory of my body to see if anything felt different—if I felt pregnant in some way. I knew it was too early to know anything, but during the cycle of my chemical pregnancy, I had noticed a few small things were amiss—like occasional ringing in my ears and light-headedness—that I was hoping for again.

"Good morning, gorgeous," she whispered.

I found her mouth with my own and kissed her gently, then whispered, "Good morning. I'm going to head to work early again. I want to finish the last of those essays, so they're not hanging over my head anymore. Is that okay? I packed Liesel's lunch. It's in the fridge." I sat up.

She brushed her hair out of her eyes. "Sure, babe." She cupped my cheek with her hand. "I love you. Have a good day."

"I love you, too, honey. See you later."

I quietly grabbed my clothes and headed to the downstairs shower, so both Cam and Liesel could sleep for a little while longer. I told myself I would swing through a McDonald's drive-thru (again) so as not to wake them with the coffee maker or microwave ... but that was just an excuse to get a breakfast sandwich and a couple of hash browns. I ate while listening to Sara Bareilles's powerhouse voice, feeling my usual mixture of admiration and jealousy. She hit a note that gave me chills, and I immediately started to cry because I couldn't share the song with my dad. Tears spilled onto my cheeks as I chewed the last of my second hash brown and pulled into the parking lot of the school.

That happens to me in unexpected moments—but usually when I'm listening to music that either he loved or that I love and am unable to share with him. Thinking about the decades of upcoming music for which this will be true takes the wind out of me.

I disposed of the evidence in my trusty garbage can and walked through the quiet, empty halls to my classroom, switching on my desk lamp—consciously avoiding my email. I only had one period of essays left to grade, so I was confident

I could get them done before first period. The name Lisa Simpson jumped out at me from the essay on the top of the pile, and I smiled at how sweet and innocent my students could be. There truly is never a dull moment.

But my computer was taunting me. What if there was another email? I gave in, pushing the essays aside yet again, and turned the computer on.

There were ten new emails in my inbox, almost all of them junk mail. I deleted most of them and then stopped at one from a "Brian A.", subject line "Re: Fwd: Kate's essay", sent at 9:38 the night before. I don't know if I was still feeling sluggishly invested in that morning's dream or what, but I didn't panic. I felt numb and detached as I clicked on it and read:

Ms. Rein-Thompson,

My wife and I received a call from Mr. Madden the school counselor this evening who proceeded to tell us that you told him to speak with Kate about the essay she wrote for your class. When he explained why he had become involved, we were appalled that you hadn't contacted us about it first.

After conversing with our daughter about this matter, it has come to our attention that you have been encouraging her to "come out" as a homosexual by insisting that she, a 15-year-old girl, reflect on who she is and who she wants to be. Because she idolizes you, she now believes that she is and wants to be a homosexual because that is what you have chosen to be.

We have heard about your being a social justice warrior and pushing your liberal politics in the classroom. We let some things slide this year, reminding Kate that she would have to deal with different viewpoints throughout her life but that she doesn't have to subscribe to them. But you have taken it too far.

We will be taking our concerns to the school board meeting next Monday evening. Mr. Dunham has been alerted, as well as our good friend on the school board, Derek Stoneman.

Mr. Anderson

I stared at the blank white space under his words for—well—I'm not sure how long. In one way, one of my worst fears was coming true; in another way, the rage I felt at his false accusation dropped a burning fire into my core—and the rage was what won in that moment.

Pushing my chair violently backward, I roared out loud. There wasn't an actual word that came out of me but more like a primal, guttural sound I didn't recognize. I stomped my feet and punched the arms of my chair and began to sob. I let it happen for a few minutes before forcing myself to breathe slowly and get control of myself. Rocking back and forth slightly, I soothed myself by saying aloud, "It's okay. It's going to be okay."

But I lost it again when my subconscious uttered the word "Daddy." Where was he? Could he see me from wherever he was? He was the only person who ever knew exactly what to say to me that was compassionate, honest, practical, and wise. He was the only person who ever truly saw me and loved every single part of me. I moaned and shook with my grief, feeling like I was swimming in an ocean of it, being tossed in its stormy waves.

The door swung open, and Dana's eyes widened at the sight of me. I gasped and frantically wiped my eyes, apologizing and shuddering and sniffling. She closed the door behind her and walked quickly to me, standing beside me and pulling my head to her middle. I started to cry again, and she smoothed my hair and whispered "shhh" over and over.

After a while, I started breathing normally again and sat up straight. Dana leaned back and looked down at me maternally. She is ten years older than I am, but that never felt especially relevant until that moment.

"I'm sorry," I whispered hoarsely. "I think I'm okay now."

She went to a student desk and grabbed a chair and then set it next to mine and sat down. "What in the world happened?" she leaned forward to look into my face.

"Madden called the Andersons and told them about Kate's essay," I said flatly.

Her eyes widened again. "Oh no. Why would he do that? Did he ask you first?"

I shook my head back and forth repeatedly, closing my eyes. "No. No, no, no. I just wanted him to check in with Kate to make sure she was okay and to see if she wanted someone to talk to who *wasn't me.*" I took a big, shaky breath.

Dana put her hand on my arm. "You haven't done anything wrong. Nothing."

"They're going to the school board," I added quietly.

"What?" She stood up. "For what? What is this—1955?" She closed her fists angrily. "Do they think they can get you fired or something? What exactly are they accusing you of?"

"Apparently," I began, "Kate likes girls because *I* like girls, and she wants to be like me."

"That's ridiculous," she spat. "That doesn't even make

sense. How does that make sense?"

I was quiet for a few seconds and then said, "Kate did mention that her parents are not exactly down with the gays. I guess they need someone to blame."

"Ha! Well," Dana ground her teeth, "then we will go to that school board meeting with armor." She looked at the clock. "Call Donna. Tell her you're going to need some union representation."

"There's more." I looked at her and then quickly away.

"What? What else?" Her eyes were expectant.

"Kate ... met me at my car the other day after school. The day she had turned in her essay. And she was upset, and I tried to make her feel better. I let her hug me." A sob threatened to escape again, but I inhaled sharply to prevent it.

"So what?" She leaned in closer to look me in the eye. "Kids hug us all the time."

"Dana," I inhaled again, my breath shaking, "someone took a video of it," I exhaled slowly, "and emailed it to me anonymously." I closed my eyes and shook my head. "I have no idea who it was, but someone is clearly out to get me." Opening my eyes, I motioned at the computer. "I thought it was one of Kate's parents who had done it, but her dad didn't mention it at all in the email I just read. Why would he send an anonymous video and then email me without even mentioning the video? It doesn't make any sense. But who—"

"Slow down." She scooched closer to me. "What did the anonymous email say?"

I threw my hands up. "It didn't *say* much of anything. They called me a," I used air quotes, "snowflake and then said they had video proof of what I had done. The end said," more air quotes, "see attached video, like some kind of formal office email."

She took a breath and then pushed it out of her nose. "Okay, there goes my theory that it was Brandon."

"I know, right?" I slumped forward. "I thought the same thing."

"What did Cam say about all of this?"

I hesitated and then sighed. "I haven't told her yet. She worries about everything so much, and she already didn't want me to be out at work—"

She put her hand on my arm again. "Josie, none of this is your fault. You didn't ask for any of this."

"I know." I groaned, startling her. "But there is yet another layer to the story."

"My God, what else?"

"Just listen. When Kate talked to me in the parking lot, she asked me if I would sponsor a GSA here at Benson" I started.

"What's a GSA?"

I sighed. "It stands for Gay Straight Alliance. It would be a school-sponsored club where kids could meet and not have to worry about being judged."

"Well," she thought for a few seconds, "are you thinking of doing it? You're thinking of doing it, aren't you?"

I turned to face her. "Do you think it would be stupid? It would be totally stupid. It would be *asking* for more bullshit."

"Now, now, I didn't say that. One step at a time, okay? Go ahead and call Donna. You definitely want to get the union involved with this one." She stood up to get ready to leave.

"Wait, what do I say to this email?" I asked her. "I can't just ignore it, like some kind of admission of guilt." I closed my eyes. "I can't respond now, though. I need to cool down first. I have gotten myself in way too much trouble in the past by not thinking before I speak."

Just as Dana started to walk away, a new email appeared in my inbox, and I gasped.

"What?" she immediately came closer to see the screen.

It was from i.see.you.snowflake@gmail.com. This time, the subject read "ATTENTION"

Dear snowflake,

Do you think you're special because you're a lesbian? That it makes you cool or "woke"? You obviously want attention. That's why you're going around telling everyone, isn't it? And the children you teach can't even use their right to free speech to tell you that they don't want to hear about it, or else they'll get suspended.

Well, you want the attention so bad, you're going to get it.

I.C. You

"What. The. Fuck!" Dana shouted as I pushed my chair forcefully backward and rolled into a bookcase.

"That's a threat." I breathed heavily. "Doesn't that last part sound like a threat?" I looked at her, eyes wide.

"Call Donna now."

- 24 -

Saturday, December 26, 2015

Tossing shoes and boots out of the way to allow for a tidier-looking living room, I gently positioned Cam in front of our plain white front door. She stood obediently and lifted her shirt to reveal her growing, five-months-pregnant belly. We had just told our families and friends the good news the day before as a special Christmas present for everyone. My mom had FaceTimed us on her break at the hospital, and she had brought her hands to her cheeks and told us how happy she was for us. We told everyone else in person—Amanda and Dad at his house while opening presents in the morning and Cam's parents and grandmother at Christmas dinner. Amanda and Dad were thrilled, and Cam's family had reacted just as I'd predicted: with polite, hesitant congratulations. In their defense, Cam hadn't been open with them about the process, so they weren't expecting it. My family, on the other hand—particularly my dad— had had to deal with my constant chatter about ovulation timing and anonymous sperm donation.

The truth was that Cam's parents were still just getting used to the idea of us being married—which we had done quickly and quietly as soon as it was legal—when we told them we were expecting. Her mother was still calling me "Cameron's roommate" to all of her friends, most of whom she knew from church. Her father was more welcoming, but he's the type of person who goes out of his way to make people feel comfortable. Her grandmother, who was also at Christmas dinner, didn't say much of anything at all, but that wasn't unusual for her. Though each of them had come a long way since Cam introduced me to them in 2007 (more on that later), I got the feeling that not one of them was exactly thrilled that we were having a baby together.

I was thinking about their stiff smiles as I backed away from Cam and centered her belly in the frame of my cell phone camera.

"You don't have to say cheese or anything. I'm just going to get your adorable little bump in the picture." I snapped a series of pictures to be able to choose a favorite later. We had decided to document her pregnancy through pictures to put into a digital album, and we were beyond excited that she was finally starting to look pregnant.

"Did you get enough? I'm cold," she said, ready to pull her shirt back down.

I reached up and pulled it down for her. "I'm sure there was a good one in there somewhere. Go ahead and sit down on the couch. I'll get you a blanket." I walked over to our basket of blankets while she walked to the couch. "Do you want to watch a Christmas movie?" I asked.

But she didn't hear me because she was looking down at her buzzing phone. "Hold on a sec. My grandma is calling me for some reason. Hey, Grandma! What's up?"

I brought our favorite colorful quilt to her and tucked it

around her legs. It wasn't like her grandma to call her—especially since we had just seen her the day before.

"Are you sure?" Cam asked her as she turned her eyes to me. "I don't think Josie would do that. No, you don't have to—" She stopped talking and listened. By that point, I was sitting beside her with my palms turned up in my lap in an effort to ask what was going on, but she had stopped looking at me. "Okay. I'll talk to her. Yes, you have a good night, too." She set her phone down on her lap and closed her eyes.

"What?" I asked. "What did I do?"

"Please tell me," she began, "that you did not post about my pregnancy on Facebook."

I hesitated. "We talked about this. I asked you if it was okay if I alluded to your pregnancy without saying too much, and you said it was."

She snapped her face in my direction and said, "I did not say it was okay. When did I say it was okay?"

Cam and I didn't see eye to eye on the topic of social media. She thought it was only for people who sought attention because they weren't getting enough fulfillment in their real lives, and I thought it was a fun way to keep in touch with family and friends. I had asked her a few days prior if it would be okay for me to announce her pregnancy—without being specific, of course—on Facebook after we had told our families on Christmas Day, and she had reluctantly said yes. I had teased her about forgetting she wasn't in a closet anymore, and she had replied seriously that she just enjoyed her privacy. Her closet was always nearby even if she wasn't in it.

"I asked you, like, three days ago, and you said it was okay. Don't you remember?" I was beginning to feel panic rising in my chest. All I had posted the night before was something to the effect of: "We hope everyone had a Merry Christmas! Ours was the best one yet because we got to tell our families we are expecting a new addition in the spring!" I was always careful not to use Cam's name, always a champion player of The Pronoun Game with plenty of practice from my classroom.

"Josie," she took a deep breath, "what exactly did you say that caused my grandma's neighbor to ring her doorbell this morning to ask about her deviant granddaughter?"

"What? Who—" I choked on my words. "I just said we are expecting a new addition in the spring. It could be a puppy for all anyone knows! I didn't even say your name. I—"

"You didn't have to! I don't understand what you don't understand about privacy. It's like you don't think about anybody but yourself!" She got up and walked quickly up the stairs to our bedroom and slammed the door.

"No," I said quietly, "what you don't understand is what it feels like to be a woman who is having a baby but nothing to show for it." I stared at the quilt while considering what to do next. I couldn't call my dad and tell him about what I was feeling because he was already so sensitive about not being biologically connected to the baby—like we were going to consider him a second-class grandparent or something. I could see in his eyes on Christmas that he hadn't quit drinking yet—even after being fired from his job for it. I couldn't put this on him. Amanda was spending the day with her boyfriend and his kids, and my mom and Sam were going to the beach. It suddenly occurred to me exactly what I should do.

I found my laptop charging on the kitchen counter. Without thinking too much about it, I logged in to Facebook, ignoring what appeared to be several notifications, went into my settings, and deleted my account. Cam was right. If we were going to parent together, I had to get my head out of my ass and more carefully consider the feelings of other people. Students were always trying to send me friend requests that I had to deny, anyway, so this would just simplify my life.

After closing my laptop, I walked straight up the stairs and quietly opened our bedroom door to tell her what I had done.

- 25 -

Wednesday, March 20, 2019

I called Donna, our union president, and asked if she would accompany me to a meeting with Mr. Dunham. He hadn't even asked to see me yet, but I wanted to get it over with. She said she would come to my classroom directly after the last period of the day, and we would talk about the situation before we walked to his office together.

I know I taught that day, but I don't remember much about that part. The last bell had rung, and students were rushing to their lockers in the hallway as I waited for Donna inside my classroom with the door closed, pacing while I considered how I would summarize the situation for her. She and I had been friendly enough in the past for her to know I'm married to a woman, so that wouldn't be a surprise. I thought I would just tell her the basics of what I was being accused of before she had to hear it from Dunham or someone else.

I glanced at the clock. 2:32. *If she arrives in one minute, that will be 2+3+3, and that's got to mean—*

There was a knock on the door, and I told her to come in. She poked her head in first and looked around to see if anyone else was with me.

"I'm alone," I said. "Thank you so much for coming."

"No problem whatsoever," she replied. Donna is a tall, confident woman with straight brown hair and black-rimmed glasses that remind everyone—students and teachers alike—that she is always one of the smartest people in the room. I've always admired her, not only because she is a damn good English teacher but because she never takes shit from anyone.

She sat on top of a student desk. "So," she prompted.

I sighed and stopped pacing to look at her and then felt too nervous to make eye contact and, instead, looked at various locations on the ceiling as I spoke, "So you probably don't know Kate Anderson because she's only a tenth grader and doesn't have any older siblings. Well, Kate wrote an essay about how she admires me, and one of the reasons was because I'm gay." I glanced at Donna to find her nodding, so I continued, "And she wrote that she is also gay. So I panicked and turned the whole thing over to Dom Madden, so he could talk to her about it. Rather than doing just that, he called her parents and got them involved, and they happen to be very conservative."

Donna continued nodding as she said, "Whew. Well, now what?"

"Now," I looked at her, "they are taking their concerns to the school board next week, and Dunham hasn't even called me down yet, but I know he's going to because her dad mentioned in his email that he told Dunham about it." I bit at a finger, thankful to find a piece of skin.

"Breathe, Josie," she said. "You haven't done anything wrong, unless there's something you haven't told me."

"No!" I said more loudly than I expected. "I mean, Kate did

talk to me in the parking lot the day she turned in her essay, and she hugged me, and I let her, and—"

"Whoa, take a breath. Did you initiate the hug?" She raised her eyebrows, and I shook my head. "Then what were you supposed to do? Push her? I'm pretty sure that would have been worse. Besides, did anyone even see her hug you?"

I panicked, both wanting desperately to tell her about the emails and wanting to ignore them entirely with the hope that they would simply go away. Isn't that what they tell you to do to bullies when you're a kid? "Don't let them see they've gotten to you, and they'll stop?"

I chose a middle ground. "I'm not sure." I paused. "Donna, I go out of my way not to talk about my home situation to students because I know there are so many conservative parents around here, and I have been trying to avoid a situation just like this one for years. His email made it sound like I've been teaching tenth grade Gay Studies instead of tenth grade English for over a decade."

"Can I read it?" she asked, and I quickly walked over to my computer, opened my inbox, and opened his message so she wouldn't see any of the other messages in my inbox. As I was moving over to give her room to sit and read, we both noticed an email notification from Mr. Dunham with the subject line "Please see me ASAP." She said, "Ignore that for now," and then took the mouse and clicked on the email from Mr. Anderson.

I watched her face as she carefully read it and wasn't expecting her to laugh dryly at one point before saying, "He's a piece of work. His words ooze white mansplainer privilege."

"I think he's actually a cardiologist," I said, not returning her amusement.

"Exactly," she retorted, closing my inbox and standing up. "We might as well go now."

Following her out the door and down the hallway, I thought about what other career choices I had. If they fired me, what would I do to make money? Our mortgage won't be paid off for another two decades at least, so it's not like I could just stop working.

She must have sensed my growing sense of doom because she said, "It's going to be okay. It would be illegal to fire you because of your sexuality. You would have quite a discrimination case on your hands that I'm sure the ACLU would be delighted to take pro bono."

I tried to smile and said, "But can't they just make up another reason why they're firing me and make it seem unrelated?"

She stopped in front of Mr. Dunham's door and turned to face me, grabbing my arms firmly, "You are a great teacher. There are no reasons to fire you. You never miss a deadline, and your test scores are fantastic. Breathe."

I inhaled deeply through my nose while she still held onto my arms. She let go, and I exhaled as she knocked quickly, and we entered his office.

Mr. Dunham looked from Donna to me and then back to Donna. "Hello, Mrs. Chavez. I wasn't expecting you." He looked at me, nodding once, "Miss Rain." I didn't have the nerve to correct him. "Please, both of you, have a seat."

We both sat in the chairs across from him as he remained behind his desk. Donna began, "I'm here as a representative of our teacher's union, by Josie's request. Please know that anything either one of you says is essentially 'on the record.'"

I nodded while staring at the floor, feeling like I was a student about to be disciplined. Unsure if I was supposed to speak first,

I waited to be spoken to.

"Josie," he began with more warmth in his voice than I had anticipated, "I'm sure you know why I asked to see you. Brian Anderson called me last night in an absolute tizzy. He said his daughter wrote an essay about how she idolizes you because you're married to a woman. Is this true?"

I looked at Donna, and she nodded. "Sort of," I told him, "but I can assure you that Kate wrote that essay having never once had a conversation with me about anything unrelated to English class, so I'm not even sure how she knew anything about my private life."

He looked at Donna before saying, "Actually, I called Kate down to my office to speak with her during her lunch period today, and she brought her friend Alexis with her because she was nervous. They both have you for fifth period. Kate was pretty shaken up about the whole ordeal and didn't say much, but her friend mentioned something to me about a journal entry in your class last week."

I froze. Why had Kate shared that with anyone? I looked at Donna who was looking at me quizzically, and I said, "Yes, she wrote a journal entry about how she had heard what Brandon Stoneman had said to me and how it hadn't been right."

"Well," he interjected, "did you know the Andersons and the Stonemans are good friends?"

"I—" I hesitated. "I didn't know until Mr. Anderson mentioned it in his email." I thought about how poor Kate was surrounded by people who might never accept her for who she is.

"Josie, did you put your hand on Kate's shoulder that day?" he asked seriously.

I pictured my hand on Kate's shoulder as I gave her a brief

pat of thanks. Before I could answer, Donna furrowed her eyebrows and said, "Mr. Dunham, I think I put my hand on about five shoulders today alone."

He ignored her and stared at me.

Why had Kate even mentioned it? Or had Alexis seen me do it? I felt exposed, like I had done something lewd. If Kate told him about me touching her shoulder, then surely she also told him about the hug.

"Yes," I replied meekly. "I patted her shoulder very briefly. But it was innocent. She had written something nice in her journal that she wanted me to read, and I didn't think it would be right if I didn't thank her for it." I leaned forward and put my head into my hands and said, "I swear I had absolutely no idea about her essay at that point. I didn't know she was questioning her sexuality." I looked up at him and then at Donna and added, "I thought she was just being a nice person! Did she ... " I hesitated. "Did she say that I had made her uncomfortable?"

My ears were on fire, and I didn't think I could ignore the lump in my throat any longer. Donna spoke, "Mr. Dunham, Josie has done nothing inappropriate, and I hope you can see that and will be able to stand up to whoever accuses her of otherwise. Remember whose team you are actually on."

He looked at her and then back to me, as tears started falling down my face, and he sighed before saying, "Josie, I trust your judgment. I personally don't think you did anything wrong, but what I think doesn't matter at this point. And, no, Kate didn't say that she had felt uncomfortable, but Alexis did mention that she saw you do it."

I felt sick, my head swimming with a concoction of shame, fear, and regret. I had no idea what to say next.

Donna stood up and pulled me by my arm to do the same. "Then we will just have to go to that school board meeting and set things straight, won't we?"

Donna and I parted ways in front of her classroom, which is about five rooms away from mine in the English wing. Before she entered her room, she told me to try not to worry—that I didn't have anything to worry about, and hadn't I gotten used to never being able to make everyone happy? The truth is I felt oddly numb to it all at that point, not sure where my emotions were going to eventually land.

As I approached my classroom, I noticed a group of students waiting for me outside the door. Many were sitting in a circle, hunched over notebooks and either reading or writing, and a few were standing and talking quietly but animatedly about something.

The slam poems. I had forgotten that some kids had asked to stay and work on them that day. I noticed that Kate was absent from the group but then shook my head back and forth quickly to center myself and said, "Well, hello there, everybody! Who's ready for some poetry?"

They all looked in my direction, most of them smiling, before gathering their belongings to prepare to go into my classroom. As I unlocked the door, Maddie approached me and said, "We are all super excited about this, Mrs. Rein-Thompson. Can we start planning our performance soon?"

I laughed. "Slow down, sweetheart. I appreciate your enthusiasm, but we're going to have to do a lot of writing and practicing and planning before then."

"Really?" Josh, a kid from my first period, chimed in. "Because I feel like a lot of us have already written our poems and might just need to practice reading them."

I turned and looked at the group as we entered the room, and many of them had heard what Josh said and were nodding. "Wow," I began, "I am truly impressed. Well, is there anyone who wants to start us off by reading what you have so far?"

Josh smiled and said, "I'll go."

I smiled back and said, "Okay, great! Let's all take a seat, and Josh can head to the front of the room." I settled into a student desk among the rest of them. Looking around as Josh got his notebook out of his backpack, I counted eight students. Lucky number eight. *Maybe I should write about trying to get pregnant?*

Josh stood confidently with impeccable posture and began to read from a black-and-white composition notebook:

"When my grandmother,
    my lao lao, used to tuck me in at night,
    she would tell me how I would someday
    be a great, powerful man.
    I would stand up,"

He slowly raised one hand, palm up, from his waist to his shoulder,

"tall

for what is right and true."

He kept his hand up.

"But what she forgot
    is that my parents are both very short,
    so I may stand for truth,
    but I cannot do it tall."

Some of the kids and I giggled as he pushed his hand slowly, palm down, back to his waist. He smiled and paused and then continued,

"Here are the truths of my life so far:
    My lao lao's optimism is an anomaly
    in a broken and ungrateful world.
    Every girl I know only sees the shape of my eyes,
    and every boy I know thinks my eyes
    can only see the inside of a book."

He took a breath.

"But I see everything.
    I see when you retreat into yourself.
    I see when you look up at the stars
    through your bedroom window.
    I see when you dream of hope while you sleep."

He stopped, and the room was silent for a few seconds before erupting into applause and shouts of approval. Josh smiled bashfully and closed his notebook and then bowed. I was speechless as I clapped my hands, but many of them looked to me to say what would happen next.

"Wow," I said again, unable to find any other words to express my amazement. "Josh, I don't know what to say. I wasn't expecting anyone to be so polished yet. Have you guys been holding practice sessions behind my back?" I teased, looking around the room.

Maddie spoke up, smiling, "Kind of! Some of us have been practicing on FaceTime. Josh has barely practiced at all, but he's already pretty damn good—sorry, pretty *dang* good."

I laughed. "I'll say!" I looked around at their eager faces and added, "Well, who's next?"

Almost all of them took turns going to the front of the room to read their poems—most with confidence but some with the shyness that comes with not being used to having eyes on you, especially when you're speaking about something that gets your heart pumping. I was thrilled and proud and so grateful to be a part of something I knew they would remember forever. For that hour, nothing else mattered, and I didn't even think about emails or the school board or anything other than those kids and their words.

Before everyone packed up to go home, I checked the district's online calendar to see when the auditorium would be available in the near future, and there was only one date open for at least a month: exactly one week from then, on the next Wednesday evening. We chatted about our availabilities and decided to go ahead and book the night. Maddie and a group of her friends started talking about making and posting flyers, and Josh said he would post about it on his TikTok account because he had what sounded like more followers than the population of a small country. They arranged for rides with each other or chose to walk home, and every single one of them thanked me as they left.

In my empty classroom, I looked around at the desks where they had just been sitting. Feeling the tears coming, I took deep breaths to prevent them. What if I wouldn't be allowed to teach anymore? What if the school board found some way to make it look like I am unfit to do this job that makes me feel so happy and fulfilled?

"Stop it," I said out loud. "Stop it right now. Go home." I followed my own command, gathered my things into my work bag, and walked out the door.

- 27 -

Friday, February 14, 2004

I sat by myself at a table for two in a smoke-filled bar called Gatsby's. My palms were sweating as I shuffled through the pages of my blue spiral notebook, trying to make a final decision about what to read at the microphone. I had signed up for this night—called "A Valentine to Myself"—over a month ago because I was in a poetry class and had a friend who wanted to do a reading, too. I had no idea how much I would learn that semester and how exhilarated poetry would make me feel as I learned how to share it with others. It was a weekly night class, and during each session, we sat in a circle and read what we had written about assigned topics throughout the previous week. I was enamored with the process—the writing, the sharing, the listening—and a little bit with my professor who was a quiet, self-assured woman whose metaphors took me to places I had never been.

My friend, Melanie, had gotten sick that day, and I thought I might not go by myself to the reading, but Cam was having dinner with her parents that night to celebrate Valentine's Day, and I just didn't have the heart—pun intended—to be alone. Dad had offered to come, and as much as I didn't mind him hearing my poetry, I definitely did not want to be the 21-year-old who had brought her forty-something-year-old dad. Besides, he had recently gotten out of a relationship and was a complete bummer to be around.

I listened and watched while people, most of them around my age, read their poetry. Many of them seemed experienced at doing it, and a few of them even seemed to have groupies. It would be my first time reading at a microphone, but I had read my poems aloud to myself so many times that I practically had most of them memorized.

There was one more reader ahead of me. She walked up the steps in her black Doc Martens with her curly brown hair bouncing as she made it to the platform—I don't think you could call it a stage—and sat down on the metal folding chair. It was the first time I looked at the chair closely, and it suddenly reminded me of the one I used to have in the basement of my mom's house when I would sit at my keyboard and write songs. That felt like a lifetime ago—pre-Cam, pre-Mom's move to California, pre-college. I missed the innocence of that time when I never thought to keep anything about myself quiet. In the last four years, since meeting and falling in love with Cam and then beginning at a local college as an English education major, I had drifted away from many of my friends because they either didn't understand or didn't approve of the secrecy of our relationship. I won't lie and say it was easy, but I understood why she was afraid. I loved her and respected her too much to try to force her out.

Looking at that folding chair, I knew which poem I was going to read. I flipped to the page and glanced over the words quickly, though I knew most of them by heart, and then snapped along with everyone else as the woman before me walked back down the steps.

I took a deep, unobvious breath so as not to appear as the newbie I was. As I climbed the three stairs, I felt everyone's eyes on the fifty pounds I had gained in the last few years, and I was hyper-aware of my stomach spilling over my jeans and poking into the yellow-and-brown-striped t-shirt I had chosen for the occasion. My hair was pulled back into a tight ponytail to contain my curls, but I could feel that a poof of it had escaped near my right ear, so I quickly tried to smooth it back as I sat on the folding chair and pulled the microphone to my mouth, setting my open notebook in my lap.

"I am a secret," I spoke into the microphone and paused as I stared down at the page and heard my amplified voice echo slightly, "best kept at room temperature, just under the surface and just past the reflection of who you wish you could be." I licked my lips and sat up straighter, eyes still facing downward. "I am unholy, stifled," I spat the last word, "a sinner in your eyes," I looked up at the audience, "in the eyes of the congregation, the masses, the host, the holy school spirit." And this is when it happened, when it felt like the words began to speak for themselves, and I didn't need to look at them any longer:

"But I am from the wooden pews
   tasting of Pledge and fingerprints,
   decorated outlandishly with rainbow flags, tattered books,
   plus-sized clothing, and scratched CDs.
   I am the Bible, dog-eared to highlight
   redemption and impossibility.
   I am searching to move forward

in a world that is unwelcoming,
trying not to be everything
you want me to be.
I am from blue carpet, rarely cleaned
and covered with independence,
from a Carebear turned gray
long after a sex change
that led to his dull eyes.
I am a child controlled
by a primal fear of happiness.
I am the loud one,
the laughing one,
swept under the rug for parties
at which the guests are respectable
but not respectful.
I am your worst fear.
I am honesty, and I am seconds away
from loving or hating you.
I am a secret that I am afraid
you will keep forever
in the pulpit behind which you preach.
I am an image of God that He loves
rarely through his messengers.
And I will change before your eyes."

My heart was thumping in my ears. The audience snapped, and I closed my notebook and stood, taking a few seconds to steady myself so as not to fall down the stairs. Hands shaking, I went back to my seat at the table by myself, and I promised myself I would do that again and again because it felt just as good as—if not better than—singing.

On my way out the door that night, I called my dad. He answered right away as if he had been expecting a call. "Yello?" he said happily.

"Hey, Dad. Do you have a minute?" I was breathing heavily, still riding the high.

"Anything for my baby girl! Happy Valentine's Day!" I could hear his smile.

"Same to you! Instead of doing something with Cam, I—"

"Oh, Cam! You mean the one who is keeping you all to herself and not letting you see your dear old dad?"

I stopped at a crosswalk and adjusted the phone in my hand. "What's that supposed to mean?"

"Do you know what I did today, Josie?" His voice sounded unexpectedly hollow. "I ate dinner with Aunt Jill and Uncle Paul, and then I went home. It was just the three of us, and it was—" Something rattled, and he muttered, "Damn it."

"Wait," I said. "Where was Amanda today? I thought she was supposed to stop by—"

"Neither one of you—" There was a crash, and then my phone beeped with the lost call. I looked at it in disbelief and looked up just in time to stop myself from walking out in front of a large green SUV.

Heart pounding, I ran to my car, which was parked about two blocks from Gatsby's. The drive to my dad's—which would have taken fifteen minutes without traffic—took thirty minutes due to a construction zone. I tried to call him back at least three times, but he didn't answer. I tried to call Amanda, too, to let her know my concerns, but she also didn't answer. By the time I got to his apartment, I was so desperate to talk to someone that I almost called my mom in California because I knew Cam was with her parents.

I hurriedly fumbled for the key to his front door and opened it. Every single light that I could see was on. "Dad?" I called.

"Josie?" he answered quietly from the kitchen. I rushed in that direction and found him sitting on the floor with his back against the under-sink cabinet and his legs stretched out in front of him, covered in an alarming amount of blood. I scanned him to try and figure out where it was coming from and saw a gash in his left arm. Grabbing a dish towel, I crouched down beside him to wrap his arm tightly in order to stop the bleeding.

"Dad, what happened?" I was breathless, applying pressure to the wound that was still actively bleeding. He pointed weakly with his right arm to a broken beer bottle under the kitchen table, and I looked from it to his face where I noticed his nose was swollen. "What happened to your face?"

He swallowed and closed his eyes. "Can you please get me some water?"

"Keep this here," I put his right hand on his towel-wrapped arm and stood to get him some water from the sink. Then, I sat cross-legged on the floor next to him and replaced his hand with my own, so he could drink the water. He chugged the entire glass and set it down beside him on the yellow tile floor before he spoke.

"I fell," he nearly whispered, breathing heavily.

"I can see that," I said gently. "How?"

"Well," he began, "I dropped the bottle and leaned down to try to catch it but smacked my face off the counter and then lost my balance and landed on the broken bottle." He closed his eyes again and winced as I tightened the towel.

"We need to get you to a hospital to see if you need stitches."

"No. I'm fine."

27

Standing up, I reached out my hand for him to take. "Come on. I'll help you up and will drive you there." He didn't even look up.

"No," he said flatly.

I threw up my hands in exasperation. "Dad! You're bleeding all over the place! You need a doctor!"

"No," he repeated. "Josie, are you going to make me say it?"

I narrowed my eyes, genuinely confused. "Say what?"

He sighed. "I lost my job. I lost my job weeks ago and lost my health insurance. I lost my job because I went to work drunk too many times. And I'm drunk right now."

Hearing him say the words left me speechless for a few seconds. All I could manage at first was a long exhale as I sat back down beside him and eventually whispered, "I knew you were drinking," I paused, attempting to keep my composure. "But I didn't know you had lost your job. Why did you start drinking again? Why? After years sober, why would you do that?"

He shook his head and blinked slowly. "I don't know. She left me and then … I really don't know. Please don't hate me." Tears filled his already-cloudy brown eyes.

I put my hand on my forehead and said, "I don't hate you. But I am definitely sad and disappointed. I thought you liked your job at the new diner."

"I did. I said I don't know why I started again."

We didn't speak for a few minutes. A clock ticked on the wall, and the furnace clicked on.

I sighed and looked down at the blood-soaked towel. "We should check that."

Untying it, I reassured him quietly, like a mother to an injured child. The cut didn't look nearly so bad then; it was probably only two inches long and no longer bleeding. "Oh," I said, "it's not so bad. Do you have some bandages and antibiotic ointment?"

He nodded. "Look in the medicine cabinet."

On my way to the bathroom, I looked at the framed pictures on the walls of myself and Amanda when we were kids. In one of them, we were standing in the kitchen of our childhood home, and Dad was sitting behind us, giving both of us bunny ears. We were all wearing tank tops and shorts, showing our tan summer skin. Walking past that picture and into the bathroom, I tried to recall that time of life when we all smiled as easily as we breathed.

- 28 -

Wednesday, March 20, 2019

On my way home that evening, I tried to call Amanda. I needed to talk to someone who was objective enough to give me an opinion about my work situation.

She didn't answer. Her voicemail spoke to me, "Hey, it's Amanda. Leave a message. Or not." *Beep.*

"Hey, Mands," I began. "I ... uh ... I had this thing happen at work that I need some advice about. Just give me a call when you have a chance. Love you."

I sighed and set my phone in a cup holder to my right. I could have called Dana, but I knew her son had soccer practice that night and didn't want to interrupt. The radio, which was tuned to an "oldies" station, began quietly playing a Beatles song, and tears immediately clouded my eyes. "Thanks, Dad," I said aloud. "I wish I could talk to you, too."

Wiping my eyes, I turned the radio off and picked my phone back up to call Cam.

"Hey, babe!" she answered. "I was just starting dinner. Are burgers okay with you?"

"Sure," I said. "How's Liesel?"

"Fine, I think," she sounded unsure.

"Why? What happened?" I felt my brows furrow.

"Didn't you read the email we got from her teacher this afternoon?"

I hadn't checked my personal email all day and immediately felt guilty. "No, I didn't look at my email today. Work was kind of crazy. Is everything okay?"

"Well, if you're asking if Liesel has mentioned anything, then the answer is no. She has not. But, apparently, Jackson said something to her today about having two moms."

My ears felt hot. "Which Jack—" I started to say but then knew immediately. "You mean Sharon's son, the one who was running around shooting people the other night?"

She laughed shortly and said, "I think so. The email said that when she told the kids their parents had all enjoyed the concert on Friday night, Jackson said Liesel doesn't have parents because she has two moms instead."

I rolled my eyes. "That doesn't even make sense. Moms *are* parents."

"Obviously." Her voice got quiet. "But I guess Liesel cried about it."

For the first moment in my life, I considered physically harming a preschooler. "I told you his mother is a bitch. She has apparently taught her son to be just as judgey as she is."

Cam muttered so quietly I could barely hear her. "We'll talk about this later." Then, she spoke normally again. "So how was your day?"

I knew I had to tell her. The issue was growing by the day. I considered whether I should tell her now or wait until later. "It was ... eventful. I'll tell you about it when I get home."

"As long as you're not going to talk to me about wedding

planning, I'm happy to listen to anything. Serena didn't shut up about her wedding all day today. She is absolutely obsessed with every single tiny detail—including how she and Ben are going to pay for it. I keep wanting to tell her that they could just go to the courthouse, like we did, and sign some papers. They've been together for like ten years, anyway, so what is even the point?"

Of course Cam hadn't wanted a wedding for us. That would be way too visible. "Yeah," I agreed outwardly. "Why waste the money?" I said because I knew that's what she would say next.

"Exactly! I'd rather spend money on, like, a trip to Europe or something. Or, maybe … " she hesitated. "Like, adoption or something."

I put on my turn signal and said, "I'll be home in a minute. I'll see you then." Then, I threw my phone onto the passenger seat—hard.

What the hell did she just say to me?

She knew I had my hopes and dreams hanging on this cycle that we were (I was) only five days into and most likely trying not to obsess about it, and she thought it was the right thing to do to mention adoption?

When Cam and I had decided to finally move in together in 2007, shortly after she had finally come out to her parents and introduced me to them, we had had a heart-to-heart about our long-term hopes and dreams. Getting married and having children—specifically being pregnant—were at the top of my list, while traveling and owning a home were at the top of hers. When we decided to move forward with trying to conceive with anonymous donor sperm, Cam was involved in the process of choosing the donor, but then she left the rest up to me—

even though she would be the first to carry our child because she is older—like arranging for transporting the vials, storing the vials, finding a doctor who would do the insemination, tracking her cycle, and telling her when to pee on ovulation tests. I made the appointments and posted on message boards and read everything I could get my hands on about timing and lesbian motherhood. She got pregnant on our first cycle of trying, and I was positively triumphant and confident that I could accomplish the same task when it was my turn.

I pulled into the driveway and put the car in park, leaving it to idle. I was and am not ready at all to talk about adoption. I mean, Liesel was technically adopted by me because we had to go through a "second-parent adoption" to ensure that I would have legal parental rights, but that was different. I practically created Liesel myself. And although it is probably too important to me that our children be related by blood, I still don't want to discuss adoption until after we have at least tried another donor or two with my body. I had no idea until the moment before that Cam was even thinking about adoption, but knowing she didn't have faith in my body—the body that I struggle so much to have faith in myself—was devastating.

The day's worries snuck into my periphery and compounded my feelings of shame and self-doubt. How could I have a conversation with Cam about what was happening at school after she had just dropped that bomb on me? I made eye contact with myself in the rearview mirror and held my own gaze for a few seconds, thinking, "You are alone. No one cares about your irrational fears and hopes. Just be practical, and go with the flow. It's not worth it to make it about yourself. Don't be too sensitive."

Taking the key out of the ignition, I planned to walk into

the house as casually as possible. When I walked in the front door, Liesel looked up from her coloring book on the living room floor and jumped up to run to me. I scooped her up and whispered, "I love you, I love you, I love you." She held onto me and kissed my cheek. When I set her down, she looked up at me seriously.

"What's up, baby girl?" I asked as I smoothed her hair down.

She frowned. "Why did Jackson say I'm not s'pose to have two moms?"

I could hear Cam clanking around in the kitchen, making dinner. I took Liesel's hand and led her to sit beside me on the couch. "Remember how Mommy and Mama always tell you there are lots of different types of families? Some kids live with two moms or two dads or an aunt or a grandpa. The possibilities are endless. But you've probably noticed most kids have a mom and a dad."

She nodded gravely. "Yeah. But Lizzy has two daddies, and Colton lives with his grandma."

"See? That's what I mean." I put my arm around her shoulders and pulled her closer to me, so her head was resting on my side. "Honey, some people don't like when other people are different from them, so they say hurtful things—sometimes without even realizing it. Remember how you told Lizzy one time that pretzels are gross, and then she didn't want to play with you anymore that day?"

"Petzels *are* gross," she mispronounced the word and wrinkled her nose.

I laughed. "You think so, but Lizzy loves them. Telling her they're gross made her feel like one of her favorite things is bad, and that's not a good feeling." I kissed the top of her head. "That's kind of what Jackson did to you today, isn't it?"

She thought about it for a few seconds and said, "But Mommy and Mama aren't petzels!" She giggled, and I decided to take advantage of the moment and started tickling her.

"Are you sure?" I asked while sticking my fingers into her armpits. "Because you're our kid, and you are rather delicious!" I made munching sounds into her ears, making her weak with laughter.

"Sorry to break up the fun, you two, but dinner's ready," Cam was standing in the entryway with a dish towel hanging on her shoulder, smiling lovingly at us. Liesel was breathless as I quit tickling her and scooped her up again, this time to carry her to our round kitchen table. As I passed Cam, she lightly slapped my butt and then followed us into the kitchen.

Liesel exclaimed, "Fench fries! Yay!" as I set her down, and she began eating immediately. I got glasses of water for Cam and myself and sat down between the two of them. Cam leaned over and kissed my cheek.

"So what happened today?" she asked, taking a bite of her cheeseburger.

"I honestly don't even know where to begin," I said, consciously starting with my broccoli. "Like ... I don't even know how to make a long story short."

She smiled. "So don't. We have time."

I set down my fork and looked at her and then back down at my plate. "Okay. So there is a student who came out to me in an essay last week. She said she admires me because I'm not afraid to be myself ... you know, because I'm also gay."

She stopped mid-bite. "What? Josie," she sighed, "I told you not to be so public about us. What if you lose your job? We can't afford this house on one salary—"

"I'm not public about us ever, Cameron. There have only

been a few times when a student has asked me privately about my relationship status, and I haven't lied—but I have never spoken openly in front of a class about it, either. I have nothing to be ashamed of, and I won't lie. Jesus, do you actually think I've done something wrong?" At that moment, I knew I couldn't elaborate too much more—and I definitely couldn't tell her that I was considering sponsoring a GSA or about the anonymous emails.

"No, I—" she paused. "I know you haven't. But people can be crazy, and I just think you could have prevented this situation somehow. How did they even find out?"

I shoved a few french fries into my mouth, picturing in my mind the name "I.C. You.". "I panicked and told the guidance counselor about her essay. This wouldn't be happening if I had just glossed over it and pretended like it didn't happen."

I touched her. Twice. I touched her, and somebody saw me.

I took a sip of water. "But how could I do that? When I was her age, I had no one to look up to. And if I had, and that person would have ignored me completely, I would have been devastated." Suddenly, I became hyper-aware of Kate's feelings. "Actually, I might be just as devastated if that person had made a huge deal of it and turned it over to the guidance counselor, who then made an even bigger deal of it." I put my hands on my forehead.

Cam put her hand on my leg. "Baby, you didn't know what to do. You did what you thought was best."

"Did I?" I shot her a look. "Or did I do what I thought was easiest for me?" I shook my head and looked down at my plate, silently counting french fries.

One, two, three, four, five, six, seven, eight, nine. I touched her. I touched her.

"Cam, you have no idea what it's like. You teach little kids who don't ask these kinds of questions and who don't need you to be a role model in that way. It's a wonderful thing, but it's also so much pressure. I don't know how to balance being confident and unashamed with being humble and quiet."

"My students' parents are well aware of my situation. You forget I teach in a school that is practically across the street from where we grew up."

"I know that, but I doubt they're having conversations with their five-year-olds about who you live with."

"I almost three!" Liesel said. "Mommy lives with me and Mama."

We both looked at her, shaken out of the moment. "I sure do," Cam said, smiling. "Don't forget to eat that yummy broccoli!" She grabbed a piece with her fork and made an airplane noise, flying it in the direction of Liesel's mouth. She smiled and opened her mouth willingly. It's true that she doesn't like pretzels, but she does like broccoli.

The moment had passed, but it hadn't taken my unsettledness with it. Watching Cam and Liesel smile at each other—their smiles so alike—resurrected my earlier disappointment at the thought of adopting our second child. *Why does everything I do feel like a failure?*

"Cam," I said quietly, but she didn't hear me above Liesel's giggles. "Cam," I said a little louder.

She looked at me. "What, honey?" Her gaze had lost its accusatory edge.

"I don't want to talk about adoption yet, okay?" I blinked a few times, willing myself not to cry.

"Oh, Jojo," she scooted closer to me and hugged me. "I didn't mean now. I meant maybe someday or maybe never but not now." She pulled me closer and nuzzled her face into my right ear, whispering, "You have had an emotional day. Why don't you go upstairs and go to bed early, and I'll put Liesel to bed? Go relax."

I looked down at my half–full plate and squeezed her back. "Not until after I finish the rest of the french fries," I whispered back.

She chuckled and released me. We finished our dinners in relative silence, except when Liesel told a story about how Lizzy had brought a cookie in her lunch that day, and why couldn't she have cookies in her lunch? I took everyone's plates to the sink as Cam explained how cookies were for special treats, not lunches, but that she didn't have to tell Lizzy that to make her feel bad. I returned to the table and kissed them both on their blonde heads and told them good night before heading upstairs and falling asleep on top of our bed in my work clothes.

- 29 -

I had a dream that I was standing in a hospital room looking down at my dad who was sitting in a wheelchair beside the bed. Staring at the floor, he looked exhausted, frail, and old—older than he had ever lived to in his life.

Suddenly he looked up at me pleadingly. "Josie, why didn't you tell me I died? I've been waiting this whole time, and you never told me."

"I'm sorry, Dad. I'm so sorry. I didn't know you needed me to tell you, or of course I would have."

"Well, what am I supposed to do now? Where am I supposed to go?"

"I don't know, Daddy. I'm so sorry. I wish I could help you, but I don't know what to do."

The skin on his face turned orange and began drooping. I didn't want to look away because I didn't want him to think that he disgusted me. I forced myself to keep facing him as the skin on his face melted off, decaying in chunks and revealing parts of his skull.

He started crying. I got down on my knees and tried to take his hands into mine to comfort him, but his hands were gone.

His skull fully exposed, he said in a robotic voice that I didn't recognize, "I see you. Do you see me?"

I stood up and started backing away slowly, watching him melt into a pile of bones.

"Josie," he whispered. "Josie, honey, wake up."

I opened my eyes to see Cam leaning over me, her face backlit by the hallway light.

"Baby, you were having a bad dream. Let's get you out of your clothes. You literally passed out on top of the comforter."

Tears spilled out of my eyes as I let her undress me. "It was my dad. He was dead, but he … didn't know he was dead. He didn't know because I hadn't told him." The quiet tears turned into a full-on sob.

She pulled me up to stand and then arranged the blankets so we could both get under them. "Come here, sweetheart. Shhhh, it's okay." I curled into a fetal position and faced her as she wrapped her arms around me.

The dream's devastation melted away after a few minutes like that, but it left guilt in its wake. Guilt that I hadn't answered my dad's phone call the morning he died, guilt that I had probably made a big mistake at work, guilt that I hadn't told Cam the whole story, guilt that I could hear her breathing slowing, but I had to wake her to tell her.

"Cam," I whispered.

"Mmmm?"

"There are some things I didn't tell you about the thing at school."

She shifted a little, as I pulled back to face her in the dark. "It's okay, Jo. Whatever it is, I'm sure it's going to be okay."

And she fell asleep.

- 30 -

Friday, December 13, 1996

I woke up early, excited about the Christmas concert at my school that day. I had been asked to sing the coveted "O Holy Night" solo that was only ever given to the best singer in eighth grade. To this day, I can still name the girls I had watched sing that verse in the years before me.

I left my bedroom to take a shower earlier than usual and was surprised to hear talking coming from my parents' bedroom. Mom was whispering, but it was a repeated, forceful sound. I couldn't quite make out what she was saying. Silently, I moved closer to the closed wooden door, but as soon as I did, she started to cry.

I jumped slightly, startled, having never heard her cry like that before. Backing away from the door, I stood with my back flat against the bare white hallway wall. *Should I go back into my room and pretend to be asleep? Should I just keep walking and go take a shower like I had planned?*

Dad's voice was suddenly closer to me from the other side of the door. "Susan, I'm so sorry. I don't know what else to say."

Afraid that he was going to open the door, I tiptoed quickly to the bathroom down the hall and closed the door behind me as quietly as I could. Breathing heavily, I took off my t-shirt and underwear and stood naked, looking at myself in the mirror. That year, I had begun to gain more weight than my friends. In hindsight, overeating had started as a pastime to share with my dad that would make him laugh about how I was just like him, and, from there, it became a habit—even an addiction. I would sneak food into my room to eat at night and then hide the wrappers in the drawers of my nightstand.

I stared at my body, critically studying every curve and bump with visceral disgust that compounded the already-existing dread inside of me. Fresh, purple stretch marks covered my sides and breasts, and when I finally reached my eyes, I was met with sadness. I watched my eyes fill with tears before my vision was too blurry to see much of anything, and I blinked to let them slide down my cheeks, satisfied by their heaviness. Closing my eyes, I pictured my parents' faces and how they had recently seemed distant from each other and from Amanda and me. I pictured how my mom's face would contort with her weeping and how my dad's eyes would be facing their brown carpet. Something wasn't right, and they were trying to keep it a secret.

I let myself continue to cry in the shower, hoping it would be enough time for me to get it all out. Dad would leave for work while I was still in there, and Mom would be putting on her makeup when I got out. Amanda would get up soon, and we would expect Mom to pack our lunches and make us something quick for breakfast, like a waffle or bagel or something we were completely capable of making ourselves, before heading off to work at the clinic. Years later, looking back, I am floored by my mom's ability to carry on business as usual while her marriage was falling apart.

When I walked out of the bathroom with a towel wrapped around me and my pajamas in my hand, I found Dad standing in the hallway with his hand resting on the doorknob of their closed bedroom door. Feeling like I was intruding on a private moment, I tried to slide past him into my room, but he turned to look at me.

He smiled sadly and said, "Morning, Joey Bean." He hadn't called me that in years, and it took me off guard. I forced a smile.

"Hey. Why are you still here?"

"I took the day off," he said. "I want to do some Christmas shopping, and I also want to come see your afternoon performance."

I had momentarily forgotten about the concert, and my stomach did an excited somersault. "Okay," I replied, trying to mask my happiness because A) he had just been fighting with Mom, and B) I didn't want to seem like a giddy little girl. It suddenly occurred to me that I had never heard of him shopping for anything—ever—so I couldn't help but be suspicious. It wouldn't dawn on me until many years later that he had taken the day off to spend it with his girlfriend, and Mom had found out about it that morning and confronted him.

Their marriage hadn't been good for years before that, so I never really blamed him for falling for someone else. In fact, they had been too young when they got married—21 years old—and they probably shouldn't have gotten married in the first place. But they wanted to "be together" and were "good Catholics," so marriage was the next logical step. My sister came less than a year after their wedding—much to my mom's dismay and to my dad's delight, as they would each remind Amanda at times. In that moment in the hallway, though, I allowed the wave of suspicion to leave me as quickly as it had come, and I told my dad I would see him at the concert.

Later that day, in the afternoon, Dad walked backstage—which was actually just a small hallway behind the church's altar—to see me before the concert.

"Hey, star of the show!" He hugged me. "I'm insanely excited for your solo. Mom will come to the evening performance. She couldn't get off early enough." He didn't meet my eyes.

"Okay," I said, too excited at the moment to see past myself.

"Break a leg!" He kissed my cheek and went to take a seat.

Throughout the performance, I don't remember thinking about anything but the music, until it was time for my solo. As I approached the microphone, an unfamiliar feeling washed over me—one that I couldn't name until at least a decade later. My feet felt heavy, like I was moving through a snowdrift. I remember the afternoon sunshine cascading through a stained-glass window portraying St. Francis of Assisi and feeling the dissonance of such a warm sight on such a cold day. I wanted to crawl into the sunshine and let it comfort me. What I was feeling was abandonment, and I would never be able to unfeel it—though sometimes way under the surface, undetected consciously—ever again.

The solo went fine—great, even. That was the year my voice became full, and I mastered the vibrato, of which I was incredibly proud. That solo was the first time I felt my voice carry across an audience in exactly the way I wanted it to, and the pride on my dad's face made me forget about the uncertainty of our family's future. I smiled at him and found myself blushing at the sight of Layla's parents sitting in the pew behind him. I barely knew them, but their presence reminded me that Layla was on the stage with me, somewhere nearby, and had just watched me sing.

Thursday, March 21, 2019

On hall duty before first period, a group of students approached me excitedly. They were quite a mix of kids I hadn't necessarily seen ever talking to each other, but I had many of them in different class periods.

Jaiden spoke first. "Mrs. R., you never told us in class yesterday if you downloaded TikTok yet.."

I laughed. "I thought you had forgotten about that. Yes, I actually did."

Savannah, the peacock lover from fourth period, pushed through the group to get closer to me. "Whoa, what's your name? So I can follow you." She whipped out her phone and opened the TikTok app.

"I didn't say I was putting anything on TikTok myself. I just downloaded it and watched some videos." Kate and Alexis had appeared on the fringe of the group, but I consciously didn't acknowledge them because I hadn't acknowledged any of the other students individually. I did, though, notice that Kate was once again wearing her rainbow hairpin.

Maddie jumped up and down from behind Jaiden. "Ooooh,

did you see Kate's TikTok about the new GSA?"

My pulse quickened, and my temperature rose. My thumb found a piece of skin hanging off of my pointer finger, but I resisted the urge to bite it. "I just watched whatever videos it showed me. I wouldn't know how to find Kate's."

Suddenly, Kate was beside me—so close that our arms were touching. I instinctively stepped away, but she moved in closer again with her phone in her hand.

It was her TikTok video. I couldn't tell where she was in it, but there was a orange, pink, and white striped backdrop behind her, and she had on her rainbow shirt and hairpin. She smiled at the camera and recited:

"Hey, hey!
Are you gay?
Then, come check out
our GSA!
Don't waste away
like a castaway.
You've got something to say,
and that's okay!
My name is Kate,
and I'm super gay!"

The video ended with Kate moving aside to reveal what was hanging behind her which I now recognized as the lesbian pride flag. The group of kids around me cheered as Kate shyly returned to the back of the group. I raised my eyebrows and nodded approvingly.

"It even has a rhyme scheme, right?" Maddie beamed. She walked toward me, holding out a piece of paper that I took from her absent-mindedly.

Savannah added, "Hashtag Benson GSA!"

"Yeah! Yeah, it's great. Nice job, Kate." I looked quickly in her direction just as a senior boy walked past her and not-very-quietly whispered the word "dyke" in her ear, and my teacher reflexes kicked into high gear.

"Whoa! Hey now, Mr. Simmons, that was completely inappropriate," I called after him, surprising myself that I had remembered his last name.

He stopped in his tracks with his back to us and turned slowly to face me. "Oh, I'm so sorry. I didn't mean to offend you. I wasn't talking to you, but I can totally understand why you may have thought I was." His face feigned innocence. "My bad!" He brought his hand to his heart and began backing away.

I tried to speak, but no words came out of my mouth.

"Jared, isn't it time you grow up? And I heard you, too. I'm writing it on a discipline referral right now and will note your harassment of both a student and a teacher."

Dana had appeared beside me, holding a discipline referral. I looked from her to Kate to Jared, who said, "I didn't say nothing—"

"Save it for Mr. Dunham. Get to class."

I could have hugged her, and I almost did, but then I remembered where I was. A hug would have been unprofessional, to start, but it also could have been recorded, and all I needed was proof of me putting my hands on yet another female.

Kate. The kids had dispersed, and I searched for her among their walking figures, but I didn't see her.

The bell rang. "Dana, I—"

"Don't mention it, Jo. Have a good day." She patted my arm and walked toward her classroom, giving me a wink before she entered it.

Looking down, I saw the paper I had been holding since Maddie had handed it to me. It was folded in half, but I could see through it to the pen written on the inside. Unfolding it, I saw a handwritten title at the top: *GSA SUPPORT PETITION*

Split into three columns were almost 100 student signatures.

- 32 -

Friday, March 22, 2019

The rest of Thursday had passed uneventfully. No more emails of significance or out-of-the-ordinary encounters with students. Just teaching and planning and grading without much time to think. Brandon was noticeably absent from my eighth period class due to an early dismissal for a basketball game.

There was a pep rally scheduled for our undefeated basketball team that afternoon, so the hallway was abuzz with excited students, most of whom were wearing our school colors of red and blue. We would be missing eighth period, which I was extra thankful for on a Friday afternoon because I didn't think I had it in me to pretend like I didn't feel Brandon watching me. I had learned that morning that part of Brandon's punishment for being suspended the week before was not being permitted to participate in the pep rally, and I was sure he wasn't happy about that. Besides, I was exhausted and just wanted to make it through the day without any more drama.

My morning was relatively normal. Each of my classes worked on their identity poems, and we read and discussed the first page of our new novel, analyzing the narrator's voice and how we can tell what her priorities are through her observations. I sprinkled in a little bit of grammar by pointing out some participles, and students looked through their poem drafts to see if they had any participles of their own, and some shared them. It was a productive learning day, and I was almost able to forget the allegations looming over me.

At the end of the day, I walked into the gym for the pep rally with a smile on my face as I saw the basketball team huddled together and getting hyped for their game. I had taught every single one of those boys, and many of them were good kids, as far as I could tell. (Although how much does a teacher really know?)

The gym was filled with the smells of sweat and floor wax mingling with excited voices that echoed off of the blue-and-red painted cinder-block walls. I had a predictable, preemptive headache but ignored it as I waved to the now-unhuddled boys and made my way over to stand along the wall next to a few other teachers.

Right before I reached the wall and was about to say hello to Bryce Flemming, the French teacher who had been hired the same year as me, I caught sight of a group of students who were in another kind of huddle near the top of the bleachers. Most of their backs were toward me, but I immediately recognized Brandon's green hoodie and mentally identified several of his friends. Just as I was about to look away, Brandon turned around and noticed me. He held my gaze for a few seconds and then leaned over to whisper to the boy next to him whom I recognized as a junior who had recently moved to the district and whose name was frequently on the school's discipline emails. They both turned and looked at me, smirking, before leaning into the center of their group and saying something that made all of them laugh and glance in my direction.

I tried to turn my attention to Bryce casually, but I know my ears told a different story. He cocked his head to the side and said, "Hey, Josie. You good?"

Leaning back against the wall next to him, facing slightly away from Brandon and his crew and slightly toward Bryce, I said, "Yeah. There's a group of kids talking about me."

He laughed and put his right hand on his hip, "That comes with the territory, doesn't it?" But when he saw I wasn't laughing, he dropped his hand and his smile and moved in closer to me. "What happened?"

"I'm surprised you haven't heard," I started, not quite able to look him in the eye. "I have parents coming after me for pushing my gay agenda."

He put his hands up in a gesture for me to stop talking. "Hold on. What? Are you, like, forcing them all to read David Sedaris or something?"

I had to smile at that. "No. But I do love David Sedaris." I shook my head to get back on topic. "No. Listen, I've been meaning to talk to you about this." I looked around to see if anyone was looking at us, but most people were watching the cheerleaders do their thing. (Side note: I never know where to look when the cheerleaders are performing. I want to show my support for them and am usually entertained by them, but I don't want anyone to think I'm looking at their bodies.) "Do you ever have kids come out to you?" Bryce is a single gay man who, like me, doesn't talk much about it in the classroom, but the kids just kind of know.

He thought for a few seconds and said, "Not really. I mean, it wouldn't come up very easily in between learning vocabulary and conjugating verbs. *Je suis une grande folle.*" He giggled and then translated, "I am a big ol' queen."

Like me, though, Bryce doesn't fall into a stereotype. Neither of us is especially feminine or masculine—more like nondescript and casual in our own ways. I smiled and said, "Those aren't words I would use to describe you, but sure!" I glanced at Brandon to discover him no longer paying any attention to me but, instead, flirting with a freshman girl whom I hoped wouldn't fall for his outward charm, so I was able to relax more. "It's a long story," I continued, more seriously. "I guess my class lends itself more to self-expression with the poetry and journaling and stuff like that. And I've had some kids come out to me before, but this was the first time one did it in writing, and her parents are not at all pleased about it."

Bryce cringed. "Yikes. I'm sorry, Josie. That sounds complicated." He ran his hands through his curly brown hair. "Want to get a drink after school and talk about it some more? I don't have any plans tonight."

I sighed. "You know, I would love that, but I'm sure my wife and kid will have other ideas. Can I take a rain check?"

"Sure thing," he said.

I looked around again before moving in closer to him. "So … there are some kids who want me to sponsor a GSA? Am I crazy for considering it?"

He raised his eyebrows. "Crazy? No. Brave? Hella."

I sighed. "There's a fine line, though. If I … decide to do it … would you be interested in participating somehow? Absolutely zero pressure. It's just that one of the kids already mentioned you, and—"

"Hmmm, I'm not sure about that. No offense, but it's a little trickier for me as a gay man. People tend to feel more

... threatened by—"

"I totally get it. I really do." I looked down at the shiny gym floor. "You don't have to expla—"

"Josie," he bent over to put his face in front of mine, "you didn't let me finish. I'd love to help with any behind-the-scenes stuff and could even attend some meetings and what not, but I don't feel comfortable putting my face on the logo, if you get what I mean."

I did. I really, really did.

Before I could answer, a bull horn sounded to signal it was time for everyone to stand and "Do the Bulldog." It looks sort of like a bull getting ready to charge, mixed with excited barking. Kids go crazy for it, and I normally participate for the fun of it, but I saw Kate watching me from across the gym. She was sitting in the front row with some of her friends, and they were all bulldogging, laughing, and talking around her, but she was looking at me with surprising solemnity.

I considered smiling sympathetically at her but instinctively looked in Brandon's direction first. He was also looking at me, but there was something else in his eyes—something that felt like quiet, confident, vengeance.

- 33 -

Friday, September 26, 1997

The beginning of high school was not an easy transition for me. Switching to public school—because my divorcing parents could no longer afford private school—left me without my friends, and I quickly became known as the slightly surly, chubby lesbian. I threw myself into any and all music programs I could find and hoped to find some like-minded people, and I did make some friends eventually, but they did not include any fellow gays.

By the end of September of my freshman year, I had settled into a lunch table of other misfits. I didn't talk much at that table, but I did have a great view of the most beautiful senior girl: Naomi Eastland. To me, she looked like a movie star. I sat sporting my braces and frizzy, sandy ponytail, unable to look away from her table for too long. But she wasn't the only reason my eyes were pulled in that direction. There were other popular kids who sat with her, and I was fascinated by their antics. I felt like I was watching a movie about the rich and famous, studying everything they did as if they and I were different species.

That morning in gym class, a girl who used to live down the street from me had approached me in the locker room. I was changing my shirt when I heard her say my name.

"Yeah?" I answered, pulling my head and arms through the holes of my tie-dyed t-shirt.

"Do you remember me? I'm Leah," she said matter-of-factly.

"Of course I remember you," I raised my eyebrows. "I'm pretty sure we played kickball in my parents' alley about a hundred times that one summer."

She shifted nervously and tried to smile, playing with the drawstring of her gym bag. "Yeah, I remember that. Do you still live there?"

"Yeah," I said. "Well, sometimes. I go with my dad on the weekends."

She looked away. "Oh, I didn't know your parents split up. Sorry."

I laughed, which surprised her into looking at me. "It's fine. They're happier apart."

She smiled. "That's good. Well," she paused for a few seconds, "is it true?"

"Is what true?" I finished putting my gym clothes in my bag and looked at her.

"Are you a lesbian?" She was looking at the bench in front of her, obviously afraid to look me in the eye.

I hesitated and then quickly decided that there wasn't any reason to be shy now when clearly people were talking about it. "Yep," I said quickly.

She looked at me. "Wow. I'm just surprised. Remember when you liked RJ and would chase him around the playground?"

I picked up my bag and my books to go to my next class. "I'm pretty sure I was just doing what everyone else was doing. And RJ still does have a pretty face."

She laughed, visibly loosening up. "He sure does!"

We walked out of the locker room together, and it felt good to be walking and talking to someone who knew me pre-misfit.

"So who do you think is pretty at this school? There are tons of girls to choose from, right?" She kept walking in the same direction as I was, so I guessed her next class was near mine.

"I don't know," I said. I hadn't even told Andrew or Layla about my crush on Naomi. They had both gone on to Catholic high schools, and we hadn't had much of a chance to talk yet since the beginning of the school year. And then I added, "Do you know Naomi Eastland?"

Leah grinned. "I definitely do. We're both cheerleaders." I hadn't realized either one of them was a cheerleader, so I was a bit taken aback.

"Oh. Cool. Well, I'm going to class," I said, walking towards the doorway to my geography class. "See you around."

"See ya!" she called after me.

I was thinking about that interaction as I sat at the lunch table and ate the turkey and swiss cheese sandwich that my mom had packed for me. Although we didn't see her much anymore because she spent most of her time with Sam when she wasn't working, she still packed our lunches every day. Feeling pleased that I had possibly made a new friend, I was surprised to see Amanda's face next to mine when I turned to look at the clock on the wall.

"Whoa!" I said. "You scared me."

She looked serious. "Are you okay?" she asked me.

I furrowed my eyebrows. "Yes. Why are you asking me

that?"

She crouched down beside me and got close to my ear. "The entire school is talking about how you have a crush on Naomi Eastland. Did you tell someone that?"

I could feel my sandwich start to come back up. Tears immediately sprang to my eyes, and I said, "I—I sort of told Leah Marsh. I didn't actually say those words. I—"

"Well, you better be prepared for people to say things to you. Naomi is pretty nice herself, but I can't say the same about all of her friends—especially not her boyfriend."

Even though I had never entertained the idea of actually dating Naomi, my shame and embarrassment were suddenly intensified by a feeling of jealousy at the thought of her having a boyfriend. I glanced in the direction of her lunch table, and there were three boys who were looking at me and laughing hysterically. Naomi was shushing them, and I could see that her cheeks were rosy from blushing. And that made me feel awful.

"I can't do this," I said quietly to Amanda. "I don't want to be at this school anymore." I tossed my brown bag in the garbage with my half-eaten lunch and rushed toward the door of the cafeteria.

A voice called after me, "Josie! Josie Rein-oceros! Naomi said she thinks you're pretty!"

- 34 -

Friday, March 22, 2019

After the pep rally, I walked directly to my classroom, grabbed my sweater and shoulder bag, and walked out the door at the same time as the students. I didn't consider the pile of ungraded papers on my desk or the fact that Monday morning's copies hadn't been made yet. I just had to get out of there. The sight of my scratched-up, reliable, tinier-than-everyone-else's car filled me with relief. I opened the door, plopped into the driver's seat, and unleashed an enormous sigh as I started the engine, ignoring the herds of laughing teenagers walking to their cars and their friends' cars, ready to embark on their Friday night adventures.

Maybe it really was Brandon sending the emails. Maybe he was disguising his tone to somehow fool me into thinking it was an adult, so I wouldn't pursue the issue and get him suspended again.

But Brandon rarely even writes complete sentences. I'm not even sure he knows how to write complete sentences. So maybe someone is helping him?

Or maybe it's someone else entirely. Maybe it actually is one of Kate's parents seeking to intimidate me into ... what? Pushing their daughter back into the closet?

It wasn't until I heard a knock on my window that I realized I hadn't actually pulled out of my parking space.

"Mrs. Rein-Thompson? Can I talk to you?"

I didn't have to turn my head to know that it was Kate.

Quickly, I pretended to be searching for something in the glove compartment. *Oh no. No, not again. If I back up and leave, maybe she'll assume I hadn't seen her. Maybe I'll just make a right out of the parking lot instead of a left, head toward the highway, and drive until I run out of gas. Cam will understand if I change my name and start a life of simplicity as a waitress at a dive bar, earning money under the—*

"Mrs. R.? I'm sorry to bother you. It's just that Brandon and his friends—"

I stopped rummaging and slowly turned my head toward her. There was something in her voice that was too familiar to ignore.

Rolling the window down, I forced a smile, "Hey, Kate. Sorry, I was looking for something and didn't see you there for a minute. Are you okay?"

She looked like she had been crying. Her mouth opened to speak, but she was interrupted by a wolf whistle aimed in our direction.

It was like someone had slapped me across the face, but I didn't bother to look around for the source. I started to roll the window up and said, "I'm really sorry, Kate. I have to get home. Have a good weekend."

She took a step back as I put the car in reverse. Though I tried not to look at her as I backed out, her small frame remained in my periphery for a few seconds. Even without looking directly at her, I noticed that her hair pin was gone.

On my way out of the parking lot, Amanda called me. I considered letting it go to voicemail but remembered I was the one who had called her first.

I answered, "Hey, Mands. How are you?"

"Hi there! I am just fine. Are you on your way home from work?"

"Yep. Exhausted. You?"

"I'm on my break. I thought I might catch you in the car. What happened at work that you wanted to talk to me about?"

"It's not that big of a—" I didn't know why I was downplaying it, but she didn't let me get away with it.

"Nope, don't do that thing where you shut off your emotions. It was important enough to want to talk about it the other day, so spill it."

She listened as I told the story, up through the pep rally that day and Kate coming up to my car again. I didn't leave anything out.

When I was done, she didn't speak for a minute or so, and then she said matter-of-factly, "So you tried to help this girl, and you're being repaid with an accusation? Can't she, like, stick up for you to her parents? By the way, I totally think it's them sending you those weird emails. Who else could it be?"

"I wish I knew! And as for her sticking up for me to them, I don't think it's that simple. They seem pretty righteous. She can't even stick up for herself let alone for me." I hoped Kate was also on her way home and that she wasn't still standing in the parking lot, sad and alone. I pushed a wave of guilt away, leaning forward to turn the fan on.

"Yeah, but you're being accused of something that isn't even true. If you mean that much to her, she should speak up on your behalf." I heard a sink turn on. "Hold on, I'm thirsty."

Can I hold it against Kate for not defending me? Does she know who's sending the emails?

Was that what she wanted to tell me at my car today?

"Sorry," Amanda said, "I have to get going. Listen, Jojo, you're an amazing person. That school board is going to see that, and this will all be a distant memory soon." Her voice was both sincere and serious.

"I don't know. Maybe I should just quit and become a recluse." I slowed to stop at the longest red light on the planet and leaned my head back on my head rest.

"No, you're going to start a GSA for those kids and ignore the haters like you've been doing for your whole gay life."

I laughed. "I wish I had your certainty, but you haven't encountered a teenager since you *were* one, so you don't exactly get it."

"Josie, think about how hard it was to be that kid. Do it for her." Someone called her name. "I gotta go. I'll call you soon. Love you!"

"Love you."

I spent the next twenty minutes of the ride alternating between being certain that I had to talk to Cam about everything that night and being certain that I should just call Kate's parents, apologize (for *what*, I wasn't sure yet), and promise to never speak to their daughter again or speak about my personal life to any student again ever for the duration of the final twenty years of my career.

Ugh, twenty fucking years. Do I really have to keep my mouth shut for that long?

That's when the Friday traffic hit full force, which did nothing to ease my anxiety. After a few minutes of aggressively tapping the steering wheel and quietly muttering profanities, I decided that the only thing that could help pass the time without making me think too much was music. I put on my favorite playlist and listened for a while, more aware than usual that every single song was performed by a female singer. Because I'm a female singer? Because I'm a lesbian?

I was about halfway through the fourth song when my phone started buzzing again. It was Cam, her smile on my phone screen flooding me with comfort.

"Hey, babe! How was your day?" I said.

"Hi there! It was definitely interesting. I got my parents to watch Liesel for the evening. Want to go on a date?"

My comfort quickly turned to gratitude. "Hell yes! Where to?"

"I thought we might try that new sushi restaurant down-town. What do you think?"

"Perfect." I looked at the time. "I'll see you in about twenty minutes if this light ever turns green."

"I should be home at about the same time. See you soon. Love you."

"I love you more!"

I turned the music back on and relished my new optimism, vowing then to spend the weekend enjoying my family without worrying about the things that were out of my control.

When I got home, Cam was just getting out of her car. I kissed her hello, and we went inside to change into jeans and more casual shirts (hers always more form-fitting than mine). I ignored my reflection in the mirror, not wanting to meet my own eyes or remember any imperfections, and it didn't take long for us to get into Cam's car and head toward the restaurant.

After a few minutes of sitting next to her as she drove quietly, I said, "So do you want to tell me what was interesting about your workday?" We always joke that teaching never has a dull moment, and I know Cam's definition of that is very different with five-year-olds than it is with me and fifteen-year-olds. I knew something had happened—maybe good, maybe bad— for her to mention that the day was out of the ordinary.

She looked at me sideways before glancing in the rearview mirror to change lanes. "Have you really not seen the news?"

"The news?" I asked, confused. "I listened to music on the way home and didn't hear anything at school today. What happened?" I shifted my body to face her as much as I could in my seatbelt.

"We were under a lockdown today," she said quietly. "Some weirdo tried to get into the front office with an assault rifle, but our head security guard wrestled it out of his hands and pinned the guy before he could make it past the secretaries."

My mouth was agape. "What? Are you fucking serious?"

"I doubt I would joke about this." She put on her turn signal and made a right on red onto the street where the restaurant is.

"Holy shit." I was speechless until a flood of questions came pouring out of me. "What time was this? Who was the guy? Where is he now?"

She expertly parallel-parked about a block away from the restaurant. "Do you think this is close enough?" she asked me.

"It's fine. Cameron, are you okay?" I grabbed her face and pulled it towards me. Her eyes were suddenly shiny with tears.

"I'm okay now, I think. I'm not sure I can say the same for my students." She pulled my hands from her face and held them in her own.

"Why? Did the lockdown stress them? What did they say over the announcements?" I couldn't stop the barrage of questions.

She sighed. "I was walking them to gym class at exactly the moment that it happened—right past the office." Her voice had gotten smaller. She let go of my hands and turned away from me just as tears started spilling onto her cheeks.

"Oh my God, baby," I started to cry for her and for those tiny students. "I am so sorry. They saw it all through the office windows? Oh my God."

She nodded as a few more tears slid down her face. "I will never, ever forget the looks of shock and panic on their little faces. And I saw the guy's face, too. His sheer determination. He was coming in to repeat Sandy Hook. I swear to God." Now her voice was shaking. I took her hand again.

"Did you recognize him?"

She wiped her face with the backs of her hands. "No. I don't even think I could pick him out of a lineup. I saw his determination and his gun, but Barry, our security guard, took him down before I could see any defining characteristics, and I tried rushing the kids into the music room to lock the door and get into a corner. Poor Mrs. Rudolph was eating her lunch at her desk, listening to Bach or Beethoven or something, and we came rushing in like a screaming mob." She closed her eyes and shook her head. "They called the lockdown right then, and we spent the next hour in the music room while the police came and took the guy away."

I couldn't tell if it was my hand or her hand that was sweating as I squeezed hers. "I'm trying to process all of this. I can't believe that I heard nothing about it. We had a pep rally, and everyone was so excited for our basketball team that not a soul was paying attention to the outside world."

"The news cameras didn't get there until the kids were dismissed at 3:30—well, the kids who were left, anyway. Word traveled quickly, and many parents came to pick their kids up early after the lockdown ended at about 2:00. You were probably in the pep rally at exactly the time they aired the news for the first time."

I shook my head back and forth what felt like a hundred times. "You were right there," I whispered. "What if that security guard had been in the bathroom or something? Oh my God." I started crying again.

She took her hand back and ran it through her hair. "I know. I can't even think about it. And not even for myself but for those twenty-two babies in my care. I can't even think about it." She exhaled loudly and said, "Let's go eat. I didn't have lunch, so I'm starving."

We got out of the car and walked down the sidewalk next to each other. I thought about taking her hand but decided against it. Neither of us has ever been much into public displays of affection—least of all Cam. I can't necessarily explain why because I doubt anyone would even notice—and, even if they did, as women, people probably wouldn't think too much about it—and we weren't anywhere near where either of us teaches. It's just not something we do often. As we walked quietly next to each other, I couldn't shake a feeling of guilt that I hadn't known about what happened at her school that day. I was berating myself for being self-centered as we walked into the restaurant.

There wasn't a wait, which surprised us. "Are we sure we have the right place?" I asked her. We looked around at what seemed like a pretty typical Japanese restaurant.

"I think so," she said. When our server came to ask us about our drinks, Cam asked, "How long has this restaurant been open? This is our first time here."

He thought for a few seconds and then said, "I just started a few weeks ago, but it's at least been here since I moved to this city four years ago."

Cam and I looked at each other, and she surprised me by bursting into giggles. Amusement flooded me with what felt like relief as my own laughter bubbled up. She looked back to him and said, "Sorry. We're not laughing at you. We're laughing because we thought we were somewhere else."

He smiled. "Ah, I bet you meant to go to the new place across the street." He raised his eyebrows. "Would you like to leave before I get your order?"

We turned to look out the window and saw at least ten people waiting outside of the new restaurant. I knew what she was thinking without even confirming it with her before I said, "We're good here. Can we please look at a sushi menu? Oh, and we will both have water to drink please."

"Of course," he said as he walked away. Cam was looking intently at me with a twinkle in her eyes, and I knew she was feeling the same gratitude that I was: for us, for this moment, and for life.

Tuesday, August 9, 2005

Cam and I sat on her parents' couch, legs overlapping, as we watched the movie *The Hours* for the millionth time. A three-quarters-empty box of pizza sat on the coffee table in front of us, and I bent forward to grab a slice with mushrooms on it.

"Why is Meryl Streep literally captivating in every single role she plays?" I took a bite while still looking at the screen.

"She's definitely talented," Cam replied, absent-mindedly stroking my leg.

"I think Kate Winslet will be regarded that way someday. She's too young now, but she's amazing already." I took another bite and looked over at Cam.

She rolled her eyes good-naturedly. "You should totally marry Kate Winslet."

Laughing, I leaned over and punched her arm. "Well, maybe she would actually introduce me to her parents if we went to the trouble of planning a whole wedding."

Cam's smile faded, and she took her hand off of my leg. "Don't start, Josie. You know it's complicated."

"I know," I said, purposely without much emotion, and

turned my attention back to my pizza and the movie.

We were in her parents' house because she was still living with them to save money, and they were on vacation at a timeshare somewhere. Actually, I had spent a lot of time in their house for someone who didn't exist to them. It never felt un-creepy when I thought about it too much—so I tried not to think about it too much.

Cam and I had been together for about three and a half years. We were at that point in a relationship when things are comfortable and easy most of the time, especially since Brad had given up stalking us in the last year or so.

That's right—the night with the cinder block hadn't stopped him.

His dedication had lessened a bit, and things got easier when I moved into a college dorm that he didn't attempt to enter, but he would still pop up here and there—usually drunk—and beg Cam to come back to him. He threatened my life a handful of other times, but I learned to pity him more than anything.

By the end of the movie, I had finished the rest of the pizza, and the summer sun had set. I stood up to go throw the pizza box away when we both heard a car door in the driveway. I spun around to look at Cam, panic flooding my veins with the uncertainty between fight and flight. Her eyes were wide, and she was frozen on the couch, legs still stretched out in relaxation.

"I'll grab the suitcases," we heard her dad's voice say.

Cam swung her feet to the floor and said, "Let's go."

I dropped the pizza box back onto the coffee table and followed her up the stairs to where all of the bedrooms are. She took me into the spare room and opened the closet door, and then she ran out of the room. When she came back, she had all of my clothes that I had been tossing on the floor of her room for the past few days, and she handed them to me and not-so-gently guided me into the closet, switching on the light before she closed the door.

This was not a walk-in closet, but it also wasn't tiny. There were old-smelling coats on wire hangers and snow boots lined up neatly on the floor. I stood holding my discarded clothing and looked around, my heart pounding too loudly for me to focus on any sounds I might be able to hear. I tried to normalize my breathing, but there was an unmistakable urge to cry underneath my adrenaline rush. Since no one could see me, I let it happen. Tears slid silently down my cheeks and onto the black t-shirt that was on top of the pile I was holding.

Just as I started to really give in to a sob, I heard footsteps on the stairs and Cam's mom's voice saying something about how the condo complex had been too crowded, and they had just wanted to come home to enjoy the local pool instead. Cam's voice was next, politely asking how their drive had been and if they were hungry.

"I see you polished off a whole pizza down here," her dad loudly teased from the living room. Over the years, I had grown to like him from afar. He never seemed to be angry and had a great sense of humor. Cam laughed and said something about eating a little bit of the pizza at a time over the past few days.

I sniffed quietly, wishing I had access to a tissue. The only thing in my pocket was my flip phone, which I quickly remembered was not on silent. Dropping the pile of clothes to the floor, I reached into my pocket and pulled it out, moving the switch on the side.

Honestly, I have no idea how long I was in there, but it felt like an eternity. The three of them went about their evening without a care in the world—although I'm sure Cam was nervous, and I hope she felt guilty for leaving me in there—while I eventually sat down on top of my clothes and leaned back against the wall behind the coats and contemplated life.

I imagined what it would be like someday when I could tell this story to her mom while sitting at their dining room table, and we would laugh about how silly it was that Cam had felt the need to put me into a literal closet—the irony being part of the amusement. We would have magazines spread out on the table in front of us, planning our wedding colors and bridesmaids' dresses. I would be in charge of the music for the ceremony and the reception. Our first dance would be to a Jann Arden song, and my father-daughter dance would be to the Beatles song that inspired my dad to give me my middle name. The flowers would be multicolored daisies, and we would each wear our own versions of white dresses. Amanda would give the toast and smile at both Cam and me, laughing about those long-ago days when she had been sworn to secrecy.

Hours later, Cam opened the door. I had fallen asleep leaning against the wall, and she crouched down to wake me gently. There was sadness in her eyes as she took my hand and helped me up. We crept down the stairs and out the back door to where she had parked the Rocket, and that's when she finally spoke.

"I am so sorry." She put her hands on my face, so I couldn't look away from her. "This isn't fair to anyone. I hate lying to them, and I hate what it does to you. I hate what it does to me. I know I have to tell them. I don't know how or when, but I have to tell them." She let go of my face and turned to go around the car and into the driver's seat.

That was the first time she had said that to me. Still half asleep, I felt giddy about the near future, my tears in the closet already a foggy memory. I was positive she would tell them soon and that all of my plans would start coming to fruition. They would love me, and we could finally really be together.

Saturday, March 23, 2019

When I awoke that morning at six o'clock on the dot, both Cam and Liesel were still sleeping. I slipped out of bed, put on fuzzy socks and shorts to go with my t-shirt, and tiptoed past Liesel's door and down the always-creaky stairs. Birds were chirping outside of the window behind the kitchen sink that faces our backyard, and the sky was just starting to hint at dawn. I grabbed my favorite coffee mug—the one that has a picture of me painted on it by Liesel (really just a circle with two arm-like things that she said was me)—and made a cup as quietly as possible, stirring in milk, sugar, and cinnamon. I carried it carefully to my favorite armchair in the living room and sat down to enjoy the birds' songs.

After about three blissful sips, I heard Liesel's footsteps upstairs and felt a mixture of disappointment, anticipation, and delight. Her door swung open, and she stomped like a herd of elephants down the stairs. I chuckled at how such a small person can make such a ruckus, and when she spotted me smiling in the dark, she ran to jump on my lap.

"Whoa, baby, hot coffee!" I warned and leaned over to set

the mug on a side table as I wrapped her in my arms. She fit her head under my chin and started rocking herself, which is always my cue to take over. I rocked her and hummed a Beatles song that my dad used to sing to me.

When I was done with the song, we sat still and silent for a few minutes. Breathing in the scent of her baby hair, I reminded myself to savor the moment because she would soon be too big to do this.

She asked quietly, "Where did you and Mommy go last night?"

"Out to dinner at a place you wouldn't like. What did you do with Pop and Gram?" I stroked her hair.

She sat up and looked at me, grinning. "Had pizza and built blocks!"

I returned her smile. "Now *that* is my idea of a good time!"

When Cam and I had finished dinner the night before, we decided to go see a movie at a cinema we used to frequent before Liesel was born. The movie was mediocre, but it was wonderful to sit next to her in the dark, holding hands and just being together as a couple. By the time we went to pick Liesel up at her parents' house, she had fallen asleep on the couch watching a Disney movie, so we scooped her up and took her home without jostling her too much, and she magically stayed asleep all the way into her own bed—clothing change and all.

Her smile faded, and she said, "I had a bad dream."

I frowned. "I'm sorry, baby. Do you want to talk about it?"

She nodded. "A witch came to take you and Mommy away. She laughed like witches laugh, like *hehehehehe*." She did her best witch impression, and I tried to keep a straight face.

"Oh my! That does sound scary. It's a good thing witches are only pretend. Right?"

She nodded again, gravely this time. "Yeah, good thing."

I hugged her to me again, but she was too awake to sit still anymore. She wiggled out of my lap and asked if I wanted to play My Little Pony with her.

"Can I finish my coffee first?" I bargained.

"Sure!" she said sweetly.

I patted her head and took my coffee back to the kitchen to reheat it in the microwave, hoping that she would forget that she had asked me to play. I am awful at playing pretend. I'm sure I did it when I was a kid, but I just cannot do it as an adult. Cam is usually good for it, and I pick up the slack with singing, dancing, and coloring. I wanted to let Cam sleep, but I was secretly hoping that she would wake up and take over when there was a knock at the front door.

"Mama, somebody's here!" Liesel called from the living room.

My pulse quickened. "Don't answer it!" I called back.

Cam's sleepy voice came from upstairs. "Who in the world …"

I rushed into the living room to be sure that Liesel wasn't walking toward the door. I must have looked worried because I saw it reflected back at me from underneath her messy morning hair. "It's okay, baby. Mama will see who it is."

On my way to the front door—which was about ten feet from where Liesel was sitting on the floor with her toys—I scanned the room for a weapon. I grabbed an umbrella and then pulled the curtain back to see who it was.

The sun was peeking over the horizon, and it was briefly all I could see. Squinting, I focused my eyes on the porch, looking straightforward, then left, right, down, and even up. But no one was there.

"Josie? Who's at the door? And why are you holding an umbrella?"

I twisted around and saw Cam standing on the stairs, rubbing her eyes and gazing at me expectantly. On the wall beside her, a photograph of smiling baby Liesel looked at us both.

And the words all came tumbling out at once, fighting each other for air time. I told her about the emails, the wolf whistle, Brandon's eyes, the GSA—everything. At some point while I was talking, she sat down on the stairs and leaned her head against the railing, watching me with an unreadable expression.

When I felt like I had told her every last detail, I finished with, "And that was just nobody at the door. I mean, it was obviously somebody, but nobody was there when I looked." I started pacing. "I didn't tell you any of this because I didn't want to worry you, but now it seems like there might actually be something to worry about." I stopped to look at her. "I am so sorry. What should we do? Call the police?"

"Whoa, slow down." She leaned forward onto her elbows. "We don't even know if the person who knocked is the same person who's been sending those emails. That would be a whole other level of crazy." She stood up and finished walking down the stairs toward me, gently taking the umbrella out of my hand. "Honey, you're shaking. Go sit down."

I went back to my armchair and sat, watching Liesel obliviously playing with her toys. Assuming Cam was going to follow me, I didn't expect to hear the front door open. I jumped up and ran to it, afraid that someone had somehow unlocked it and was walking in.

Instead, I saw Cam coming back in, holding an Amazon package. She smiled warmly, "Special delivery. Is this that new coffee you wanted to try?"

I looked from Cam's face to the package and back to her face. "Jesus, why would the delivery person knock on the door so goddamn early in the morning?"

She shrugged, still smiling. Glancing at Liesel, she said, "Come sit with me in the kitchen. We can talk about everything while I make some coffee."

Following her, I questioned why it had taken me so long to confide in her. Had I been worried about her worrying, or had I been worried about her making me feel even guiltier than I already did? Was I afraid she would confirm that I had somehow ruined our family's lives by opening myself up to this level of scrutiny?

Yes. I was afraid that she was going to be angry, not worried. But the smile on her face that morning had to be a good sign, right?

I sat at the table while she walked to the Keurig and made herself a cup. Unlike me, Cam doesn't say the first thing that comes to her mind, and I could tell she was considering what to say next.

She sat down across from me and took a sip of her coffee before saying, "Has anything else happened other than the emails? Have you felt threatened by anyone?"

I thought about it. "No. A few kids have made comments here and there, but I haven't actually felt threatened." I was trying to read her expression.

"Well," she continued, "someone is clearly pissed off, but they're not pissed off enough to physically approach you. That's a good thing." She took another sip and thought as she swallowed. "Do you think whoever it is has shown the video to anyone else?"

My stomach twisted as I pictured myself looking around to see if anyone was watching before putting my arms around Kate. "I have no idea," I said flatly, shifting my gaze to the wood grains on the table, absently searching for a pattern.

"Josie," she smacked the table lightly to bring my attention back to her face. "Josie, you haven't done anything wrong. Does this complicate your life a bit? Yes. But you haven't actually done anything wrong. The school board is going to see that. It's 2019, for God's sake. They can't fire you for being a lesbian! Do I wish you somehow could have prevented this from happening? Of course I do, but I've been thinking about Kate's essay since you told me about it, and you know what? You really didn't ask her to write about you, and you especially didn't ask her to come out of the closet in it. When I was hugging my kids in that music room yesterday, it was hard *not* to think about what actually matters in life." She paused, and we both heard Liesel quietly singing nursery rhymes. "Like her." She nodded toward the living room. "And us. And our life together that no one can take away from us."

I watched her, marveling at how her face still looked like it did nearly twenty years ago—those eyes that had startled me that first night, still as bright as ever.

She continued, "You were right before. It's easier for me with little kids because they don't think about my private life. They're only thinking about what's in front of them, and for all they know, I sleep under my desk every night." We both chuckled. Then, she looked at me more seriously. "Listen, if you didn't tell me all of this because you thought I would be mad, I'm sorry. I'm not mad." Her eyes were warm but concerned. "I am, however, worried about you. Are you considering moving forward with the GSA idea? Don't you think you should just try to put all of this behind you?"

I felt sudden conviction. "But how can I? Now that everyone knows, what would even be the point of trying to pretend anymore? Wouldn't that just make me weak? Wouldn't that set a terrible example for these kids—queer and straight alike?"

She sipped again. "Maybe. I don't know. Look, I can tell you're overwhelmed with all sorts of emotions about this, and I get it. Actually, I probably *don't* get it, but I can imagine. I'm your wife, and I want you to know that I'm going to support you no matter what you decide to do. I trust you to make the right decision."

I closed my eyes and rubbed my forehead, wishing I hadn't gotten out of bed so early. She was right that I was over-whelmed, but something in me felt a little lighter. I sighed. "I already feel better after telling you. I didn't realize how much keeping it from you was getting to me. I'm sorry." I looked at her and took her hand from across the table. She squeezed my fingers.

"This week might really suck, babe. But we will get through it." She stood up and walked over to me, pulling my head to her middle. I reached my hand up the back of her sweatshirt and slid it across her warm, bare skin.

"Mmmmm," I pulled her in closer to me, inhaling her sweet morning scent, when Liesel's voice was right next to us.

"I'm hungry!" She was standing in the doorway of the kitchen, holding a pony in one hand and a purple marker in the other. The marker snapped me to my senses.

"Oh, hey there! Were you making some art, baby girl?" I got up and walked toward her while Cam grabbed a bowl from the cabinet to get Liesel some Cheerios.

"Yep! I drew a pony on the pillow!"

Following her into the living room, I thanked the universe for washable markers.

Sunday, March 24, 2019

On Sunday morning, as Cam, Liesel, and I ate a breakfast of eggs and bacon together, we made plans to go to a playground across town that one of Cam's students had recently mentioned. All Liesel had to hear was that it had a "giant rainbow slide," and she was all in. Since Cam had already done her training run the day before, she was free to hang out with us all day. Although I had grocery shopping and grading to do, I told myself to live in the moment and enjoy the time with my family.

When we got to the playground at mid-morning, it was already crowded. Kids ran and screamed, and we told Liesel to go have fun as we found a spot to share on a bench. It was one of those spring days that reminds you of why you've been waiting for spring in the first place—sunny and breezy with just the hint of a chill. Cam and I sat close to one another and smiled as we watched our daughter easily make a friend and ask her to play in the sandbox.

Cam looked at me and then back at Liesel. "So, do you want to talk about anything? The GSA? Tomorrow's board meeting?"

I wished she hadn't mentioned either subject and had been trying really hard to forget the fact that the board meeting was happening the next day. "Not right now," I said, not taking my eyes away from Liesel, whose blonde hair was practically glowing in the sunshine. "I just want to enjoy the morning."

"Okay, babe." She patted my leg softly.

"Miss Rein-Thompson?" I turned to see Matt, a student from my first period, smiling shyly down at me from behind our bench.

"Hey, Matt!" I said cheerfully, feeling the familiar vulnerability of being seen in public with Cam by a student, combined with the guilt of still not grading his essay from the other day. "Shoot, looking at you is reminding me to finish grading those essays today!" I smiled up at him, hoping our interaction would be quick.

He shrugged and then pointed to the sandbox. "Is that your daughter?"

I looked where he was pointing and nodded. "Yep, that's Liesel."

"She's playing with my little sister, Maggie." The two little girls were laughing and singing something about princesses.

"Well, that's a coincidence!" I said, smiling up at him again, just as a woman with red hair like his joined us. "You must be Matt's mom." I stood up and stuck my hand out to shake hers. "I'm his English teacher, Mrs. Rein-Thompson."

She looked from her daughter in the sandbox to me and then took my hand and shook it quickly, not meeting my eyes. "I know. I've heard a lot about you."

Her shortness surprised me, and I laughed nervously and looked at Matt. "Good things, I hope!"

Matt looked uncomfortable, and I saw his mother glance down at Cam before saying, "Jessica Anderson is my cousin." She cupped her hands around her mouth and shouted, "Maggie! Time to go home!"

Maggie, whose auburn hair was a much subtler shade of her mother's, looked up, disappointed. My phone buzzed a few times in my back pocket, but I didn't think it would be an appropriate time to look at it. Liesel followed Maggie's gaze and saw that Maggie's mom and I were standing next to each other, so she jumped up and ran over to us.

"Hi, Maggie's mom! Maggie and I are friends now because we both like princesses and don't like petzels." She spoke quickly and enthusiastically.

Maggie and Matt's mom smiled politely at her. "Well, isn't that nice?"

Maggie made her way to us and stood next to Liesel. "Yeah, we're best friends now, even though she's not three yet, and I'm four. Can we have a playdate?"

I felt nauseated at my worlds colliding, and this was not eased by the woman's quick "no."

Maggie persisted, whining, "But Liesel said both her moms would be fine with me coming to their house."

"That's *enough*, Margaret." Her mother took her by the hand and led her away from us. Maggie looked back at Liesel, her expression confused, and Matt glanced back at me with what looked like pity.

"What was *that* about?" Cam asked. "Did she say Anderson?" She suddenly realized. "Oh. Yikes." She took my hand and pulled me back down onto the bench. My pulse was still racing, and her touch soothed me a bit, but my gratitude was tinged with paranoia. I looked around to see if there were any other familiar faces who might bring any more unpleasant surprises, but my eyes locked on Liesel. She, thankfully, had already forgotten about Maggie and was happily running to get in line for the tall, multicolored slide nearby.

I pulled my phone out of my back pocket and saw I had missed an unfamiliar, local number, deciding it couldn't have been important if no one had left a message. Still on edge, I sighed.

"Hey," Cam said, putting her hand on my arm. "That lady clearly had some anger issues." She turned to face me. "We've met so many wonderful people who are perfectly fine with our family. Don't let a few assholes get to you. We've talked about this already. Your job isn't in jeopardy. They don't have a legal leg to stand on."

I sighed and semi-successfully pushed away a bubble of resentment, wondering how she could so casually dismiss "a few assholes" when she had spent so much of her life running from them. "It would be different if those few assholes didn't make me feel like my existence is somehow rated R."

We both looked toward the slide as Liesel shouted blissfully while coming down it. Clapping and grinning, I said, "Let's just forget about it for today. There's nothing I can do. I'm going to go home and grade some papers to remind myself of why I got into this business to begin with."

We spent the next hour or so watching Liesel have fun with various kids as we casually socialized with their various parents—none of whom batted an eye about us being two moms. I knew Cam was right and that most people were accepting—or, at the least, too self-absorbed to care. I made a silent decision on that park bench: I was going to go home and write a school board proposal for our school to start a GSA.

- 39 -

Friday, August 12, 2005

Cam and I—pretending like the closet incident hadn't even happened—were going to spend the weekend together. The following week would be the first week of school for that year; it was her fourth year teaching kindergarten in the district where she still teaches now, and I would be doing my student teaching at a neighboring district. We had taken out a map of the state and chosen a new city to visit by closing our eyes and pointing to a random spot. We were basically going to the middle of nowhere to a cheap hotel, but it had a pool, air conditioning, and free breakfast, so we didn't care where it was.

I had packed my lavender corduroy backpack with toiletries and clothes and was adding my toothbrush when I heard Cam's ringtone on my phone. By the time I finally fished it out of my bag, she had hung up. I called her right back, but it went straight to voicemail. I tried a couple of more times, and the same thing happened. Looking at the time, I told myself she would be picking me up in fifteen minutes, anyway, so I would talk to her then.

But fifteen minutes came and went. I gave her a five-minute grace period before I started calling her again. This time, her phone rang like normal, but she didn't answer it.

I texted: *Is everything okay? Weren't we supposed to leave at noon?*

I stared at my phone for a few minutes, but she didn't text back. That wasn't like her. I tried calling one more time—still no answer—before I decided to get into my car and drive to her house. The A/C in Woody didn't work, so I rolled the windows down and tapped the steering wheel as I drove, a bundle of nervous energy. What would I do if I got there and saw her car and her parents' cars there? I surely couldn't just walk up and ring the doorbell.

My emotions went on a roller coaster ride in the five minutes it took to get there. I was worried about her, but then I was angry that she wasn't talking to me. I was excited about our trip, but then I was devastated that maybe she didn't want to go anymore.

I pictured the inside of that closet door.

By the time I turned onto her street, I was sweating in the August heat and fully unprepared to see her car, her parents' cars, and Brad's white pickup truck.

I slowed to a crawl, attempting to peer into the front window. I could see the back of Cam's head and the back of her mom's head. They were both sitting on the couch looking straight ahead—sitting on the couch that Cam and I had sat on together countless times, holding hands, cuddling, kissing, talking, laughing.

The mixture of confusion and jealousy made me feel sick. *Why is Brad there? Why is he allowed in there, and I'm not?* She hadn't spoken to him in months—at least that I knew of. I hadn't seen him at all that summer and was hoping he had finally moved on.

But there he was. I could see him walking into the living room, Cam's and her mom's heads turning to face him.

A car horn sounded behind me, causing me to jump and instinctively step on the gas pedal, jolting the car forward. I sped to the stop sign at the end of the street, slammed on the brakes, and kept driving to an unknown destination.

About fifteen minutes later, I found myself in a Wendy's drive-thru, ordering two meals and a frosty. I ate every last morsel while driving aimlessly in any direction, listening to nothing but my own chewing and Woody's struggling engine. If I went home, my mom would ask why we hadn't left yet. If I went to my dad's, he would ask the same thing. Maybe I would just keep driving forever, and no one would miss me.

I pulled into a gas station to throw away the garbage, and when I opened the door to get back in the car, Cam was calling me. Seeing her name on the digital screen flooded me with a swirl of relief and apprehension. I didn't know if I should answer angrily or give her a chance to explain.

"Hey," I said sadly—which was not an emotion I'd expected.

"I'm sorry," she whispered. "I can't talk long. Brad showed up and told my parents everything—about you, about me ... just ... everything." She breathed heavily.

"What? Why now?" I put on my turn signal to make a U-turn and head back to my mom's house for her to pick me up.

She was a little louder this time. "I have no idea, Josie." She paused. "Listen ... " She paused again. "My mom is really upset. She won't talk to me. I can't tell if she's madder that I'm a lesbian or that I lied." Pause.

Feeling giddy at the prospect of her finally coming out to

her family, I had the phone pressed to my ear so hard that my elbow was starting to hurt, but I was having such a hard time hearing her. "Cam, I can barely hear you. Are you coming to pick me up? I'm not home yet—"

"Josie, I can't do this anymore."

The frosty threatened to come back up into my throat. "What do you mean? Do what?"

She breathed audibly again. "It's too confusing and too hard." More pausing. "You deserve better than this."

"Are you breaking up with me over the phone right now?" An unfamiliar combination of hysteria and humiliation exploded in my chest.

"I'm sorry." She was whispering again. "Maybe someday but not now. I love you." Her voice broke. "Please don't call me."

And she hung up.

Monday, March 25, 2019

Dana was waiting in my dark classroom, her face illuminated by the light from her phone. She was sitting at my desk with her travel mug in front of her.

I flicked on the lights. "Hey," I said.

She looked up. "Hey."

I walked closer to her and set my bag on the floor. "What's up? Everything okay?"

She was following me with her eyes. "Yeah. I just wanted to check on you. I thought I might hear from you this weekend to … like … talk through some strategies for the board meeting or something."

I sighed and sat down on top of a student desk. "Sorry. I finally told Cam about everything, and then I didn't feel like talking about it much after that."

"Oh, okay." She wasn't meeting my eyes.

"What? Why are you being weird?" I raised my eyebrows.

"It's just … " She hesitated. "People are really talking about you on Facebook. Some of it is positive from students and parents of students and even former students. But there are some people who just can't let go of the fact that you touched

Kate's shoulder in class." She finally looked at me, sadly, and added, "It's not fair that anyone is judging you, and I just wish this wasn't happening. If you hadn't touched her—"

Narrowing my eyes, I interrupted, "It was completely innocent. Do you know how many shoulders I've touched in all of these years?"

Startled by my volume, she winced. "Yeah, but maybe that wasn't the right moment to do it. I mean, maybe Kate's wasn't the shoulder to touch."

I flinched. "Are you kidding? How was I supposed to know she likes girls? I may have a relatively accurate gaydar, but I may also have left my psychic powers at home that day." My ears were hot. I got up and started pacing before adding, "I can't do this right now." I stopped pacing and looked at her. "And I definitely don't need you telling me to feel guilty about something I've already lost sleep over." I turned to walk away and stopped, turning back around to look at her. "Wait. Is anyone talking about me hugging her in the parking lot? They're just talking about her shoulder?"

"From what I saw, that's it. Listen, Josie, I'm sorry. I'm not trying to be unsupportive or un … sympathetic." Her eyes were pleading, but I was too defensive to hear what she was saying.

"I just wish for your sake that you hadn't touched her because you haven't done anything else that anyone could consider to be inappro—"

"*Nothing* I've done was inappropriate. Nothing."

The bell rang, and she got up—the irony not lost on me when she put her hand on my shoulder before walking toward the door. When she got there, she turned around slowly and said, "I'll be at that meeting to support you. I'll always have your back."

She turned and walked out as students began entering sleepily. I felt my pocket buzzing and took out my phone to see the same local number that had called the day before. I declined the call and wondered if they would leave a message this time.

The kids seemed especially quiet—even for a Monday morning. I tried all of my song and dance tricks to get them interested in participating, but nothing worked until I mentioned our poetry slam that would be coming up on Wednesday evening.

Several of them perked up and mentioned that they thought many people were coming, based on what the buzz was on social media. Josh reached into his backpack and pulled out a colorful paper that boldly read "SLAM POETRY JAM" in all capital, graffiti-looking letters, followed by smaller, bold black letters that read "Wednesday March 27 @6pm in the auditorium."

"I've been putting this up everywhere there's empty space," he said proudly.

I nodded, impressed. "That is good-looking! Can I have one to hang up on my door?"

He handed one to me and asked, "Can we practice today after school? I know of at least five more kids who want to participate, and I can text them to tell them we're having practice if you say it's okay."

"How about tomorrow? There's a ... ummm ... meeting tonight that I need to go to." I got out some tape from a desk drawer to hang the flyer on the outside of my classroom door, purposely not meeting anyone's eyes. When I came back in, many of the students had taken out their identity poems, so I went with it. "We might as well spend the last fifteen minutes working on our poems. Go ahead and take it out if you haven't already."

While they got to work, I pulled my phone out of my pocket to check my calendar to be sure I was, in fact, free after school the next day, and I saw that I had a voicemail from that local number. Worried that it might have something to do with Liesel or Cam, I said to the class, "Hey, guys, I have to check my messages real quick. I'll just be in the hall."

I walked out into the hall, leaving the door ajar in order to hear any horseplay, and pressed the voicemail icon. A female voice said, "Hi, Josie. My name is Adelaide Foster, and I'm a reporter with the Dispatch. We got a call about your situation, so I checked out the school's Facebook page to get an angle, and I just got confused. Would you mind talking to me to clarify some details? I'd like to write about it in tomorrow's edition … after the school board meeting tonight, of course. Give me a call to set something up. Thanks!"

My heart was racing. What did she mean by my "situation," and what were the multiple angles she was choosing from? I took a few journalism classes in college and am not a stranger to how reporters spin information to suit their biases. Was she trying to sound supportive, or was she just nosy? Was she being objective, or was she, like, a friend of the Andersons or Stonemans?

I thought for a few seconds and decided that if she was going to write the piece with or without my input—and it sounded like she would—that I should at least defend myself. If she was going to quote me, though, I had to be sure about what I wanted to say. Without significant premeditation, I normally end up oversharing, and that's the last thing I wanted to do and have it end up in writing.

Almost forgetting why I had looked at my phone in the first place, I walked back into the classroom, checking my calendar to confirm I was free after school the next day—and I was. I told Josh to go ahead and spread the word.

I spent the rest of class walking around the room, helping kids with their poems and kicking myself for not doing a similar activity in years' past. I was thrilled by their willingness to open up and play with words and spacing—even students who normally didn't write or speak much.

With about two minutes left in class, there was a knock on the door. Josh offered to get it, and when he turned around after opening it, he was holding a bouquet of red roses.

"Uhhh, Mrs. R., these are for you." He walked toward me and handed them to me, smiling shyly.

I took the roses from him, my eyes narrowed in their direction. *Cam wouldn't send me flowers at work. She's never been that kind of girlfriend or wife. Who else would—*

A small, white, rectangular card fell out onto the floor. Josh reached to pick it up just as the word "snowflake" caught my eye. I dove in front of him, our heads bumping together, and snatched the card.

"Sorry, honey!" I stood back up quickly, out of breath, holding the card in the palm of my hand facing away from everyone.

Josh rubbed his head and grinned. "Yikes! So am I!"

The bell rang, and the room emptied. Before my second period students arrived, I quickly scanned the card:

Dear snowflake,

Since you want so much attention, I hope 100 people ask you who these are from. Good luck at the meeting tonight.

I.C. You

Second period couldn't go fast enough. As soon as the kids left my room, I closed the door and pulled out my phone, googling "Freedom Florist." The first website listed was for a local flower shop that I had probably passed a million times but just hadn't noticed. I clicked the link to the website and then the phone number at the top of the page.

"Freedom Florist, how may I help you today?" a friendly voice answered.

"Good morning. I received some roses from your shop this morning and was hoping you could tell me who sent them to me. The card doesn't mention a name, and I want to be able to thank whoever it is." I sat down in a student chair and tapped my foot quickly on the floor.

"Yes, ma'am," she said. "I'll do my best, but some folks don't give names on purpose."

"I get that," I tried not to sound irritated, "but this is … important." Closing my eyes, I brought a finger to my mouth and bit off some loose skin.

Her fingers clicked on a keyboard. "Where are you located, ma'am?"

"I'm at Benson High School. The order was for a dozen red roses." I had set the roses on my desk horizontally, and no one in my second period class had noticed them. Looking at them now, I was struck by how expensive they had probably been.

Some more clicks. "Are you Josephine?"

"Yep, that's me." I rubbed my forehead, feeling a headache coming on.

"All I can tell you is that it was a female. My boss took the order, and he mentioned in the notes that, quote, 'she was adamant about remaining anonymous', and that's all I can say."

I forced a quick laugh. *A woman. Now we're getting somewhere.* "Well, I know it wasn't my wife because this isn't her style. Any other notes on that order? Thanks again for checking."

She was quiet for a few seconds and said, "Um, I really can't help you. Have a good day." My phone beeped with the end of the call.

"Hello? What the hell? Talk about lousy customer service."

I took my phone away from my ear and stared at it for a few seconds. It was still displaying the florist's website. This time, I noticed the title on the top of the page: *Freedom Florist, Patriot Owned and Patriot Proud*, backed by an American flag. Intrigued, I scrolled down, past some Easter specials and photos of sample bouquets. The bottom of the page read: *A traditional family owned business since 1992*

I thought about the words "traditional family" and shook my head, knowing those words were code for "Take your queer business elsewhere." I.C. You—whoever *she* was—was clearly happy to patronize such an establishment, and who would be surprised by that? Not me.

But, seriously ... what harm was she actually doing? What harm was she meaning to do? By mentioning the school board meeting, was she threatening to do something worse then?

I pictured the projector screen slowly descending from the ceiling behind the board members' table. They would look around at each other with questions in their eyes: Did *you* press the button? Was it *you*? All chatter in the audience would die down as a giant version of my and Kate's bodies appeared. My head would turn back and forth about twenty times in some sort of freakish edit of real time, and then the camera would zoom in on my hands resting on Kate's back. Everyone in the room would gasp with horror and demand that I be fired on the spot.

"Josie! Shut. Up!" I said aloud.

But how unrealistic was that scenario, really? Besides the firing part. I didn't think they could actually fire me for something so innocuous as a quick hug—unless it's edited to seem longer than it was?

I was pacing again. *Get a grip. I'm serious. You have the original video in your email, remember? If someone would show some kind of doctored version, you could show that one in response.*

I walked to my desk and stared down at the roses. Did she think I would display them in some kind of vase in front of the room? What would stop me from putting them right into the garbage? She may have been dedicated to trying to intimidate me, but she clearly wasn't the sharpest tool in the shed. Yeah, my first period students saw them, but so what?

So. The fuck. What. With renewed conviction, I grabbed an old Benson Bulldogs water bottle from a drawer and took it out to the hallway to fill at the water fountain. It wasn't a pretty vase, but it was all I had on hand. I put the roses in the bottle and set them beside my computer monitor before I opened my saved document titled "GSA Proposal." I read it over:

To: Board of School Directors
Benson High School

Club Name: Gay Straight Alliance
Grades: 9–12
Duration: September–June

Overview:
This proposal has been prepared as a result of Benson High School students' interest in creating a Gay Straight Alliance, which currently exists in most neighboring school districts. This club will meet weekly and will aim to provide safe social opportunities for our school's LGBTQ students and their friends and will be offered to any students in grades 9–12.

Attached is a scanned petition that has been signed by ninety-nine students at Benson High who have pledged their support of the club.

Mrs. Josephine Rein-Thompson, tenth grade English teacher, is willing to sponsor this club.

I looked it over twice. With the board meeting being that night, I knew that getting it onto the agenda was a long shot, but it was, as they say, now or never. I grabbed the folded petition from under my keyboard and quickly threw it into my scanner. As the machine hummed, my eyes were drawn to the roses.
Maybe something beautiful will come out of this after all.

- 42 -

Sunday, July 6, 1997

In the choir loft above the congregation, I always felt special. It was like I could see my voice carrying all the way to the altar, bouncing off of the stained glass windows and washing over everyone sitting in the pews. Our choir director sat me in the front as the lead soprano, and I took my role seriously—never missing a word or note, relishing especially in a descant.

But in the time between songs, my mind drifted. Ever since my dad had moved out six months before, I had lost my belief in God. The homilies did little more than bore me, and, at most, they irritated me. My parents were getting divorced, and I knew that was a sin. I also knew that a loving God wouldn't have let it happen in the first place.

That summer was the last time I ever sang in a church choir, and I sometimes miss the music so much that I look songs up on YouTube and sing along. They still take me to a peaceful place when sunshine filtered through the multicolored saints, and my mom and dad were kneeling next to each other, waiting to get in line for Communion.

In the choir loft that day, Layla sat directly across from me. She was the lead alto, and if I concentrated hard enough, I could hear just our two singular voices harmonizing together. Her posture, as always, was impeccable, and her voice was rich and full. She was wearing a floral sundress and black, platform Mary Janes. Occasionally, she crossed or uncrossed her slender legs, and it made me feel light-headed—or maybe it was the heat? No, by that point, I knew what my body was telling me. The clenching intensified and butterflies grew larger when I started to recognize them more and more throughout the previous school year—my last year in Catholic school.

The priest was talking about the Seven Deadly Sins, focusing on gluttony, which he defined as an excess of anything, like money, food, or material things. I inwardly scoffed and thought about the secret family size bag of Lays potato chips I would be eating later that night as I watched reruns of *Mad About You* and salivated over Helen Hunt.

"Surplus," he said, "in all instances, is sin. God wants us to have what we need, but he doesn't always want us to have what we want." He paused. "Anything extra, unnecessary, superfluous should be given to someone who needs it. Pass on that second serving, and give it to the poor."

I pictured myself jumping in Layla's swimming pool with all of my clothes on to avoid being seen in a bathing suit. My wet, oversized Madonna t-shirt would hang heavily all around me, my jean shorts clinging to my thighs. I was bigger than all of my friends in all ways—wider, taller, and louder. I felt like a sore thumb among girls and a nonentity to all boys. And it wasn't that I was interested in the boys, but I wouldn't complain if one of them was interested in me.

Not liking the train of thought that gluttony had awakened, I called my attention back to Layla's legs, now crossed at her ankles and tucked under her chair. I imagined what it would feel like to touch her smooth skin. The setting in my mind shifted to a Coach bus like the one we had recently taken as a class on an overnight field trip.

It's pitch black outside, and Layla is sitting in a seat across the aisle and back a few rows from me, chin pushed downward so that her eyes look up at me seductively. She crawls over seats to get to me, just as hungry to kiss me as I am to kiss her.

The organ played the first chords of the next song, sucking me out of my fantasy. As I stood to sing, I was aware of the elastic in my waistband cutting into my skin, and my shirt felt wet under my arms. I deserved to be punished for my gluttony. I deserved to be unwanted forever.

- 43 -

Monday, March 25, 2019

Not one student had asked me where the roses were from. Not even Kate. She saw them, but she didn't ask. This was par for the course, though, in my career as a closeted teacher. Most kids either didn't have the nerve or respected me too much to ask questions.

I kept busy that day, *finally* finishing grading those essays over my lunch and actively walking around the classroom during every class, helping kids with their poems.

By the time Brandon walked in for eighth period, I was pretty much on auto-pilot, just trying to make it to the end of the day. I couldn't name my feelings about the meeting that night because there were too many of them, but I had to admit that they weren't all negative.

"Nice flowers," Brandon called from the back of the room. "Who are they from?" He was clearly trying to sound casual, so I matched him.

"Aren't they beautiful? I actually don't know who they're from. I must have a secret admirer!" I grinned at him and then wiggled my eyebrows at some of the other kids who were smiling back at me.

But he didn't back down. "Huh. How's your wife gonna feel about that?"

The class collectively held their breath. I thought of that petition which had surely made its way to the superintendent's office by then. "Probably guilty for not buying me flowers more often!" I pivoted. "Okay, everybody, we're going to work on some poetry today. Go ahead and take out what you have so far."

What an absolute adrenaline rush—to knock his fastball out of the park like that without any hesitation. I purposely didn't approach him for the rest of the period. I could see that his paper was blank, but nope. I wasn't going there again. If he had a question, he could ask. I mean, if he had *another* question—the next one hopefully about English class.

With about ten minutes left in class, the school's lockdown alarm sounded.

"Shoot," I muttered, scrambling to my desk to open my email for a memo I must have missed. But there wasn't one. With only eight minutes left before the final bell of the day, it was an odd time for a drill. If it *was* a drill, it would be quick.

I got up out of my seat and went to the door to lock it from the inside with the new key that had been provided to all of the teachers. It can lock any of the school doors from the inside and was colored red, so we could distinguish it from all other keys. Just as I was locking it, Mr. Dunham panted over the loudspeaker, "Until further notice, we are on lockdown."

That was it. He didn't say anything else.

Why had he sounded out of breath?

I pictured Cam's face as she told me about the intruder at her school last week. That guy was in jail, right? He had to be.

What if I.C. You had come to the school and officially gone

off the deep end, shouting threats at the secretaries about how she was going to come kill me? Had a woman ever done that? Have there been any female school shooters?

I took myself to the corner down the wall from the door and stood with my back against it, listening intently for any sounds in the hallway. The kids followed me and huddled nearby, most of them appearing relatively unfazed but knowing that they had to remain silent.

I remembered sitting on my mom's couch as a sophomore in high school, watching the news footage of the Columbine shootings. Ever since, those black-and-white images of the kids hiding under tables pop into my mind at odd moments, sometimes completely unrelated to school or even violence. Sixteen-year-old me cried alone in our living room that day, imagining what it would be like to spend your last moments petrified on a cold tile floor, praying to a God who would let that happen.

The silence was too much. I took my phone out of my pocket and texted Dana, even though I still hadn't forgiven her for that morning's accusations:

What's going on? Have you heard anything?

I waited, wondering if I should try someone else. Going back to my text homescreen, I composed a message to Cam: *Ugh, lockdown time. And the email weirdo sent me flowers today. Yes, you read that correctly.*

Dana texted: *No. Dunham sounded nervous.*

Me: *I know. That's not like him.*

Cam: *Flowers? Lockdown? Are you OK?*

Dana: *These kids are restless. Not sure what to tell them.*

"So, what, are we supposed to believe that you're going to save us if some psycho comes in here with a gun?"

It was Brandon, asking another question.

I put my phone in my pocket and looked him dead in the eye. "Yes, Brandon, you are. Because that is my job."

He scoffed. "Yeah, okay, the only student you'd be willing to save is Kate Anderson."

I blinked. He nudged the boy to his left who gave him a half smile but was clearly uncomfortable.

Brandon continued. "I mean, unless anyone else in here is gay. You'd probably save all of the gaybos, right?" He turned away from me and stepped out to face his classmates. "Raise your hand if you're g—"

"Brandon, shut up." Trent, a fellow athlete who normally got along with Brandon just fine as far as I could tell, said through his teeth. "If there's a shooter, your voice is going to lead him right to us, you asshole."

Other kids muttered their agreement.

Trent, emboldened, added, "And Mrs. Rein-Thompson never did anything to you. Let it go, man."

Just then, Mr. Dunham's voice was back on the loudspeaker, this time calmly stating, "The lockdown drill has concluded. Please resume regular classes."

My eyes were still on Trent as kids made their way back to their seats, my heart pounding.

With two minutes until the bell was going to ring, I went back to my computer and saw a message from the superintendent, Dr. Michaelson:

To All Staff:

Today, we completed an unannounced lockdown drill in an effort to sort out complications that could arise in the event of a real lockdown, as was experienced by a neighboring school district last week. We apologize for alarming anyone, but it was for the greater good. All seemed to go well.

Yours in education,
  Dr. Anita Michaelson

The bell rang, and the hallways exploded with students who needed to burn off their nervous energy. By the time thirty seconds had passed, they were laughing and carrying on as if nothing out of the ordinary had happened—as if the threat of imminent death were just a regular, everyday possibility.

I took my phone out of my pocket and texted Cam: *Just a drill. See you at home.*

The school quieted within minutes, and I closed my door and turned off the light. In the dimness, I noticed the voicemail light was blinking on my classroom phone. How I had missed the phone ringing, I wasn't sure. Picking up the receiver, I quickly entered my passcode: Dad's birthday 0506. *5+6=11, 1+1=2—*

"Hello, Miss Rein. This is Derek Stoneman. Brandon told me you've been advertising yourself all over the school on some kind of flyers, and Jessica Anderson told me a reporter called her last night, so I'm calling to let you know there's to be absolutely no media present at the meeting tonight. It's for community members only, with you as the exception since you live ... uh ... elsewhere. You should know that there are many who are upset about your lack of discretion. Be prepared to defend your decision to put your hands on Kate." *Click.*

Putting my hands on Kate? Does that mean he has seen the video, or is he talking about my hand on her shoulder?

And advertising myself on flyers? He had to mean the poetry slam flyers, but my name wasn't even on those. This had Facebook written all over it. One of the things Cam and I had decided was that I should prepare myself for the meeting by reading some of the comments being left on the school's

Facebook page, but since neither one of us had an account, we couldn't see anything. I almost asked Amanda to join the group but then thought her last name would be too obvious. There was only one other person I would feel comfortable enough asking.

I dialed Dana's classroom, and she answered immediately. "Oh, I'm so glad it's you. I feel awful about making you feel bad this morning."

On a mission, I pushed my feelings aside. "It's fine. Can you do me a favor?" I looked at the clock and saw that I could stay for twenty more minutes in order to have enough time to go home and change before the meeting.

"Sure. What's up?"

"Come here, and bring your phone with you. I want to read the Facebook comments about me." I opened my email inbox to see if I needed to tend to anything before I left for the day, and a message from Mr. Dunham caught my eye. "Ugh, and I got an email from Dunham. Can you just come over here? I'm a bundle of nerves today."

"I'll be right there." *Click.*

About thirty seconds later, she walked into the room, holding her phone in one hand and a glazed donut in the other. "For you," she said, bumping the door closed with her hip before walking toward me and handing me the donut. I took it gratefully and ate it in three bites.

She pulled a student chair up beside me and opened her Facebook app, scrolling to the school's account and past congratulations for the basketball team, eventually landing on an article shared with the group with the headline "Schools forcing children to read books featuring homosexual parents."

My stomach twisted, and Dana looked at the scowl on my

face. "Some of this won't be easy. Are you sure you want to see?"

I exhaled through my nose. "Yes. I need to know what I'm walking into tonight."

So she clicked on the comments section of the article. The person who had originally shared it was Brian Anderson, whose profile picture was of himself with a woman and Kate. They were all smiling in a formal family photo, posed in front of a blue backdrop.

His initial comment had read: *Over my dead body.*

There were several likes on his comment, but someone pretty quickly stepped in (Sarah Dander) and said: *Kids should learn about different types of families.*

That comment had more than double the likes, and that made me feel a little better until I saw the way he responded: *My Bible tells me otherwise.*

The next ten or so back-and-forth comments were arguments about what the Bible actually says about homosexuality (news flash: not much that's meant to be taken literally if you ask me). Dana scrolled past them and said, "After this argument is when he brings you up."

"Anderson actually says my name himself?" I looked at her.

"Not exactly." She was squinting at the screen. "Look." She pointed.

Brian Anderson: There is no place for indoctrination in a public school. My daughter's English teacher recently tried pushing her gay agenda. Believe it!

Sarah Dander: Oh give me a break! Your daughter's English teacher is a kind woman who just so happens to like other women.

My son had her last year, and he learned a ton.

I looked at Dana. "Who's her son? I don't recognize the name."
"I think she's Truman's mom. He has his dad's last name."
I pictured Truman's easy smile and nodded, unsurprised that his mom was a good person. I continued reading.

Brian Anderson: Don't you tell me. She told my daughter to write an essay about how to be "gay." I have the essay to prove it.

Tim Li: My son Josh has the same teacher this year and she has really excited him about writing.

Brian Anderson: Yeah she's a little too excited about my daughter. She even touched her in class

Sarah Dander: what's that supposed to mean

Donna Chavez: That's enough. This is inappropriate. It's one thing to complain about a teacher in private, but doing it on this public forum is wrong.

Brian Anderson: I'm going to be even more public at next week's school board meeting.
That "woman" touched my daughter's shoulder to try to persuade her. I won't change my mind.

Maddie Bronson: Mrs. R is a great teacher! She's letting us do a poetry slam next Wednesday, and we can't wait!

Jaiden Hammond: she touched my arm once too because she's nice

Savannah Morrison: English is boring but she is always smiling and actually looks like she likes her job.

Donna Chavez: We will see you at the school board meeting, sir.

I sat back. "Good ol' Donna. Remind me to hug her." I sighed. "Is there more? It's pretty much what I expected, so I don't think I need to see more. It doesn't seem like anyone has seen the video." I smoothed back my hair. "I can't believe Savannah stuck up for me. Did I tell you about the day she didn't stop talking about peacocks?"

She smiled and nodded. "The rest of the comments are more of the same. Derek Stoneman gets in on it a little later, and someone tells him he shouldn't be biased as a member of the school board, so he shut up real quick." She scrolled a little further. "There are also a bunch of other kids who come to your defense and maybe only two other parents who complain about you being quote-unquote too liberal. The only kids who say anything negative are Brandon and his friend Trevor, who you didn't even teach."

"I saw them together at the pep rally on Friday." I thought for a second. "I do want to see what Brandon said."

"Are you sure?" She looked like she was ready to close the app.

"Yes. Like I said, I just want to be prepared." I reached for her phone.

She squinted and scrolled some more. "Here it is."

Brandon Stoneman: All that teacher ever wants us to do is talk about our feelings and act like we care about other peoples that is the definition of gay

I chuckled. "Is that it? One lousy run-on sentence?"

She smirked. "I think so."

"Remind me to talk to him about punctuation." I sat back in my chair. "You wouldn't believe his nerve eighth period today. He was on fire asking questions about my wife and if I would save any straight kids from a school shooter." I shook my head, wincing slightly. "But I'm actually proud of myself for not backing down from him. And the other kids didn't humor him, either. I guess that's a win?" I looked at the clock. "Did I mention I sent the proposal for the GSA?"

She clapped her hands together. "What? No! Josie, that is so awesome. These kids are never going to forget it."

I shrugged. "Yeah, well, neither will I." I paused. "Thanks for coming over."

She stood up slowly. "I really am sorry about today. I was worked up about the comments and just wished I could make it better for you, but then I just ended up making it worse." On her way to the door, she turned back around to face me. "Do you want me to post a comment about anything on your behalf?"

I shook my head. "Nah. I'm going to have to speak up for myself at that meeting tonight, so I'll just wait until then."

"Okay," she said. "Go eat some dinner. You don't want to be nervous *and* hungry." She turned and walked out.

I looked down at my phone and searched my recent missed calls for Adelaide Foster's number, hoping she hadn't called me from a landline. I texted:

Hello, Adelaide. This is Josie Rein-Thompson. Sure, we can talk. I'm supposed to tell you that you can't come to the school board meeting because it's for community members only. Sorry!

Almost immediately, my phone vibrated with a text:

What if I told you I live across the street from the school and have a son in your seventh period class?

- 45 -

Friday, June 16, 2006

Tara and I had been dating for about six months. We spent most of our time in her apartment, eating takeout and watching movies. If I ever mentioned Cam in conversation, Tara would narrow her hazel eyes at me and then turn her face away, tossing her curly brown hair in my direction. Eventually, I decided that the ensuing silent treatment wasn't worth it, so I kept my Cam thoughts to myself.

By trade, Tara is an actor. I was drawn to her dramatics at first, but they soon began to irritate me to the point of near-hatred. I stopped singing because she thought I was competing with her voice. I hadn't written poetry since Cam and I had broken up because I couldn't bring myself to access any deep feelings, even though Tara often asked me to write about her, but I couldn't. I let Tara take the lead on most things—from telling me which soap to use to how to style my hair—and I even let her hide me from her parents. After all, what other life did I know?

It was her twenty-fifth birthday. We were getting ready to go out to dinner for the occasion when she turned to me, backed me up against a wall, and said teasingly, "Ugh, look at those eyebrows. What is this—a circus? Let me go get my tweezers."

What she didn't know was that, the night before, I had had a dream that was still sitting in the pit of my stomach. In my dream, I was on the patio of a beach condominium, looking down at the ocean, watching it for any signs of a storm. Everyone knew a tidal wave was coming, but we weren't sure when. All I could think about was where Cam was. Was she safe? How could I let her know to get away from the ocean? I woke up just as I saw the giant wave coming toward me—right before it was going to break over the building.

All day, I was fighting the urge to call Cam. After that day she had told me not to call her anymore, I had respected her wishes—mostly. There were times, mostly in the middle of the night, when I would block my number and call her just to hear her voice. I had considered doing it that morning, but I resisted.

She used to do the same thing, too. In fact, it had become a sort of game for us—a silent game that nobody was winning. Anytime I saw a private number calling me, I would answer immediately. Sometimes, I would say something out loud like "I miss you" or "I hope you're doing okay," but sometimes I would just sit and enjoy knowing she was sitting there on the other end with me.

With my back against the wall, I glared at Tara as she entered her bathroom to retrieve the tweezers. Across the room, the early-summer sun was shining on the bright green trees outside of her sliding glass door. I remembered how Cam and I had taken one of many road trips one summer with no air conditioning in the Rocket, and we had gotten stuck in traffic on a highway. The day was sweltering with no airflow and the sun beating down on us, and I took pictures of the emerald green trees to our right against their backdrop of a cloudless sky. We laughed about how sweaty we were, and I took a picture of Cam sticking her tongue out at me, panting like a dog. We kissed in her idling car, listening to Jann Arden, not caring what strangers saw us.

"No," I said. "My eyebrows are fine."

"Oh, just let me even them out," she said, walking back toward me.

"No," I said more firmly, feeling the familiar disgust bubbling inside of me.

The truth is that I had started dating Tara way too soon after the breakup. In fact, I started dating any girl who would look at me twice about a month after my final conversation with Cam. During that first month, I had spent most of my time in bed at my dad's apartment, unable to eat or sleep and practically unable to move. I went to classes when I had to and went through the motions of life—even successfully completing my student teaching—but when I came home, I went straight to my bed. Dad would talk to me through the door, trying to gently encourage me to come out. He offered pizza, karaoke, Scrabble, trips to Paris—but I just couldn't do it. When the fog lifted after that month, I was on a mission to find someone to take my mind off of her. I went on dates with about five different women before I met Tara, and she entertained me to the point of it sticking.

She raised the tweezers to my face, and I sidestepped her and backed into the small kitchen decorated with Italian chefs. "Tara, I mean it. Leave me alone."

"What's with you?" She pouted. "It's my birthday. Don't be mean to me on my birthday."

"Mean to you? You pretty much just told me I look like a

sideshow freak." I bit a piece of skin hanging off of my finger.

"I was joking!" She walked closer. I wasn't lightening up. I allowed the heaviness to stay with me until I thought about what it would be like to walk out of her apartment and never see her again.

"I can't do this anymore." I looked her in the eye. "I'm an asshole to do this on your birthday, but I'm not happy. And you aren't, either. I know it's killing you to lie to your parents every day."

She flinched. "I told you I'm not ready to tell them yet. My brother just came out last year, and they've had a hard enough time—"

"I know. I'm not blaming you. I'm just not happy for a lot of reasons, and I think I need to spend some time by myself." I thought about how she would get angry with me if I would exercise because she thought I was trying to look better than she did—how she made me watch horror movies when I told her they gave me nightmares. "Maybe we can try again sometime, but this isn't working for me right now." I walked past her and into her bedroom, picking up the clothes I had left on her floor.

When I walked down the steps and got into Woody, I felt a potent mixture of guilt and relief. Who breaks up with someone on their birthday? But who stays with someone just to ... be with someone? I knew it was the right thing to do, even if the timing might be wrong.

Getting onto the highway to go back to my dad's apartment, there was no question what I was going to do next. I rolled the windows up and dialed *67 before Cam's number.

She answered after two rings. "Hey. I was just thinking about you."

I stayed silent, wondering if she could hear the hum of the engine, and then, without warning, I started to cry. I tried to do it as quietly as possible, hoping she wouldn't be able to hear me, but it was obvious she could when she said, "I know. I am so sorry. I know."

We stayed that way for a few more minutes until we both stopped altogether. Before she hung up, she whispered. "I love you."

- 46 -

Monday, March 25, 2019

On my way home to change my clothes, I called Cam. She answered in her car, and I could hear Liesel whining from the backseat.

"She okay? Did she take a nap?" I asked.

"Big girls don't take naps!"

"I guess I'm on speaker phone." I laughed. "Hi, baby! How was your day? Did you have fun at school?"

But she was back to whining, clearly missing that nap. I heard shuffling as Cam took me off of speakerphone and brought the phone to her ear.

"She's miserable. I'm hoping she falls asleep in the car for a little bit to take the edge off. Sheesh."

I smiled. "How was *your* day?"

"Surprisingly fine. None of my kids even brought up the scary stuff from Friday, so I don't know if they've just forgotten, blocked it out, or got tired of talking about it with their parents over the weekend."

"Maybe all three?"

"Yeah. Hey, what was with your lockdown today?"

"I'm pretty sure they did it because of what happened at your school. Something about working out kinks with procedures?"

"Makes sense. And did you say your email friend sent you flowers? Should I be jealous?"

I was grateful that she was starting to find some humor in the situation, too. "No, but Brandon Stoneman actually asked me that same question in front of his entire class."

"Ugh, that kid really is a total douche. What did you say?"

I chuckled. "That you'd feel less jealous and more guilty that you hadn't been the one to send them yourself."

"Ha! Wait ... do you want me to send you flowers? I can send you flowers."

"No! That's not the point. But if you ever do, you know they should be—"

"Daisies. Duh."

I smiled and then spoke without thinking. "Listen, Cam ... do you want to come to the meeting with me tonight?" I snorted. "Oh man, that sounded like I was asking you out, didn't it?"

Liesel wasn't whining anymore, and I hoped that she was asleep. Cam's car was so quiet, in fact, that I thought she either hadn't heard me, or the connection was bad. "Cam?"

"I'm thinking." She was quiet again. "With everything going on, do you think it would be wise to parade me around tonight?"

"I was thinking less parading and more sitting next to you, but okay." She didn't want to come. She was okay to support me from afar, but she wasn't okay with the spotlight being on her.

"If you really want me to, Jo, of course I will."

But the key word was "really." She would do it if I absolutely needed her to, but it wouldn't be because she wanted to.

There I was again, lying by myself on the exam table at the

fertility clinic.

"You're right," I said as casually as I could. "I shouldn't draw too much attention to myself. After all, everyone's already paying attention to me, anyway."

"Speaking of," she changed the subject, "what are you planning on wearing? What statement do you want to make?"

I hadn't thought about it. "Hmmm, well, I currently have on gray corduroys and a cream polo shirt. Should I go for more ... I don't know ... feminine?"

"Maybe? I mean, you don't want to not be yourself, but maybe the board will be more inclined to go easy on you if you're ... conventional looking?"

"Ew, that sounds ridiculous. What does that even mean? Like wear a dress? I haven't worn a dress to school in about ten years. They'll see right through me."

"But your legs are so—"

"Cameron! I don't want to be sexy. I want to be professional yet ... sympathetic. Normal? Not-deviant? Ugh ... "

Neither of us spoke for a little while, each of us clicking turn signals at intervals, getting closer to home from different directions.

"I know," she said. "You have that really pretty navy blouse with the tiny red roses on it."

I gasped. "You are *brilliant*. That will show her I'm not afraid."

"*Her*? Is there something you're not telling me?"

For the rest of the ride home, I filled her in about the florist. We laughed together about the woman hanging up on me and laughed even harder when I gave her my description of the website. By the time I pulled into the driveway, I was warm with acceptance and love.

When Cam's car pulled up, I got out of my car and walked to Liesel's door. Reaching in, I unbuckled her from her car seat and lifted her gently, resting her head on my shoulder. She breathed evenly into my neck as I carried her into the house.

The sun was just considering its descent when I was on my way to the school board meeting. Liesel had woken up shortly after we went inside the house, so we were all able to sit and have dinner together. Before I left, Cam kissed me and told me she was proud of me. For what, I wasn't sure yet.

If I lost my job, we would survive.

If I lost my job, we would still be a family who loves each other.

Now, on my way back to the school, I called Adelaide. She told me that her son, Ellis, is in my seventh period Honors English class and that she had first gotten wind of the situation through Ellis himself, who doesn't normally say much about school at all but had mentioned some kind of "teacher scandal" that had piqued her interest as a reporter. He was vague about the details, though, so when someone called in the story the next day, she was eager for more. When the caller—Brian Anderson himself, apparently—described what had happened, she knew there had to be more to it. That's when she went to Facebook and "couldn't make heads or tails."

Ellis is a sweet, quiet kid who gets good grades in my class but would definitely rather be doing math—which I would never take personally, obviously. According to Adelaide, he was upset about some people saying negative things about me because I am "always fair and nice." I thought about how that word kept coming up everywhere: nice. *What does it even mean? Is everyone defining it the same way? Is it a good thing that I'm nice, or am I too nice because I sometimes touch a student's shoulder or—worse—let them hug me?*

I told Adelaide what Derek Stoneman had said to me about not having media at the meeting, and she had said, "Ha! It's funny, then, that his friend Brian was the one who called me. Maybe he should have told Mr. Anderson his rule, rather than you." She went on to explain that, as a community member, she was welcome to attend the meeting and that she would identify herself as both a local and a reporter. They wouldn't be able to kick her out.

The questions she asked me were direct, and I tried to answer them honestly without saying too much. I couldn't tell yet what her spin was going to be, but I had nothing to hide.

While I was pulling into the school's parking lot, a robin swooped down in front of my car and landed on the grass near the outside of the district office where the meeting was being held. I took a deep breath and prepared to thank my dad for the sign that he was with me when the grass suddenly filled with more robins.

I counted them quickly: thirteen. Smiling, I knew he was reminding me that not only was he with me but that I am like my beloved birthdate—not everyone's favorite thing, and that was absolutely okay.

I turned off the engine and closed my eyes, silently giving myself a new kind of pep talk: "You have a family who loves you. You are a good teacher. You are who you are."

Someone knocked on my window, and I jumped and looked

up to see Donna leaning forward to look at me. "You ready?" she asked, raising her eyebrows.

I took off my seatbelt and got out of the car, taking in the fresh spring air. "I think so," I said to her, and we walked toward the door together.

Looking around, I was surprised to see so many cars there. My stomach sank. "Why are there so many people here? Maybe I'm not ready for this."

She shrugged. "This has been kind of a thing on social media, so it's probably a bunch of people being nosy. I would definitely prepare to have anything you say posted all over the internet."

"Can they do that?" I stopped walking and looked at her.

"By law, the board can't stop them from recording. I'm not saying it's going to happen, but I definitely wouldn't be surprised." She walked ahead of me and opened the door, holding it for me.

I thanked her and walked in. There was a chair set up right inside the entrance that had a sign taped to it:

THE SCHOOL BOARD MEETING HAS MOVED TO THE HS AUDITORIUM.

It had been a while since I was at a board meeting, so I wasn't sure if this was usual or not. I looked at Donna.

She tilted her head to the side and said, "Well, I guess there *are* a lot of people here." Then she waved me to the left to head toward the auditorium.

As we got closer, we could hear the mumblings of a crowd. Some students were gathered outside the doors, and when they saw us, a few of them waved. I gave them a closed-lip smile and a small wave before opening the door.

The board had set up a table in front of the stage where an orchestra pit would be during a stage production. They sat behind it, facing the audience, who took up about a quarter of the seats. The audience members were of various ages, but most seemed to be teenagers and people who would be their parents' ages. Some of them turned to look at us, and many of those people turned quickly away like they didn't know if they should acknowledge me or not. Dana smiled and waved from among a group of teachers who had shown up, all of them someone I would at least consider an acquaintance. Although Donna was walking with me, I felt alone—like a singular spotlight was on me, following me down the aisle.

"Where should we sit?" I asked Donna through the side of my mouth, worried people would be reading my lips and would know how nervous I was.

She stopped walking at the fourth row from the front. "This should be good. We don't want to be too close to the board because then nobody else will be able to hear us. We definitely don't want to sit in the back and seem distant."

Nodding, I followed her into the row, trying not to look around too much. My ears were hot, and I was blinking like a madwoman. Donna sat down and looked up at me, "It's going to be okay. You haven't done anything wrong. These people are out to get you because they need someone to blame. Now sit down and breathe."

I obeyed. Wiping my sweaty hands on my grey dress pants, I looked at the board and waited for them to begin.

- 48 -

Monday, August 28, 2006

It was the first day of my first real teaching job. I had my own classroom, which Dad and I had spent much of the previous week organizing and decorating. He told me that he liked my room number because it was 229, and 2+2+9=13, and the number thirteen had always reminded him of me. He said it had to be a good sign.

During the previous year, after graduating and while substitute teaching around the area, I had spent my evenings serving tables at the bar my dad was managing at the time. I made a ton of money in tips and was able to get an apartment in a decent neighborhood. That apartment was my pride and joy, and I lovingly decorated it, painting the living room walls a bright orange and the bedroom walls a soft purple. I bought tan microfiber couches from a discount furniture store, and my mom sent me my first ever bookshelf that I filled to bursting. Even though I had also bought a used burgundy hatchback—and cried when I said goodbye to Woody—I didn't feel like a real live adult until I got the call that I had been hired to teach tenth grade English at one of the best districts in the area.

On the morning of that first day, I put on the outfit I had set out days before. There were two in-service days the previous week when I had worn khaki pants and light, airy blouses, but I wanted to wear a skirt for my first day with students. It was important to me that they view me as feminine, though I'm still not sure why. I wore skirts and high heels for most of that first year, in fact, until I came to my senses and opted for comfortable chic instead.

As I headed out to my car in the dark, my phone vibrated in my leather work bag (also purchased by my mother). I was surprised to see a private number on the outside of my flip phone. *Why was Cam calling that early?*

"Hey," I said, getting into the driver's seat. Of course, she said nothing. I started the engine, pulled out of my complex's lot, and said, "I got my first teaching job. I'm on my way there now. Remember where your cousin Simon went to high school? It's there. I'm so nervous I might throw up, honestly."

She was still silent, so I continued. "What if they don't like me? What if they make fun of me behind my back—or worse, to my face? What if they call me fat or think my sense of humor is too corny?" I took a breath, swimming in questions. "What if they find out that I'm gay? I'm not dating anyone right now, so they wouldn't have a reason to see me out anywhere or anything, but what if they just, like, guess? Oh no, what if they ask me if I have a boyfriend? Should I lie?"

I heard her take a breath. "Josie, slow down." I practically melted at the sound of her voice and immediately had to blink back tears. Our silent phone calls had become less frequent over the past few months; I didn't know why she had stopped calling as often, but I know I had stopped because it was just too hard. I had spent the two months since breaking up with

Tara alone, and it had been good for me. I lost weight, read a ton of books, and reconnected with old friends. When I heard Cam's voice, I felt weak, so I tried to avoid calling her more than I felt I absolutely had to.

I had stopped talking, so she said, "Are you still there?"

"Yeah." I sniffed quietly. "Sorry, I wasn't expecting to have a conversation with you after over a year of our weird one-sided exchanges."

She laughed. Oh, that laugh. I closed my eyes, and she said, "Josie ... " and hesitated. "Josie, I'm ready. I want to be honest with my family, and I want to be with you."

"You ... what?" I stopped at a red light and pressed the phone tighter to my ear.

"I'm so sorry it took me so long. I even tried to date a few guys. Those poor things." She chuckled and then turned serious. "I have never once stopped thinking about you. Can you ever forgive me?"

The light turned green, but I didn't notice until the person behind me beeped. I was silently weeping. She said, "Are you okay? You there, Jojo?"

"I'm here," I said shakily. "I ... I just was not expecting this at all today."

"You don't have to answer me now. You probably hate me on some level for not doing this years ago. But please know that I just wasn't ready, and I was so afraid of disappointing my family. I'm the only one they have."

"I don't hate you, Cam. I could never hate you. I've spent the past year trying unsuccessfully to replace you ... but it has always been you. Always." Tears were streaming down my face as I pulled onto the highway.

She was crying now, too. "I am so, so, so sorry. I want to

spend the rest of my life making it up to you." She sniffled and continued, "Can I see you? You'll be exhausted this week, I know. Can I see you this weekend?"

The soaring in my chest matched the acceleration of my car. "Yes. God, yes. I have an apartment now. I'll text you the address, and you can come on Friday evening."

"Okay." She was smiling. "I hope you have an amazing first week."

"Thank you. Are you starting today, too?" My heart finally started to slow down, falling into a more comfortable rhythm.

"We started last week already. I'm already knee-deep in their snot and love."

"Still in kindergarten?"

"I love it. I hope they never move me. They are so sweet and innocent, and on most days, they make me want my own kids so much that my uterus practically hurts."

We both fell silent, surely thinking about the same thing—the same potential, uncertain future. I got off the ramp to go toward the school and said, "I'll text you soon. Cam, I ... I am so happy you called."

"So am I." She was smiling again. "And, Josie, they are going to love you. How could they not?"

Now I was smiling. "Maybe."

"Don't take any shit, okay?"

I huffed. "I'll try not to."

"Talk soon?"

"Absolutely." I was smiling so big that my face hurt.

"Good. Now go knock their socks off."

Monday, March 25, 2019

"I am calling to order the regular meeting of our school board." Martin Temple, the school board president, spoke into a microphone. He adjusted his glasses and looked down at a paper in front of him. "All members are present. In addition, we are joined by superintendent Dr. Anita Michaelson and high school principal Mr. William Dunham. Everyone, please stand for the Pledge of Allegiance."

We obeyed and said the Pledge together, looking at the flag standing on the stage above the board members. Afterward, they went through a roll call in businesslike tones while we all listened politely. Then, Mr. Temple said, "We will begin by giving the opportunity to any community members who would like to speak."

I gasped quietly, not expecting him to say that so soon. Donna took a copy of the printed agenda out of her bag and pointed to the order that the meeting would follow, and I kicked myself for not mentally preparing in that way.

Mr. Temple continued, "Following any community members who choose to speak, we will have a brief student recognition for the recent regional science fair. We'll have updates from our student school board representatives, and then our superintendent will share some good news about the basketball team and give us updates on a number of financial projects. We'll approve the consent vote agenda, which we reviewed earlier this month in committee."

Clutching my thighs, I tried to prepare for what was coming next and allowed a thought to pass about whether or not the GSA had been added to the agenda. What had I been thinking? Why had I picked now to send in that proposal? What if the meeting went horribly wrong, and then what—as they were dragging me through the mud, they would bring up a proposal for an actual gay club? I winced and clutched my legs more tightly.

"Finally, we will adjourn. Are there any questions or com-ments at this time?"

Nobody spoke. "Okay, is there anyone from the public who would like to speak?" I swear he looked at me briefly and then directed his attention to someone near the back and said, "Yes, sir. Please state your name, address, and reason for speaking. We ask that you limit your comments to three minutes or less."

I couldn't bring myself to turn around, though most other people did. I heard, "Brian Anderson from 2828 Cherry Hill Drive, here to voice concerns about an inappropriate high school teacher."

I crossed my legs and bounced my foot repeatedly, unable to sit still. *2828. Dad died on the 28th. Is that a good sign or a bad sign?*

Mr. Temple nodded. "You may proceed."

"My daughter, Kate Anderson, is in tenth grade. In her English class, the teacher recently told the class she is a homosexual and encouraged students to quote/unquote 'come out' if they also believe themselves to be homosexual. She took a special, inappropriate interest in my daughter, causing her to be confused and upset."

Mr. Temple was nodding periodically, but not as quickly as my foot was bouncing. Donna put her hand on my knee to stop it. I was willing myself not to put my fingers in my mouth instead.

"Please elaborate on what you have called a 'special, inappropriate interest,' Mr. Anderson."

"She had her write an essay about it and has touched Kate intimately."

Several people gasped, and I slammed my hand onto my lap and turned to look at him. Sitting in his row were his wife (whom I recognized from the Facebook photo), Kate, Brandon Stoneman, and who I assumed was Brandon's mother. Kate was staring at the chair in front of her, and Brandon was doing something on his phone. The women were looking up at Mr. Anderson like he was preaching some kind of holy truth. He looked at me and then back to Mr. Temple, who said, "That is a very serious accusation that could result in a teacher's suspension or even termination. Let's take one thing at a time. What was the essay prompt, and was it just for Kate or for all of the students in the class?"

He looked at his wife who said something quietly to him. Appearing irritated, he looked back at the board and said, "It was apparently a prompt for Women's History Month, and the essay was supposed to be about a woman who has inspired them."

"Them, sir? So this essay was assigned to everyone?" He was looking over his glasses, and I could feel my nerves calm a bit. Anyone could see now that the essay assignment itself wasn't inappropriate.

"Well, yes," Mr. Anderson continued, "but in a class with a teacher who is constantly speaking about her deviant personal life, Kate felt obligated to write about her teacher as her inspiration."

Mr. Temple furrowed his brow and then turned directly to face me. I instinctively flinched. "Mrs. Rein-Thompson, would you like to explain this assignment further?"

I looked at Donna, who nodded slightly, and then I stood to speak. "Yes, sir, I would."

Many people in the audience began mumbling to each other, but I willed myself to keep my eyes on the board members as I stood to speak. "It's a prompt that I have used for years. Many students choose to write about their mothers and grandmothers. One that made me laugh this year was about Lisa Simpson and how she's smart and not afraid to be different."

Some of the board members smiled—not including Mr. Stoneman, at whom I chose not to look directly. Relieved to see that most of them weren't taking the Andersons' accusation seriously—at least not yet—I continued, "And, for the record, I have never once spoken about my romantic relationship in my classroom because it's irrelevant to my content."

Mr. Temple nodded and looked back to Mr. Anderson, "So your daughter chose to write about her inspiring teacher for this assignment, and you are bothered because that teacher happens to be a lesbian?"

I sat down quickly, ears burning at the sound of that word in front of everyone. Donna patted my arm comfortingly while Mr. Anderson said, "The essay was all about how she wants to be just like *her*." I figured he was pointing at me but didn't turn around to confirm it.

"If I recall correctly, Mr. Anderson," Mr. Temple took his glasses off to clean them with his sleeve while he spoke, "an essay does not contain one reason but, rather, three reasons. Surely all three reasons were not about this woman's sexuality."

At that point, I had to turn to see his face. He looked at his wife again who blinked up at him before reaching into her purse, pulling out a folded piece of paper, and handing it to him. He scanned it silently, and I couldn't tell if he had read it before.

Mr. Temple asked, "Can you please read us her thesis statement?" Then, he looked at me. "It's been a long time since I've written an essay. Is that what it's still called?"

I smiled and nodded and turned back around as Mr. Anderson read quickly, "She has had a positive impact on my life because she is kind, successful, and true to herself."

Mr. Temple scratched his salt-and-pepper hair. "Well, now, that sounds lovely." He looked at me. "I'm sure you were flattered, yes?"

I blinked and then gave a small nod, not wanting to appear too excited by her words. He continued, looking back at Mr. Anderson, "So which part is about her sexuality? I assume it's the being true to herself part?"

Mr. Anderson looked back to his wife who was clearly losing her patience with him. She pointed aggressively at the paper in his hands and said, "Read it for yourself!"

My eyes went directly to Kate. Was he about to read aloud her private coming-out paragraph? She surely wasn't ready for such a public display—in front of adults, at least. As he was looking for the paragraph, I stood and looked at Mr. Temple. "Yes, the paragraph about being true to myself did reference my sexuality. She admires me for not trying to be someone I'm not, even though this meeting right now demonstrates why it isn't easy."

His eyes smiled a bit. "Yes, indeed. Well, Mr. Anderson, I think your daughter is fortunate to have a teacher who is a positive role model for her."

Mrs. Anderson stood up furiously. "You haven't even asked us about that woman touching her. Kate now thinks she's … different … because that woman touched her in class." She pointed at me.

I was still standing, and without thinking, I put my hand up as if to block her. Turning back to the board and looking directly at Mr. Stoneman, I said, "I patted her shoulder once because she wrote in her journal about how what Brandon Stoneman had said to me in class wasn't right."

Mr. Temple looked at Mr. Stoneman and said, "What did he say?"

Shaking his head, Mr. Stoneman said, "It's irrelevant. This isn't about Brandon." It was difficult to hear him because he didn't have the microphone.

Looking back to me with curiosity, Mr. Temple continued, "Would you mind telling us what Brandon said?"

I looked at Donna again, feeling my eyes narrow in a question. Before I could answer him, a woman's voice called out from behind us.

"You leave Brandon out of this! He has already been punished for executing his First Amendment right to free speech!"

Without turning around, I knew it had to be Brandon's mother.

She continued, "That woman has no right to force her views on our children! When did it become okay to allow a teacher to teach students to—"

"That's enough," Mr. Temple spoke firmly into the microphone. Then, more quietly, he said, "I'd like to speak with Mr. Stoneman in private. Let's take a fifteen minute break. Please return to the auditorium at 7:45."

I headed straight for the restroom, feeling light-headed. In a stall near the wall, where I hoped no one would notice, I sat with my eyes closed and attempted to go to one of my happy places: Lying face down on a beach towel, listening to music. Sitting next to Dad on a couch, watching *Look Who's Talking*. Holding Cam's hand on a road trip. Cradling baby Liesel in my arms.

People moved about the restroom, chatting in hushed tones about who was right and who was wrong. I tried not to listen.

Until I heard Kate's voice.

"Mom, I can't let you guys make her seem like a bad person. She's not a bad person."

"You are too young to understand right from wrong in this context, Kathryn Amelia. She took advantage of you."

"She did *not*. She hasn't asked for any of this. It's *me*. *I'm* the one who wrote the essay. You're mad at *me* for being gay."

"Shhhhhh." Her mother paused and then forcefully whispered, "Stop calling yourself that. Someone is going to hear you."

"I'm pretty sure everyone already knows! This whole meeting is about—"

Mr. Temple's amplified voice spoke from a distance, "Everyone, please take your seats."

I waited until I heard the restroom clear out and stepped out of the stall, surprised to see Kate's mother standing silently in front of the mirror.

"Excuse me," I said, reaching past her for some soap. She watched me in the mirror as I pretended to not know who she was while washing my hands, grabbing a paper towel, and leaving.

I didn't realize until I walked out of the restroom that I had been holding my breath. Releasing it through my nose, I headed back to my seat next to Donna, who gave me a thumbs up with her eyebrows raised as if to ask if I was okay. I nodded and sat down next to her.

"I would like to resume the meeting," Mr. Temple spoke into the microphone. "Mr. Stoneman has told me his version of what happened in his son's English class last week, but I would like to hear Mrs. Rein-Thompson's version of the story before I make any judgments about the situation." He looked at me. "I'm told that you accused Brandon of being lazy, so he retorted with a comment about your sexuality. Is this true?"

Of course he had twisted it.

I shook my head slowly and then looked back at Brandon, who was no longer playing on his phone but looking right at me. I met his gaze and then turned to face Mr. Temple. "When I tried to help him with his essay—that same essay, in fact—he told me his mom had told him not to get too close to me, or he might turn out gay. I was caught off guard and shot back about him being lazy. It was unprofessional of me, and it won't happen again."

Mr. Temple looked back at Brandon and his mother and then to his left at Mr. Stoneman. He leaned over and whispered something to Mr. Stoneman, and a woman's voice spoke from behind me.

"You're damn right it won't happen again! If you are so easily triggered, maybe you shouldn't be a classroom teacher," she paused, "*snowflake.*"

My eyes widened as I turned to face Brandon's mother who was standing in front of her seat. Was that a coincidence?

No. She was shooting fire at me with her eyes, and I knew it wasn't.

Several people were muttering again. Smirking, Mr. Temple mumbled, "Mrs. Stoneman, it sounds like your son, as they say, 'started it.' And while I agree that Mrs. Rein-Thompson's retort was inappropriate, Brandon had no right to say such an ... asinine ... thing to his teacher. Did you *say* that to him at home? Was he telling her something true?"

Mr. Stoneman stood up and grabbed the microphone, looking out into the audience. "This is a public school where indoctrination is prohibited. A teacher should not be permitted to influence our children in this way. Our conservative values—"

Mr. Temple's voice sounded distant without the microphone. "I'll take that back." He motioned with his hand, and Mr. Stoneman hesitated before leaning over to return it to him. Mr. Temple looked from him to Mr. Anderson and said, "While you have the right to your own beliefs, this teacher has the right to live her life, and it isn't fair to put her under a microscope or hold her to any kind of different standard than her colleagues. Mr. and Mrs. Anderson, did your daughter tell you that Mrs. Rein-Thompson had touched her inappropriately?"

I turned my head and searched for Kate's face. She looked mortified. Our eyes met, and she widened hers briefly before turning to her mother, who had sat back down beside her, and was muttering something. Mrs. Anderson replied to her firmly, but I couldn't make out what she said. Suddenly, Mrs. Anderson stood and announced, "It doesn't matter if my daughter thought that the touch was inappropriate. Teachers should not be touching their students regardless. That woman should be fired."

I flinched and turned to face forward.

What is today's date? March 25th. 3+2+5=10.

Wait, it's 2019. 10+2+1+9=22. 2+2=4. 4 is half of 8.

I moved a hand to my stomach and closed my eyes for a few seconds.

Mr. Temple sighed. "Ma'am, a pat on the shoulder hardly constitutes inappropriate touching." He turned his face slightly. "Kate, has Mrs. Rein-Thompson done anything to make you feel uncomfortable? Anything at all? Is there a reason why you told your parents about Mrs. Rein-Thompson touching you in class? Please be honest."

I turned to look at Kate. What was she going to say? She shifted in her seat, her eyes fixed on the chair in front of her. Her mother returned to the seat next to her and nudged her elbow. Kate moved her eyes to Mr. Temple, took a deep breath, and shook her head firmly. Then, she stated more loudly than I had ever heard her, "No." She took another breath. "And I didn't tell them she touched me. My friend saw her do it and told the principal because she thought she was helping. He told them."

Mr. Dunham spoke up from the table in the front. "I simply relayed the information given to me by both Kate and the friend who accompanied her to my office." I turned to look at him as he turned to look at Mr. Temple. "If I may add?"

Mr. Temple nodded, so Mr. Dunham continued, "Josie Rein-Thompson doesn't deserve any of this. For God's sake, she's being punished for being a caring teacher. I don't normally speak out against a student's parents, but this isn't right, and I have a duty to defend my teachers when necessary."

By this point, he had moved his gaze to the Andersons, so I did, too, my eyes watering at Mr. Dunham's words.

Through my tears, I could practically see Mrs. Anderson's blood boiling. I wiped my eyes, overwhelmed with gratitude, but I could sense that this wasn't over for her. Mr. Anderson sat down, looking more confused than anything.

And then Mrs. Stoneman stood up and pushed her way across the row, stepping over legs and almost tripping into the aisle.

"Marjorie—" Mr. Stoneman said.

"No, Derek. They have to see this." She was marching toward the board's table, a look of sheer determination in her eyes and her phone in her hand.

The video. She was going to show the board members the video.

I wanted to indicate to Donna what I knew was happening, but I was frozen. All I could do was watch as Mrs. Stoneman reached Mr. Temple and pressed play.

There wasn't even a whisper from the audience as everyone tried to stretch their hearing to the front of the room, but I could have told them that the only sound they'd have heard was the distant song being practiced by the marching band. It was what you could see that counted.

Mrs. Stoneman's hand was shaking as Mr. Temple looked up at her from his seat.

"Mrs. Stoneman, did you ... take that video? Were you spying on them?"

She brought her phone to her chest, clutching it like a prized possession. "Well, I wouldn't call it *spying*—"

I felt myself stand up and slam my palms down on the seat in front of me. "Not only has she been spying on me, she has been sending me anonymous emails meant to ... what," I looked into her eyes, " ... intimidate me?" I looked back at Mr. Stoneman. "I don't need to see that video because I've already seen it. She sent it to my school email address."

"I'm sorry," Mr. Temple looked from me to her and raised his eyebrows, "you've been sending Mrs. Rein-Thompson threatening emails?"

She didn't answer at first. She just stared at me, and it was the first time I was able to really look at her. Her makeup was heavy. Her brown hair was short in the back and then angled longer to the front. She was wearing wedge heels with skinny jeans and an oversized white button-down shirt that did not cover her bulging middle like she thought it did.

I clutched my own bulging middle as she continued staring, using my other hand to finger my shirt cuff where I knew a red rose was printed. *Rhinoceros.*

Rhinoceros. Rhinoceros. Rhinoceros.

Rhinoceros has ten letters. R 1. H 2. I 3.

"Mrs. Stoneman—" Mr. Temple prompted.

Like a feral cat, she lunged in my direction. I instinctively sat down and covered my head with my arms while she screamed, "You are what's wrong with this world! Why do we all have to bow down to *you*?! Why do *you* get to have an agenda?! How are you special just because you're *gay*?!"

Her voice was getting farther away, and I looked up to see why. Charlie, one of our security guards, had her by the arm and was leading her toward the auditorium exit.

From the table, Mr. Stoneman yelled, "First Brandon and now her! You're infringing on our right to freedom of speech!"

She continued, not to anyone in particular, "Are we all supposed to live in a PC commie world for the rest of our goddamn lives?" And then to Charlie himself, "I bet you're a libtard, too! Get your hands off me!" She tried to pull away, but he kept a hold of her arm and led her through the double doors.

- 51 -

Monday, December 23, 1996

Almost two weeks after I heard my parents arguing in their bedroom, Amanda and I sat silently in our living room, each of us absently looking at the multicolored glow coming from the lights on our Christmas tree. In a room that was usually off-limits, the stiff, burgundy couches were less than inviting. The tree—covered in handmade ornaments and sparkling, golden garland—was positioned in the center of the front window of the house, and even though it was only six o'clock in the evening, it was dark outside. Sitting at the top of the tree was a caroler made of red and white felt whom we always called "the angel," though she didn't have wings or a halo. I guess it was because she looked so cherubic with her rosy cheeks and lips formed into a singing "oh."

We were alone in the house and had just voiced our fears to each other for the first time, each of us picking up on things here and there between our parents over the prior few months. Ever since the afternoon Christmas concert that my dad had attended, he had hardly been home. When he was home, he slept on the couch. Mom was working extra hours at the hospital, so we barely saw her, either. It didn't feel like

Christmas without us all spending time together, watching movies, singing carols, and baking cookies.

Something was wrong.

I told Amanda about hearing them whisper-arguing, and she told me about the Friday night the month before when I had called from the movies to ask if I could sleep at Layla's house. Mom had said no harshly and quickly and hung up the phone, and Amanda said that, about two minutes before I called, she had arrived home from dinner with friends to find our parents screaming at each other in the kitchen. There was even a broken plate on the floor that Dad was trying to clean up while yelling something about Mom being "a control freak," and Mom yelled something back about being thankful she's not an asshole like him. When they realized Amanda was home and stopped talking.

The morning of the last day of school before Christmas break, Mom had left a note on the kitchen table that told us to have a nice last day and that she and Dad would be home that night to talk to us about something.

And we just knew.

The motor of the garage door clicked on, and we looked at each other in the near-dark. Amanda had gone to basketball tryouts that day, and her dark hair—which looked black in the darkness—was pulled back into a sweaty ponytail. She was hoping to start as a point guard and had been training all summer and fall. She had found out that day she'd made the team but would forget to tell our parents until a few days later.

We could tell by the heaviness of the car door slamming that Dad was the one home first, but just as he was opening the door to enter the family room in the back of the house from the garage, we heard Mom's car door shut from the front of the house. I wiped my damp palms on my sweatpants, aware of the Cheeto residue on my fingertips.

"Hello?" Dad called.

"In here!" we answered in unison.

He walked into the living room and squinted at us. "Hey, girls," he said quietly, stepping onto the cream-colored carpet. He looked around the room, uncertain where to sit and eventually choosing the spot on the loveseat next to me. Patting my leg, he said, "How was school?"

He smelled like fried food, as usual, and his eyes looked both tired and sad. Before either of us could answer his question or spend too much time hoping that maybe they were going to tell us something fun and surprising, Mom opened the front door, looking startled to find all three of us sitting there together in the dark.

"Hey," she said, hesitating. She looked especially small in her puffy white coat and Grinch scrubs as she leaned to the side and dropped her purse to the tile entryway floor with a thud.

"Hey," I said, the only one to answer her. Looking back and forth between the couches, she headed to the spot by Amanda and sat down without taking her coat off.

Dad sighed. "Girls, your mom and I have something to talk to you about." He cracked his knuckles while he spoke. "This isn't easy to say. I've been thinking about how to—"

"Your father is leaving," Mom said flatly, and both of our faces whipped toward her. "He's moving out the day after Christmas." Her eyes were fixed on the cream-colored carpet, her posture stiff.

Even though I had suspected it all along, the reality of losing him hit me like a punch in the stomach, and I began to sob.

He tried to take my hand, but I wouldn't let him. "Baby, please don't cry. It's not about you two at all." He looked from me to Amanda, who had also started crying. "I love your mother, but I'm not *in* love with her anymore. But that doesn't make me any less your dad."

Mom's voice was choked by her own tears. "Tell them what else—"

"Susan," he cut her off. "They don't need to know every single thing. Have a heart."

"*Me?* Have a heart?" She raised a shaky hand to her chest. "Don't you *dare* make any of this about *me* not having a heart, Thomas." She took the hand from her heart and pointed it at him accusingly. "*You* are the one who is tearing this family apart." Then, she stood up and walked up the stairs to her bedroom and slammed the door.

Amanda and I sat sniffling while he looked at his lap. A car passed by, its shadow crossing the ceiling, and I wondered if the person driving it was having a normal day or if their lives had also just been changed forever.

That night, I slept facing away from the window in my bedroom, suddenly terrified that a lunar eclipse would blind me. Even though I knew the eclipse had happened months before and that it was actually a solar eclipse that could hurt your eyes, I spent months sleeping that way, afraid of the moon.

- 52 -

Monday, March 25, 2019

The auditorium was abuzz with chatter. I was still staring at the exit, waiting for Mrs. Stoneman to somehow reappear.

"Holy shit. What the hell was that?" I had forgotten that Donna was standing beside me.

I shook my head slowly and slightly, still watching the door. "Well, now at least I know who was sending me those emails."

My eyes landed next on Mr. and Mrs. Anderson. Like the rest of us, they wore their shock plainly on their faces. Kate had one hand over her eyes like she had been watching a horror movie, and Brandon stood with his arms folded over his chest, eyes cast downward. Was he embarrassed? Pouting? I couldn't tell.

Mr. Temple spoke. "All right, everyone." He cleared his throat. "All right."

Much of the noise died down. When I turned to face him, I saw that Mr. Stoneman practically mirrored his son—arms crossed and teeth clenched.

He continued, quietly, "I have lived in this school district for my entire life. And while I know there are differing political opinions about various topics, someone's humanity should never be on the table." He scratched the stubble on his chin.

262

"In the interest of transparency, I'd like to tell you all that the video Mrs. Stoneman showed me was of Kate Anderson hugging Mrs. Rein-Thompson in the school parking lot."

I expected the audience to erupt into commentary, but there was hardly a sound.

He continued, "And there clearly wasn't anything lewd about it. Not to mention that Kate was the one who had initiated it."

I hoped that Kate wasn't embarrassed by that but didn't think it wise to turn around to check. I was working hard to keep my eyes on Mr. Temple, not allowing them to drift to the right to Mr. Stoneman.

But then Mr. Temple looked at Mr. Stoneman. "Sir, I hope you do some real soul searching after tonight. The First Amendment does not give you or your family—or *anyone*, for that matter—the right to harass someone for any reason." He looked at me. "And I believe that's what's been happening: harassment."

Mr. Stoneman didn't speak, and I still didn't look at him.

Mr. Temple looked to his right.. "Thank you, Mr. Dunham, for speaking up on behalf of Mrs. Rein-Thompson." He turned slightly. "And thank you, Kate. I do apologize for this mess. I'm sure it hasn't made this time of your life any easier." Finally, he looked at me. "Mrs. Rein-Thompson, I haven't heard any evidence of you doing anything against school policy. While it is your duty to be objective in the classroom, it is also your duty to care for your students, and it sounds like that is what you were doing with that essay prompt and the subsequent turning in of the essay to the guidance counselor, um ... " He shuffled through some papers. "Dominic Madden. I imagine that your position as a gay teacher has been difficult, but I want you to know that you are not in any kind of trouble today." He raised one eyebrow. "But I assume that you will be much more careful in the future about touching students because ... " He chuckled briefly. "I don't think you want to deal with this again."

I nodded respectfully. "Yes, sir. Thank you."

He smiled and said, "Okay." He looked toward the rest of the audience. "Are there any other community members who would like to speak?"

"I would." I recognized her voice before I saw her. "My name is Adelaide Foster, and I live at 260 Hannity Road, just across the street from here. Full disclosure, I'm also a reporter for the Dispatch."

Mr. Stoneman, who had been sitting grim-faced and staring at the table, shot her a look and then looked at me. I tried to focus my attention on Adelaide while he bore a hole into my cheek.

She continued, composed, "I came as a concerned citizen, having learned about Mrs. Rein-Thompson's situation through my son, who is one of her students." I stole a glance at Mr. Stoneman, and he was looking at Adelaide with his jaw set, tapping his finger on the table. I wondered if he would interrupt her or if he would have something to say to me afterward about the media being allowed in. At that point, though, I no longer felt nervous.

I turned around and, for the first time, took in who was there. The entire slam poetry group had shown up, and several of them waved or gave me a thumbs-up. Around them were many other students—past and present—at various levels of attentiveness. Some were so attentive that it appeared they were taking a video of the meeting, which I was surprised was allowed. I smiled at them all as a group, and many of them smiled back.

"Please state your concerns, Mrs. Foster," said Mr. Temple.

"*Ms.* Foster," she corrected him. "Sometimes we forget how much that title matters to a woman." She looked at me and winked subtly, and I couldn't help but smile.

"I apologize, Ms. Foster. Please continue." He looked slightly amused, smiling again with just his eyes.

She nodded and continued, "I send my children to public school so that they can be exposed to all different types of people—including bigots, unfortunately." She looked directly at Mr. Stoneman, who had suddenly found the agenda notes to be very interesting. "I moved to this school district because it's one of the best in the area, and part of that is the quality of the teachers. Mrs. Rein-Thompson is dedicated, challenging, caring, and—yes—just so happens to be liberal and gay. But guess what: My son has at least two other teachers who I would consider conservative, and just because one of them even mentioned recently that abortion should be illegal—God help us—I didn't contact the school about it. Want to know why?" Her voice was rising. "Because it's a free country, and I teach my kids to think for themselves. If one of them came home and told me they agreed with that teacher and that abortion should be illegal, I would give my two cents about why I disagree, and then *I would let them make up their own mind.*"

She paused, and the entire auditorium was silent. I looked back at my students, all of whom were either looking at Adelaide or looking at their phones that were recording Adelaide, and finally at the Andersons. Mrs. Anderson was scowling while her husband shook his head back and forth over and over again.

I went to turn my attention back to Adelaide but quickly realized I had forgotten to look at Kate. I turned back around to find her watching Adelaide quietly with what appeared to be conviction on her face. I was proud of her. She looked strong, and I knew at that moment that she was going to be able to take care of herself somehow, even in the midst of a family who might shun her.

Mr. Temple asked, "So your concern is not about any particular teachers at the high school?"

"Yes," she began quickly, "it is. My concern is for the well-being of Mrs. Rein-Thompson, who deserves to be acknowledged and respected. I wasn't sure what my angle was going to be with this story, but after interviewing several students and adults, and after hearing the people speaking at this meeting, there are no questions in my mind. I just wanted to let everyone know I will be publishing the article online tonight. Thank you." She sat down.

The meeting continued as planned, but I didn't hear much else. I cheered for the basketball team and was happy to hear about the passing of some renovation projects, but my focus was mostly inward. I couldn't wait to tell Cam about all of the people who had come out to support me. But, more than anything, I wished I could call my dad.

- 53 -

As the meeting was winding down, Donna leaned toward me and whispered, "You okay?"

"Yeah," I nodded. "I think so. I mean, it could have gone better, but it could have gone way worse." I shrugged.

She exhaled briefly with amusement. "Listen," she turned to face me, still speaking quietly, "if you want to pursue charges or something about the harassment, I will totally back you up."

I thought for a few seconds, picturing the hate in Mrs. Stoneman's eyes. But then I thought of those thirteen robins.

Shaking my head and returning her gaze, I said, "No. There are always going to be people who don't," I used air quotes, "believe in my lifestyle." I gave a short laugh. "I stayed in the closet all these years to avoid them, but now that the door has been opened, there's nothing I can do about people like that." I wiped my hands on my pants again. "Besides, she didn't actually do anything illegal, did she? I mean, aside from spending way too much money on a dozen roses."

She jerked her head back. "A dozen roses?"

"Motion to adjourn. All in favor, say 'aye,'" one of the board members, whose name I still forget, spoke into the microphone.

I chuckled and said to Donna, "Long story." We both reached down to the floor to grab our bags.

"Excuse me," Dr. Michaelson said in the front row, her hand raised. Jane, her secretary, was standing in front of her, holding a pile of papers. Dr. Michaelson stood and repeated more loudly, "Excuse me, Mr. Temple."

He looked at her and then reached to retrieve the microphone. "Yes, Dr. Michaelson?"

"I apologize for interrupting," she said, "but it appears that we missed something on the agenda for this evening."

I looked at the pile of papers that she was now holding, and my heart sped up. Could it be? It had to be.

She approached the table and handed the papers to Mr. Temple, who looked over the top paper silently. Flipping through the pile, he found copies for the rest of the board members and passed them down the table accordingly.

The people around us were gathering their things, probably assuming that the new item was something boring like a request for a field trip or a conference attendance. I looked at Donna who was also holding her bag and sending a text, ready to leave, and put my hand on her arm.

"I think that's from me," I said quietly.

"What is?" She looked up at me and then at the board.

"The new proposal that the board is reading right now."

"A proposal? For wha—" she interrupted herself and turned back to me. "You did it? *Already?*"

I shrugged and slumped down a little in the chair, closing my eyes.

"You are a glutton for punishment, my friend," she snorted and shook her head.

"I had my reasons," I muttered, trying to read the board

members' faces.

With my eyes closed, I could hear that many people hadn't even noticed the board still in session.

Mr. Temple spoke with more volume this time. "Since you all don't have a copy of this addendum, I will read it to you."

The auditorium quieted, and I opened my eyes. My entire body cringed as he read my proposal aloud—especially when he got to my name. I watched him and the rest of the board through squinted eyes as he said, "All in favor, say 'aye.'"

Then, the most amazing thing happened. Almost every single one of them said "aye" in succession. I sat up straighter.

"Anyone opposed?"

Mr. Stoneman raised his hand, his eyes remaining on the papers in front of him.

And the auditorium exploded with applause—including my own. I looked around me at all of the smiling faces, many of whom had upgraded to standing ovations. I turned to look for Kate and found her parents shuffling her up the aisle toward the door, but not before she could turn around and grin at me.

Donna nudged me with her shoulder and smiled. "Well, what do you know? That was really freakin' easy." She laughed.

I shook my head in disbelief and smiled, leaning forward to grab my bag. As I went to stand up, my eyes landed on Mr. Stoneman, who was watching me with ... sadness? I met his eyes and nodded once. A truce was probably out of the question, but I refused to stoop to his—their—level.

On my own way out, Maddie stopped me. "Mrs. R., you were absolutely amazing! You are, like, so brave."

I chuckled, "Thanks, Maddie. I'm just, you know, existing."

"Quick!" Savannah ran up to me. "Dance with me!"

She showed me some moves that involved her hips going in

one direction and her arms going in the other, and I copied her, both of us giggling. A crowd of students had gathered around us and were cheering us on.

"Okay!" I announced, out of breath. "I don't know about you guys, but I am beat. We have to be back here in, like," I checked my watch, "ten hours, and I need my beauty rest."

Josh appeared at my side as I continued walking, "Okay, so, Kate mentioned something to me about using the poetry slam as a fundraiser for the GSA. Do you want to, like, sell tickets to it or something?"

I hadn't planned that far ahead. "I don't think so. That might prevent some people from coming, don't you think?"

We stepped out into the lobby with the rest of the crowd. He said, "Maybe. So, like, a raffle?"

I held the door open for him and the group of kids who was still walking with us and called after him, "We'll think of something!"

On my way to my car, I caught sight of the North Star. Immediately, I heard my dad's voice singing, like he used to when I was little, "When you wish upon a star, makes no difference who you are ... " I took a deep breath and sent a silent thank-you to the universe, knowing he was out there somewhere.

Monday, March 28, 2016

It was fourth period, and I was reviewing state test-taking strategies with my class. There was a multiple-choice question that referenced a microwave on the interactive whiteboard. I don't know why, but I will always remember that.

My classroom phone rang, and I ran to pick up, saying breathlessly, "Rein-Thompson!" I leaned over to scratch my knee and then held up a finger to a student whose hand was raised to give the answer to the question on the board.

"Josie, someone named Mia is on the line," Phyllis, one of the secretaries in the main office, said. "She said it's important."

I turned around to face away from my students, briefly noticing there was a chip in the wood of the door. Mia was my dad's too-young girlfriend who had never once called me for any reason. "Okay, put her through. Thanks, Phyllis."

"Josie?" Mia sounded nervous.

"What's wrong?"

"I'm so sorry. Your dad is in the hospital. He was in an accident—"

"What happened? Where is he?" I could feel the panic rising inside of me.

"We had a fight, and he got into his car to drive ... I don't know where to. He had been drinking—"

"What? Why? He hasn't—"

"I don't know why, Josie. Just come to East Side Hospital. Come now."

She hung up, and I held the phone to my ear for another few seconds. When I turned to face my students, many of them were looking at me with concern in their eyes. Sydney Freeman, whose face at that moment I will never forget, said, "Mrs. R., what can I do?"

"Go get Mrs. Wilson." I knew Dana had her prep that period. Sydney ran out the door as I went to gather my coat and bag. She returned with Dana a minute later, and I said, "I have to go. My dad was in an accident." Tears filled my eyes.

"Go," Dana said. "I'll call the office and tell them you're leaving and to get someone to cover you." She squeezed my arm and repeated, "Go."

I ran out the door and got into my car, thinking about how he had called me that morning, and I hadn't answered because I had been listening to an audiobook that I wanted to finish. I was planning on calling him back after school. *Why am I so selfish? I could have finished the book after school and answered his phone call this morning. What the hell is wrong with my priorities?*

I weaved through traffic and ran red lights, somehow making it to the hospital in only twenty minutes. Amanda had texted me on my way, saying that she would get there around the same time as I would. The nurse at the front desk told me that Thomas Rein was in room 506, and I immediately started to cry because May 6th was his birthday and Liesel's due date.

When I walked into the room, Aunt Jill and Amanda were already there. Dad's face was bandaged and bloody, and he was unconscious with a ventilator breathing for him. I crouched down beside his bed and took his hand, which appeared to be the only part of his body unharmed.

"Daddy, no, no, no, no, no," I murmured over and over.

Amanda began weeping behind me, and Aunt Jill put her hand on my shoulder. "The nurse was just in here. He's bleeding internally, and they're going to transfer him to the ICU. It could be a long night."

I stood up, and he lifted his hand. I grabbed it and squeezed, saying, "It's going to be okay. You're going to be okay." But he didn't squeeze back.

While he was being transferred to another floor, I called Cam and told her what I knew. At that point, she was eight months pregnant and struggling to keep up with her kindergarteners. "He seemed fine when we had dinner with him the other night," she said, small voices laughing and talking in the background. "Why do you think he was drinking?"

"I don't know." My voice sounded cold. "Can you please come here after work? I don't want to do this alone."

"Of course. I'll bring you some dinner."

"And some comfortable clothes please. I'm going to stay here as long as it takes."

Amanda, Aunt Jill, and I rode the elevator to the ICU and took seats in the waiting room. We stared at the nearly-silent TV on the wall where a woman in a pink dress was talking about the week's weather forecast. None of us said a word for hours, until Mia walked in.

I sat forward in my seat. "What happened? How did you

know he had been in an accident?"

She sat down in a chair across from the three of us, under the TV. "We argued about something silly this morning, and I told him I was going to take a shower. By the time I got out, he was drunk." Her eyes never met any of ours.

"Then why did he leave?" Amanda asked, clutching the armrests on either side of her.

Mia looked at the floor. "I told him I couldn't deal with his drinking anymore and that I thought we should break up." She put her hand on her forehead. "I had no idea he would take it that hard. We haven't even been dating that seriously or for that long." She covered her face with both of her hands.

A doctor came out and called, "Amanda Rain?"

Amanda and I both stood and walked over to him. "Is he okay?" I asked.

There was sympathy on his face. "I'm afraid not. We're going to do everything we can, but he has a great deal of internal bleeding."

Cam walked up beside me, holding an overnight bag. "Can we see him?"

He looked at her and then down at the chart in his hand. "Are you another daughter?"

Cam hesitated, looking at me and then back at the doctor. "No, I—"

"Family only." He looked back at me as I put my hand up to explain, but Cam beat me to it.

"I'm Josie's wife." She took my arm, and I reached for her hand to squeeze it, the warmth of recognition slightly dulling my panic.

"I'm sorry." He was looking at me. "It's hospital policy to only allow immediate family. His two daughters can come back for a few minutes, but he isn't conscious." He turned and held the door open for Amanda and me.

Leaning forward to kiss my cheek, Cam whispered that she loved me and walked slowly over to sit beside Aunt Jill.

Amanda and I held hands as we walked into his room. He was hooked up to what seemed like a hundred machines, different ones buzzing and beeping in their own ways. His eyes were closed, and his chest rose and fell unnaturally with the ventilator. Looking more closely at him this time, I saw that his left eye was bandaged, and his head had been shaved and was also partially bandaged. His left arm—the one he wrote with—was in a cast, and I couldn't see what was under the blanket that covered most of his body.

We got closer, both of us crying. "We're here, Daddy," I said. "Amanda and I are both here, and we love you so much."

He didn't move at all, aside from the artificial rising and falling of his chest. I broke away from Amanda and walked to his right side to hold his good hand. He didn't squeeze or acknowledge me at all. I leaned forward and said quietly to him, "You have to pull through this, Dad. Liesel will be here in a month, and she needs her PapPaw." He had chosen that name for himself, spelling and all.

Still no reaction. The doctor walked in and said, "We will keep you updated. Please know we are doing everything we can. His paperwork indicates he is an organ donor and does not want to be resuscitated if something should happen."

I felt numb. How could this be happening so quickly? He had just called me that morning. *Why did he drink today? Why did he drive?* I was angry with him for taking a breakup so seriously—especially a breakup with someone whom he'd only been dating for a few months.

Not able to stand there any longer, I bolted out of the room and back into the waiting room—straight to Mia, who was still sitting under the TV. "Why did you let him leave? He's going to die, and it's all your fault!" She cowered as if I was going to hit her, and all I could see was her frizzy, bleach-blonde hair.

Sliding out from under me, she stood and turned to look at me. "He left while I was getting dressed. By the time I realized he wasn't there, he had been driving for at least five minutes. I jumped into my car and tried to guess what direction he had gone in." She sat down in a different chair and leaned forward with her elbows on her knees. "I found his car upside down in a field outside of town. I called 911 and tried to talk to him to soothe him, but I don't think he was conscious even then. When the paramedics got there and pulled him out of the car, I couldn't believe the amount of blood—"

"Shut up!" I shouted. "Get the hell out of here! You barely even know him!" I was stomping my feet and pounding my fists on my thighs. "Shut up and leave! *Go!*"

Cam came up beside me and wrapped her arms around my waist, pulling me to her. I fought for a few seconds but then let it happen. She pulled me down into an oversized chair and held me as I shook and wailed, still yelling obscenities in Mia's direction.

Eventually, I calmed down. Cam offered me the cheeseburger she had brought me, but I wasn't hungry. Aunt Jill was on the phone with Uncle Paul when the doctor came back out. We could all tell by his face that Dad was gone.

Amanda screamed, and Cam grabbed my arm and practically cut me with her fingernails. I had no reaction at all, aside from the need to vomit. Thankfully, there was a trash can nearby.

The rest of the evening is a blur. We paid for parking like

it was any other day. We drove our cars like the world hadn't changed. It was dinner time around the city, and people laughed and talked on the sidewalks, and I wanted to tell them all to go home. I hated them for their carefree smiles and hated myself for letting him die.

- 55 -

Monday, March 25, 2019

As soon as I got in the car, I called Cam. "Hey! Sorry, were you asleep?"

"Kind of," she said drowsily. "But I want to know how it went. Are you okay?"

"Yes. I'm perfectly fine. The school board president wasn't having any of their bigotry. He barely entertained them at all. Lots of kids showed up, too. Actually, it was kind of nice."

She yawned. "That's wonderful, babe. Be careful driving."

"Wait. Don't go yet. Wanna guess who my stalker has been this whole time?"

"What?" I heard her fumbling to sit up. "How do you know? What in the world happened now?"

I told her about Marjorie Stoneman trying to attack me and how she was basically karate-chopped out of the room by Charlie the superhero security guard.

"So now what? Will she leave you alone?"

I sighed, noticing that my dashboard was warning me that I was low on gas.

"Shit, I have to stop and get gas. Yes, to answer your question. I think she will leave me alone, especially now that everyone knows what she's done. I told Donna that I wasn't thinking about pressing charges or anything. I mean, she didn't actually, like, *do* much of anything to me."

She was quiet for a few seconds. "I guess not. See," she paused, "I told you that shirt with the roses on it would bring you good luck."

I smiled. "I guess so." Spotting a gas station, I put on my turn signal. "There's one more thing, and then I'll let you go back to sleep."

"Yes, love?"

"They approved the GSA."

"Whoa. Are you serious? I didn't even know … I didn't think you had turned in a proposal for that yet."

"I know what you're thinking. It's okay. I'm going to be okay. Did I tell you that ninety-nine students had signed a petition in favor of it?" I pulled up to a gas pump.

"You said there were a lot of them, but you didn't say how many. Listen, Jo, if you feel like this is something you have to do—"

"I don't *have* to do it. I *want* to do it. These kids deserve a confident, positive role model to help them through the most ungodly time of their lives."

My phone beeped with another call as I was getting out of the car.. Adelaide was calling me. "I'll see you soon, babe. Adelaide's calling. I'm going to get gas and then will be on my way. Love you!"

I switched calls. "Hey, Adelaide." I was ready to be done with everything but remembered she was going home to work on the article, so maybe she needed some more details.

"Hi, Josie. I just want to let you know the article will be published tonight by midnight, so you might want to prepare to see it on social media."

"I don't even use social media, so I'm good."

"Not at all? Not even Facebook?" She sounded genuinely shocked.

"Nope," I said, feeling more tired by the minute.

"Okay, then I'll email it to you myself. I think you'll appreciate the angle."

I smirked. "Thanks."

"And maybe the social media thing is for the best because there were lots of students there taking videos, and I guarantee they're already all over the internet—particularly TikTok."

I tried to picture what the videos would even look like. They were relatively far away from most of us who were speaking, so I couldn't imagine any videos were of great quality. "I don't know about that. It wasn't all that exciting. Except maybe when Mrs. Stoneman lost her shit. Oops, sorry. Keep that off the record."

She laughed. "You got it. Hey, thanks again for talking to me. You did great tonight."

"Thank you. I had no idea what to expect, but I survived."

"You sure did. Take care."

"You too."

I put my phone in my pocket and waited impatiently as gas filled my tank. Watching the numbers tick up slowly, I tried to recall the events of the evening in the order they had happened.

"You're the gay teacher," a male voice spoke from behind me.

I jumped. Turning my head, I saw a teenage boy putting gas into a muddy Jeep. He was wearing a red baseball cap that shaded his face from the fluorescent lights above us, so I had to squint to figure out his identity.

It was Trevor, Brandon's friend. It was too late to pretend like I hadn't heard him, but I wasn't sure what to say. I just stood there and blinked, his eyes remaining on mine.

He continued, "I'd like to see what you do behind closed doors." He looked me up and down, leering.

The gas nozzle clicked. I hung it up and walked quickly around to get back into my car. On school property, I don't think he would have had the nerve. Out in the world, he thought he had the right.

That's enough for tonight, I thought as I sped out of the parking lot and toward my sleeping family.

The house was silent. I slid in as quietly as I could and stood in the entryway for a minute, letting my eyes adjust to the familiar darkness. Kicking off my shoes and setting my bag down on the floor, I crept toward the living room couch and pulled a blanket on top of me.

Outside, a distant siren echoed, and I was struck by a replay of Charlie pulling Mrs. Stoneman out of the auditorium. If he hadn't grabbed her, would she have attacked me? It was hard to imagine but definitely not out of the question.

I shook my head to shake away the possibility. Knowing I was too amped to go to sleep, I took out my phone to check the weather for the next day, planning to turn on the TV to watch something mindless, when something told me to open TikTok.

What was the hashtag Savannah had told me to search for? Bulldog GSA?

I tried it. The search results took me to several videos of bulldogs doing hilarious things, particularly riding things like Roombas and skateboards. I scrolled through at least fifty videos before remembering that she had said *Benson* GSA, not Bulldogs.

The results were immediate and overwhelming. The first

one, with over 10,000 likes, showed my smiling face.

I was wearing the same shirt I had on—the navy button down with the red roses on it—and there was Savannah to my right.

I clicked.

Savannah and I were dancing in the auditorium, surrounded by several cheering students. But the video quickly cuts away to a closeup (*how*, I don't know) of Mr. Temple reading the proposal for the GSA, the board voting yes, and the auditorium filling with applause. It ended with Maddie standing in the lobby, smiling and forming a heart with her hands, stating calmly, "Love. Is. Love."

Ten thousand likes. Wait, now it was eleven thousand. Who in the world was watching this? Like, the *entire* world? I looked at the hashtags: *#bensongsa, #loveislove, #gayteachersoftiktok, #part2*

"Part 2" of what? I clicked on the profile picture (Savannah with her tongue out, wearing a t-shirt that displayed a peacock) to look at her other videos. The video next to the one I had just watched showed Marjorie Stoneman's angry face and the back of my head.

I clicked again and immediately saw her come at me as I ducked for cover. Charlie swooped in as she twisted in an attempt to get out of his grasp, shouting, "You are what's wrong with this world! Why do we all have to bow down to *you*?! Why do *you* get to have an agenda?! How are you special just because you're *gay*?!"

Savannah's phone camera followed them to about the middle of the auditorium before flipping and showing Savannah's face, saying, "Big Karen energy." Then she curved her hand around her mouth and announced, "Meltdown on aisle three. We've got a spill. Bring your mop to soak up those boomer tears." She giggled and lost control of the phone, showing a brown auditorium chair, then the floor, and then her face again, whispering, "Stay tuned for part two."

She knew it couldn't end there. I smiled, thinking about her choosing which parts to splice together for the second part.

I clicked on the comments section. The top comments were:

That teacher feared for her gay life for a sec

yass queen, push that gay agenda

ummmm, yes, being gay is special

This video had almost as many likes as the other one. I wondered about the legal ramifications from the Stoneman family. Would Savannah be sued for some kind of defamation? Did that even exist anymore with the internet? Since the school board meeting was public, wasn't anything said there allowed to be public knowledge, anyway?

I leaned my head back on the couch and closed my eyes, not knowing whether to laugh or cry.

"Honey, you need to get some sleep."

I opened my eyes to see Cam standing in the doorway to the living room, hair messy and "Viking basketball" shirt askew. She looked so warm and real and perfect that I had to stand, pull her to me, and kiss her.

Afterward, she pulled back and said, "So this is what school board meetings do to you. I think I like it."

I laughed and took her hand, pulling her toward the stairs.

Wednesday, March 30, 2016

Amanda and I were tasked with planning Dad's funeral because he wasn't married. It was one of the most surreal experiences of my life that I wouldn't wish upon anyone. My mom had flown into town to help, but she was purposely emotionally distant from the whole situation.

Dealing with an untimely death is not something anyone can prepare for. Getting a returned phone call in the middle of the night from a funeral director, letting you know the body will be picked up and transported as soon as possible, is not something anyone can prepare for. Walking into your middle-aged dad's apartment after he has died and finding a basement filled with discarded, full garbage bags is not something anyone can prepare for. Choosing the music to be played at your middle-aged dad's funeral is not something anyone can prepare for. Looking through a catalog of caskets to pick one for your middle-aged dad is not something anyone can prepare for.

Tuesday evening was the viewing. People I hadn't seen in many years showed up—distant relatives, his high school friends, my high school friends. Everybody mingled against a backdrop of music coming from my laptop—songs he had shared with me throughout my life. Music had been our mutual wavelength—a place where we could meet and leave the outside world behind. I stood off to the side and watched people chat with each other, unable to say much myself, and spent a lot of time staring at the burgundy-carpeted floor and listening to artists like Elton John, Barry Manilow, or Paul McCartney.

Wednesday morning was the funeral service at St. Francis, where I hadn't been in many years. We sang some of Dad's favorite hymns, like "On Eagle's Wings" and "Morning Has Broken." The priest gave a generic eulogy while I scolded myself for not getting up to speak, knowing I would be too emotional to get through it. While he blathered on, I studied the stained glass window to my left, even though I had seen it from a distance a thousand times as a kid.

Leaning over, I whispered to Cam, "Look at that. I never noticed that robin at the bottom of the window. See the tree in the corner?" I pointed, and she nodded. "Did I ever tell you the story about Dad running from a mother robin? He was such a pain in the ass as a child." I suppressed a giggle-sob.

"Tell me later," she whispered, putting her hand on my black stockings. "We're supposed to be listening to the priest."

I turned my attention back to the priest, who was saying what he probably said at everyone's funeral: the gates of heaven, yadda yadda, God's welcoming arms, yadda yadda. I wondered how welcoming God could be if he was willing to kill a middle-aged man who never seemed to catch a break. I knew what Dad would say if he could speak to me, though: It was karma for breaking up our family. He had always felt guilty about that.

Aunt Jill had arranged for a man in a kilt to play bagpipes at the cemetery before lowering Dad's casket into a plot next to Grandma Louise. I stood in the early-spring chill with Cam on one side and my mom on the other. They each held my hands, and I squeezed as hard as I could while the bagpipe notes floated "Amazing Grace" into the miles surrounding us, our palms all slick despite the cold.

For the rest of my life, I will wonder what would have happened if I had answered his call the morning he died. Would I have somehow prevented him from drinking or from driving? Where was he actually going? When I consider that maybe he had been driving to see me, I lose all of the air in my lungs. It doesn't even make sense because I was at work, and he wouldn't come to interrupt me teaching, but the possibility still haunts me.

On our way home from the funeral, Cam drove my car. When she went to push on the radio, I stopped her hand, "No. I can't listen to music right now. Can we just have silence?"

"Of course." She took my hand, and we rode home without a sound until I remembered I wanted to tell her the robin story.

"Oh, I almost forgot," I began and then told her about little-boy Dad who had taken the blue robin's egg from its nest to show his mother. Cam hadn't met Grandma Louise before she passed away, but she had heard stories about how tough she could be.

When I finished talking and was shaking my head and smiling with tears dripping down my face, she said, "He was a sensitive soul, Jojo. That doesn't just go away. I bet you'll see him around you in all kinds of places now."

In bed that night, after we had been sleeping for an hour or two, she grabbed my hand and pulled it to her protruding belly.

Liesel was moving all around, and I could feel her elbows and knees pushing and twisting. Forgetting my grief for a moment, I grinned in the dark.

"I want to change her middle name," Cam whispered.

"To what?" I asked, my hand still resting on her.

"Robin." She pulled me closer, and I buried my face under her chin, unable to hold back tears of longing and gratitude. And that's how our daughter became Liesel Robin Thompson.

- 58 -

Tuesday, March 26, 2019

Without constant anxiety in the back of my mind, I had an exceedingly normal school day. I made myself avoid Adelaide's article that morning because I didn't want to distract myself from the tasks at hand: teaching, moving on, and planning for the next day's poetry performance. I wrote on my board in the morning that we would be having poetry practice after school, and I still had to return a phone call from a local bakery who had offered to donate cookies for the occasion—among all of the rest of my teacherly duties.

After the final bell rang, I left my classroom (where Brandon had been oddly quiet, by the way) to go grab my snack out of the faculty room. On my way, I called the bakery's number.

"Sweet Treats!" a voice answered cheerfully.

"Hey, Sweet Treats!" I reached into the refrigerator for my cheese stick. "This is Josie Rein-Thompson returning your call."

"Hey there! I read your article this morning and saw you on TikTok last night. We are thrilled to support you." She spoke to someone near her, saying something about "that teacher from the article."

I wasn't expecting them to mention the article and wondered briefly how they had found out about it. "Great! We are very thankful. Can you drop the cookies off at about six tomorrow evening? We'll take care of setting them out for people after the performance."

"Sure thing! We'll bring a variety of types and make sure the boxes are labeled for anybody with allergies."

"Thanks again. This really means a lot to me and to the kids."

"You're doing so many special things for those kids. It's the least we can do. Also, we want to suggest that you sell the cookies at intermission to raise money for the new GSA. We would have charged one dollar per cookie, so maybe you could do the same?"

I smiled. "Did any of my students call you guys? Because you're pretty much reading their minds right now."

"Nope! We came up with the idea all on our own."

"Well, then, I think I will have to take you up on it. It's a great idea. Truly, thank you."

They hung up, and I unwrapped my cheese stick and took a bite on my way back to my classroom, where the poets were waiting for me at the door—a number that had steadily grown over the last week to include students in various grade levels.

I swallowed and smiled. "Hey, guys! Ready for our last rehearsal? I actually was able to snag the auditorium, so we can practice with the sound system. Who's in?"

They picked up their bags and followed me down the hallway, chatting excitedly about various things. I finished my cheese stick and wished for another as I flicked on the auditorium lights and led them down to the front to sit in the first few rows.

"Mrs. R., we were so proud of you at the meeting last night." Josh ran to catch up with me. "And that article is perfect."

"Thanks, Josh. I actually haven't read it yet." I jumped up onto the stage and pulled a microphone stand from behind the blue, velvet curtain. Setting it in the center of the stage, I switched it on and said, "Testing. Can everybody hear me?"

"You haven't read it?" Josh called from the floor while several kids gave me a thumbs-up. "You might be the only person in the state who hasn't." He took out his phone and clicked around for a few seconds. "Look at this." He faced the screen toward me. "It has over 20,000 likes and 5,000 retweets."

"What?" Forgetting I was standing behind a microphone, my loud voice startled me. I crouched down and squinted at his phone screen. "I don't even know how to use Twitter, so I have no idea what I'm even looking at. Who are these people who are liking and retweeting?"

He laughed. "They're anybody. Lots of people are coming out—no pun intended, I guess—talking about how they are either gay teachers or students who wish they had gay teachers. You're kind of an icon right now."

I reached out my hand. "Do you mind if I look? I'm having a hard time processing this."

"Not at all." He handed me his phone. "Take your time. I'll read at the mike first and then will just ask who wants to go next."

I took his phone and sat down in the front row as he ascended the stairs to the stage. He wasn't exaggerating. There really were that many likes and retweets. The headline of the article read "Teacher forced out of the closet by conservative parents," and the accompanying photo was me from last year's yearbook. I cringed a little because my face looked chubby, and the striped shirt I was wearing did not do me any favors. Without thinking too much, I clicked on the article link that took me to the Dispatch's website.

Teacher forced out of the closet by conservative parents
   ADELAIDE FOSTER
   Mon., March 25, 2019, 11:24 p.m.

Accused of influencing a female student's sexuality by the girl's parents, Josephine Rein-Thompson, a tenth-grade English teacher at Benson High School, spoke on her own behalf at tonight's school board meeting held in the auditorium to accommodate an unexpected number of attendants. The girl's parents claimed that Mrs. Rein-Thompson "tried to make her a homosexual" by assigning an essay honoring Women's History Month wherein students were to write about an inspirational female.

The student in question wrote about Mrs. Rein-Thompson because she is "kind, successful and true to herself," the last part referring to the teacher's identity as a lesbian. Mrs. Rein-Thompson has a wife with whom she parents a daughter. According to her, she does not discuss her personal life in her classroom because it is "irrelevant" to English class.

School board president Martin Temple dismissed the family's accusation, calling the essay "lovely" and "flattering."

"That family had a clear agenda," Mr. Temple said following the meeting. "When it came out that Mrs. Rein-Thompson is being harassed by a student and his mother—both family to a school

board member, no less—it was obvious to me who the victim in the situation is. And it isn't the little girl with the gay teacher."

When asked for comments, the accusing parents had none.

Also unreachable for comments were Derek Stoneman and his wife Marjorie Stoneman, who has been accused of ongoing harassment toward Mrs. Rein-Thompson. Mrs. Stoneman had verbally attacked Mrs. Rein-Thompson at the meeting, calling Mrs. Rein-Thompson a "snowflake" and citing her "agenda."

Without federal legal protection, many LGBT teachers live in fear of losing their jobs, so they live lives of virtual silence. While most teachers hang pictures of their spouses and children in their classrooms, thousands of LGBT teachers shy away from public displays of their private lives. Understandably, Mrs. Rein-Thompson was worried about being fired because of a false accusation.

"She admires me for not trying to be someone I'm not, even though this meeting right now demonstrates why it isn't easy," Mrs. Rein-Thompson said tonight, in reference to the essay in question.

Several students attended the meeting to show support for their teacher. Many of them called Mrs. Rein-Thompson "nice" and "dedicated," and one mentioned that "she never talks about her wife in class."

But shouldn't she be able to? In 2019, what are people afraid of?

If you want to show Mrs. Rein-Thompson your support, you won't find her on social media. Instead, start a conversation with the people around you about love and acceptance.

Josh was done reading at the microphone and had come off of the stage to wait patiently for me to finish reading. When I looked up, he said, "Do you want to read the comments? They are overwhelmingly supportive." He reached for his phone.

I handed it to him. "No," I answered. "But thank you for letting me read the article. I'm afraid the comments would be too much, and I'm just not interested in seeing anything negative right now. I'm ready to move past this."

He nodded. "I get it."

Kate was sitting quietly in the row behind me, down about ten seats. I glanced back at her, feeling thankful that Adelaide had chosen not to mention her specifically or to even mention her parents' names. She had been to all of our poetry practices but hadn't read anything of her own yet, so I thought that maybe she was just hanging out to support her friends. Suddenly, I knew what I had to say.

"My wife is going to be so happy the article is positive." I was looking at Josh but hoping that Kate was listening. Adelaide was right. It's 2019, and it's time to normalize something that is undeniably normal for so many people.

Kate looked over at me quickly and then looked away. Madison had just finished reading her poem, and kids were snapping. I stood up and said, "Who's next? Wait until you hear your voice carry throughout this entire room. Isn't it awesome?" I looked at Madison as she jumped down from the stage, grinning.

"I'll go." Kate was sitting up straighter and looking at me. Was that a new sense of confidence in her eyes? I hoped so.

"Sure, Kate." I smiled. "I was hoping you were going to speak up."

She stood up, and the weight of my words floated in the air, traveling with her up the stairs and to the microphone. Adjusting it to her shorter height, she spoke into it, "Hello." When she heard her own echo, she smiled and took a deep breath.

"Every sunrise has its own beauty,
   even when no one is awake to see it.
   The colors mingle in the sky,
   swirling like paint on a canvas."

She was focused on the back of the auditorium.

"Sometimes the moon sticks around
   to see the sun's show,
   feeling envious
   and forgetting its own beauty."

Her eyes drifted toward the ceiling.

"Moon, you are alone,
   but you are not lonely."

She shifted her gaze to the other side of the ceiling.

"Sun, remember each morning
   that the moon has come before you
   to remind the world how bright you are."

Her eyes dropped back to the audience.

"I am the sunrise,
     but I used to be the moon."

She looked right at me.

"I am a new day filled with color."

Smiling softly, I snapped my fingers along with everyone else, impressed by her nerve and her figurative language. She had clearly been practicing on her own because she had the piece memorized.

Not only was she going to survive this time in her life, but she was also going to grow up and be just fine. Maybe her parents would come around; maybe they wouldn't. The important thing in that moment was she was owning her transformation, and she wasn't afraid to show it.

Wednesday, March 27, 2019

I was running late in the morning because Liesel had a cough and had struggled to sleep, so Cam and I had played what we like to refer to as "musical beds" throughout the night. By 2:00, and the third time I'd been awakened, it took me forever to fall back to sleep. You know how all of your small daytime worries turn into huge nighttime fears? My heart was pounding at the thought of Sweet Treats forgetting to drop off the cookies, and that led me to repeat my performance poem over and over in my mind, making sure I had it memorized.

I hadn't told anyone—not even Cam—that I was planning on performing a poem. Honestly, I wasn't sure I would actually have the nerve to do it when the time came, so I kept it to myself. I wondered if Kate's parents would be there or if Brandon would be staring me down from the front row. There were too many variables for me to be certain.

At some point, I drifted into a restless sleep and then had a terrible time waking up with my alarm, uncharacteristically hitting snooze a few times. When I walked into school fifteen minutes later than usual, I could see from down the hall that there was a piece of paper taped to my door. Deciding it was probably a note from Jim, the awesome custodian who cleans my room each night, I didn't think much of it until I got closer. Written in all capital letters on jaggedly-ripped lined paper, it read:

JUST BECAUSE PEOPLE ARE NICE TO YOUR FACE DOESN'T MEAN THEY DON'T THINK YOUR DISGUSTING BEHIND YOUR BACK

I tore it off of the wood and looked around to see if anyone else was looking.

Flooded by snapshots of my high school's cafeteria, Naomi's red face, bright purple stretch marks on my sides, Tara's tweezers, kids calling out *rhinoceros* in the endless hallways—which at some point turned into "dyke-oceros"—I had to steady myself against the doorframe, feeling light-headed. Shame and self-doubt filled my blood and pumped to every part of my body.

No. Like my interaction with Trevor in the gas station, I was going to ignore the note and move on with my life. Whoever wrote it—who probably was not Trevor because he had made it clear that I did the opposite of "disgust" him—wanted to make me feel paranoid, and I was not going to let them.

In fact, I decided at that moment I was going to do the opposite. I was going to speak my poem on stage that night, no matter who was in the audience.

Taking a deep breath, I crumpled the paper in my hand, picturing its incorrect usage of "YOUR." Inside my classroom, I tossed it into the green recycling bin and promised myself I wouldn't take it back out.

In my classroom, the voicemail light was blinking. Sighing, I dropped my bag to the floor and picked up the receiver. A robotic female voice stated, "Message received at seven-oh-eight PM on Tuesday, March 26th."

"This is Brian Anderson. Regardless of what the board decided last night, my wife and I do not want our daughter to have any unnecessary contact with you. It has come to our attention that you recruited her to read some kind of poem on a stage tomorrow, but she is not permitted to do so." *Click.*

Not permitted? I hadn't thought to get parents' permission to participate in the poetry slam. Did Kate know her parents had forbidden her? Was I supposed to stop her from getting up onto the stage? Did her parents know about her TikToks that were getting more views than could possibly fit into the auditorium to watch her read a poem?

A thought struck me: *Don't acknowledge the message.*

A twinge of guilt appeared in my stomach but was quickly replaced by a protectiveness for both Kate and for myself. What would I say to him, anyway? Surely they had told Kate themselves and weren't relying on me to tell her.

If she showed up at the slam to read, she was disobeying them. And that wasn't any of my business.

- 60 -

Thursday, May 5, 2016

Cam started having contractions—big, painful, regular ones— while we were watching TV in our living room. I had just known the answer to Double Jeopardy and was about to do a triumphant dance when she grabbed her belly and looked at me, wide-eyed.

"Our suitcase is packed and in the car," I said, literally jumping into action. "We have our birth plan printed out, and we will play our Jann Arden playlist on my laptop. Let's call the doctor's office to let them know."

We were told to come to the hospital as soon as we were ready since the contractions were already so close together. Driving down the highway, I called Amanda and told her to call our mom, and then I called Cam's mom to meet us at the hospital. When I put my phone down and looked at Cam, she was smiling.

"It's happening, babe." She grabbed my hand, immediately squeezing it hard and grimacing to get through a contraction. I squeezed back and reminded her to breathe. The windows were down, and the loveliest spring breeze was washing over us, the sun making its way slowly toward the horizon, even though it wasn't quite dusk yet. I wondered if this was what photographers often referred to as "the golden hour" because everything around us seemed illuminated by a pure yellow glow. Cam had never looked more beautiful to me.

At the hospital, they quickly took us into triage to check both Cam's and the baby's vitals. She was already five centimeters dilated, so they admitted us right away, leading the way to a labor and delivery room, where an anesthesiologist arrived within about twenty minutes to administer Cam's epidural. After that, her hand squeezing lessened significantly, and she spent the next hour or so with her eyes closed, breathing consciously. I set up the music and made sure that the songs—our songs—would play on repeat for however long it took.

At about ten o'clock, our favorite doctor—Dr. Thomas— walked in the door. "Ahhh, the Thomas once again meets the Thompsons!" He was grinning, and his sandy brown hair looked a bit messy like he had just been taking a nap.

Dad's name was Thomas. Dad, I know you're here.

"Hi! Oh, we're so glad it's you." I returned his smile.

"You're in luck, ladies." He sat down in front of Cam's stirruped legs. "I'm leaving for vacation tomorrow morning, so your timing couldn't be better."

Something about the twinkle in his eye reminded me of my dad, and I had to hold back tears. Dad had barely been gone a month, so I was still prone to unexpected bouts of weeping. There were even times when I would be teaching, and I'd have to turn away from the kids for a minute and pretend like I was looking for something, just so I could let out a few tears. Honestly, that still happens to me sometimes now.

Cam was looking at me, steadily breathing. "Are you okay, Jojo?"

I looked down at her and smiled, crinkling my eyes. "Me? You're about to give birth, honey. I am absolutely fine." I sniffed as subtly as I could.

She nodded and put her head back, closing her eyes again. Dr. Thomas looked at me and said calmly, "I think she's ready to push."

I took a deep breath and then leaned over to kiss her shiny forehead, whispering, "Are you ready, baby?"

Eyes still closed, she nodded. Two nurses I didn't recognize walked in and erased the names that were on the whiteboard. "Hi, girls!" one of them said pleasantly. "I'm Caroline, and that's Robin."

My eyes shot toward the woman who was helping Dr. Thomas prepare for the birth. She had a dark brown bob and looked to be about twenty-five years old. Cam giggled breathlessly and looked at me. "Robin? Okay, Josie, now that is more than a coincidence."

Robin looked at me and raised her eyebrows. I said, "It's a long story, but Robin will be our daughter's middle name."

I hear you, Dad. Hang out here for a while please.

"Well, how about that?" she said, smiling.

Cam was shaking. I moved her hair away from her face and said, "It will be over soon. You totally got this."

She started pushing. The first visible sign of Liesel was a little spike of blonde hair at the top of her head about a half hour later, and I was already in love. Cam was so strong and pushed her out within forty-five minutes, when Dr. Thomas announced that she had been born at 12:05am on May 6th, 2016.

I was already sobbing with joy, but when I realized that Liesel had been born on my dad's birthday, my tears turned bittersweet. She would never know him except through stories. He would never know her.

Are you still here, Daddy? Please watch over her always.

They moved us to a more comfortable room and told us to try to get some sleep with Liesel in her little see-through bassinet. She slept most of the night, and we tried to do the same amid all of the beeping and talking and babies crying. I sat up in a panic at least three times throughout the night to make sure Liesel was still breathing, and all but once, Cam was sitting up in bed, watching over her, too.

"She's amazing. *You're* amazing," I said, getting up from the pullout chair to sit on the edge of the hospital bed and lean my head on her shoulder. "How are you feeling?"

She sighed and kissed my messy hair. "I'm fine. I can't seem to stop looking at her, though."

"I understand, but I guarantee we're going to have visitors in the morning, so you need to rest." She nodded, and we lay still and silent together for a while until we both fell asleep.

Cam's parents came to the hospital as soon as visiting hours started in the morning, and although we were both exhausted, it was wonderful to see the joy on their faces. Any fear I had about them not loving our baby was wiped away, replaced by a fear that they didn't see me as an equal parent to Cam, but I tried to push that away to reflect on later. Dana stopped by in the afternoon, followed Cam's friend Serena from school, and Amanda a little after that.

I was just starting to tell her about all of the coincidences the night before when I saw that our mom was trying to FaceTime me. When I answered, she was in purple scrubs with a big smile on her face. "Let me see my beautiful granddaughter! I'm flying in over Memorial Day weekend. Did I tell you that?"

Cam was still nursing, so I said, "I'll show her to you in a minute. She's absolutely perfect, Mom. Are you at work?" I tried to figure out what was behind her.

"Yep. I'm on my lunch break. Sam booked my flight for Saturday the 28th. Will you be around to pick me up?"

"Of course. Do you want to stay with us?" I looked over at Cam to see her burping Liesel by holding her little face and patting her back, and I said, "Oh my goodness, look at that face!"

"Show me! Show me!"

I turned the phone to show her Liesel's squished cheeks, just as she let loose the biggest burp of her life so far. All four of us laughed hysterically, but Liesel wasn't amused—more like very sleepy. Amanda leaned in front of my phone and waved.

"She is absolutely gorgeous! You look great, too, Cam ... and Mandy!" I turned the phone back to me. "Do you mind if I stay with you when I come in a few weeks?" Mom continued. "I'd love to help with the baby and let you two get some sleep."

I looked at Cam, who nodded, and I said, "Sure! That would be great."

"Wonderful. I have to get back to work, but I'll talk to you soon. Love you."

"Love you, Mom." I set down my phone and looked at Cam. "That's the most she's spoken to me since Dad died. Looking at me must remind her of him or something."

"Or maybe that's the most *you*'ve spoken to *her*?" Cam raised her eyebrows while she rocked Liesel to sleep. "You always go straight to shutting your mom out when you're feeling vulnerable. You should remember now that you only have one parent left, so maybe try a little harder with her."

I knew she was right. The truth was that my mom had tried

for years to get me to open up to her in order for us to be closer, but I think I always held it against her for moving away when I went to college. Dad's apartment never felt like home, and it was like she was trying to escape us—when my rational mind knew she was just trying to escape the memories of my dad.

"You're right. She's Liesel's Grandma Susan, and it's time for me to show up."

- 61 -

Wednesday, March 27, 2019

A pink van labeled *Sweet Treats* in curlicue letters pulled up to the front entrance of the school at about 5:45, just as the seats in the auditorium were filling up. I was chatting with Madison's cousin Mary—the one who had introduced Madison to slam poetry a couple of weeks before—thanking her for sparking a new passion in some of my students' lives. Mary is a college student studying creative writing, and I felt a twinge of envy when she told me that before I reminded myself that I should be thankful for the writing opportunities I do have.

I set the cookies down on a table in the lobby with a sign that read, "Please save these $1 'Sweet Treats' until after the performance! Proceeds go to our school's brand new GSA! Thanks!" I set a donation box next to them and hoped the honor system would get our funds started and then headed down to the front of the auditorium to make sure all of the kids who wanted to perform were sitting in the first row. When I got down there and glanced at the audience, I did a double-take, surprised to see so many people—especially so many unfamiliar faces. I looked for Josh and went to stand in front of him.

"Whoa, you did a good job getting the word out. I'm impressed." I raised my eyebrows.

He shrugged and said, "Lots of people on Twitter and TikTok said they were coming to support us for being a welcoming school who doesn't let homophobes have their way. Word spread pretty quickly that you were the one in charge of this whole thing."

My eyes widened, and I scanned the audience again. This time, I saw Cam standing in the back, holding Liesel. They were both waving and smiling, so I did the same. Looking back at Josh, I said, "Well, here goes nothing."

Turning around, I headed toward the stage. As I climbed the stairs, I tried not to think about how my butt looked in my navy pants or how many cookies I hoped to eat in the near future or how many people were there because they were nosy about who I was. I stepped to the microphone and signaled for Dana—who had generously offered to help out—to turn on the spotlight and turn down the house lights. The spotlight nearly set my eyes ablaze, and I put my hands up instinctively and then laughed, hearing several others laugh with me. Dana shouted an apology and dialed down the brightness.

"Yikes," I said into the microphone. "Okay, thank you, everyone, for joining us this evening. The kids have been working really hard on perfecting their readings, and I know you're going to love them. In case you've never been to a poetry reading before, you might not know that the Beatniks started the tradition of snapping instead of clapping. So rather than applauding, we will snap our fingers after each reader." I looked down at the front row and smiled at our group of poets, quickly and silently counting them. There were fifteen of them ... including Kate.

I flinched quickly when I noticed her, swearing that she hadn't been there thirty seconds before. I hesitated but reminded myself that her disregard of her parents' wishes had nothing to do with me.

"Well?" I smiled at them. "Who wants to start?"

Josh unsurprisingly stood and waved at me. I nodded, and he jogged up the stairs confidently, introduced himself, and began reading the poem he had written about his identity as a Chinese-American. I watched from offstage, thankful for my view of him and the audience. The line about his short stature made many people laugh, and I could see the energy flowing through his body as he worked his way to the ending: "Every girl I know only sees the shape of my eyes, and every boy I know thinks my eyes can only see the inside of a book," he paused, "but I see everything. I see when you retreat into yourself. I see when you look up at the stars through your bedroom window. I see when you dream of hope while you sleep."

The audience was silent for a few seconds, feeling the weight of his words, and then they began to snap. He smiled and bowed before jogging back to his seat.

Madison came up next. I wasn't sure what to expect from her piece because she had changed it so many times over the previous week, so I was eager to hear the final product.

"I'm Madison Bronson." She waved, and a few people in the back cheered. After smiling briefly, she closed her eyes.

"When I was a little girl,
    the only thing I feared was the dark."

Bringing her hands up to mimic feeling around without being

able to see, she kept her eyes closed.

"I was sure someone
    or some*thing*
    was waiting for me in all that blackness."

She dropped her hands and opened her eyes.

"Now, it's the light that I fear."

She brought her hands to her cheeks.

"Will the light show my pores
    or a pimple under my foundation?"

She dropped her hands.

"Will it drag me out of bed
    from a dream I'll never finish?
    Will it show everyone
    I'm the only one
    who is still awake in the house,
    overthinking that stumble in the hallway
    that nobody saw but me?"

She closed her eyes again.

"Darkness is safety.
    It's where I can hide
    like a joey in her mother's pouch,
    safe and warm."

The snaps were faster to begin this time. Madison's smile overtook her face, and when she passed me, she mouthed, "Thank you." I blew her a kiss and then froze, looking out into the audience to confirm no one was looking at me. All I needed was for someone to accuse me of kissing students.

The snapping died down, but no other student arrived. I leaned out onto the stage to check if any of them were approaching, and I saw Kate standing in front of her seat, taking a deep breath.

Before I had time to worry too much, she walked up onto the stage as our third reader. I had purposely avoided looking for her parents in the audience, but there was no way around it now

as her mother appeared on the other side of backstage across from me. She was shooting daggers at me with her eyes, and I struggled internally with the desire to please her and a steely resolve against her bigotry.

Kate, however, hadn't noticed her at all.

She approached the microphone, her hands shaking, and took a deep breath. Leaning forward she spoke, "I am Kate Anderson." And then she began. Though her poem didn't reference anything specifically about "coming out," her imagery did a great job of implying it. I tried to keep my eyes on her, but they drifted briefly to her mother's face. She looked like she was in pain, and I hoped that meant she was wrestling with her beliefs in order to learn how to accept her daughter.

When Kate finished, the audience erupted into applause—

real applause. Kate was startled, and so was her mom. She looked from Kate to the audience and back to Kate, who was smiling from ear to ear, still not knowing that her mom was watching her.

Mrs. Anderson hesitated before bringing her hands together and clapped slowly, breathing heavily in what appeared to be an effort to hold back tears.

Judging by the intense blushing on Kate's face, she hadn't been expecting so much attention. I joined in the clapping and watched her walk down the stairs, looking a bit like she'd like to curl herself into a ball and hide. I could relate so much that I had to catch my breath and refocus as the next reader came up to the microphone.

The next ten or so readings flew by, and I had a final decision to make. Picturing the note that had been taped to my door in the morning, I felt a surge of anger that brought with it a sense of conviction. I was going to do it.

After the last student reader, I walked back out onto the stage and returned to the microphone. Some of the audience had started talking to each other, assuming the show was over, and I was only going to thank them for coming. An image flickered in my mind of the school board sitting at a long table that was no longer set up beneath me. I wavered for a few seconds but then saw Liesel's eyes on me. She had run down one of the aisles and was standing next to Dana, watching me like my next words would stay with her forever.

"I am double the age of my students,"

I started, and most of the talking in the audience died down, "but a time traveler in any moment."

I stood up straighter, knowing I had their attention.

"I love grammar, numerology,
    and the color orange.
    I can't sleep without
    a fan on, and I can't sleep
    after I've caught someone else's fears
    like a flu."

Pause.

"I've been told my whole life that,"

I sped my voice up to list things,

"my voice is too loud,
    my nails are too bitten,
    my eyebrows are too honest."

I paused again, looking to the back of the auditorium where I met Cam's eyes.

"But I've kept a secret
    for a long, long time."

I waited, letting those words sink in and refocusing on a neutral part of the back wall.

"I see words in my mind,

but I don't always say them."

another pause,
Oh, I want to speak plainly,
but I fear that my fidelity
to what is true will overwhelm you.
My truth is freckled
and vulnerable. It is pale
and primal and unexpected.
It is human
when I am expected not to be.
It will exist,"
pause,
"even when,"
pause,
"I no longer do."

Cam was smiling, and then so was I. I said, "Thanks again for coming, everyone."

The sudden explosion of cheering and applause nearly knocked me over. My ears burned, and I grinned as the students in the front row jumped up and congratulated each other with hugs, high fives, and fist bumps. Someone held up a sign in one of the middle rows that displayed a rainbow with the words, "LOVE IS LOVE." Someone else in the back held up another colorful sign that read, "Gay teachers rock!" I truly didn't know what to say or do, so I descended the stairs and walked straight to Liesel, picked her up, and squeezed her.

"Mama, you a rock star!" she squealed.

I laughed and carried her up the aisle toward Cam. At the end of one of the rows, Adelaide stood smiling at me. Cam was walking in our direction, so I waved her closer to where Adelaide was. "This is the reporter I was telling you about. Adelaide, this is my wife, Cameron."

They shook hands, and Cam said, "Thank you so much for writing such an optimistic article. As you can guess, we've been a bit stressed by the whole situation recently."

Adelaide chuckled and then motioned to the people around her. "I think it's safe to say you don't have anything to worry about."

"Well," Cam said, looking at me with soft eyes, "we have come a long way."

- 63 -

Thursday, March 28, 2019

No, the robin doesn't have any answers for me this morning, but I know someone who might.

I pick up my phone and press my mom's smiling picture.

"What's wrong?" she answers. "Josie? What happened?"

"Nothing, Mom. I'm sorry it's so early." My voice catches in my throat.

"It's okay." She clears her throat, and I hear her feel around for her glasses. "Oh my. It really is early. Did something happen?"

I can't speak for a few seconds, and then all I can do is whisper. "Dad died today."

She breathes. "I know." Neither of us says anything for a little while, and then she repeats, "I know."

I whisper, "How has it already been three years? How have I already lived three years without him?" A sob escapes, and I cover my mouth, not wanting to wake Cam or Liesel.

"We always somehow keep going, don't we?" She is quiet, probably trying not to wake Sam.

I look back up at the robin and then close my eyes. "I'm sorry I haven't called recently."

316

"Oh, it's fine, honey. Are you getting ready for school?"

"Not quite. I wanted to call you because I'm about to look at something, and I don't want to be alone when I do it."

"What is it? Are you okay?"

I look down at the white stick sitting on the white sink and say, "I think so." Then, I take a deep breath, steadying my hands and stifling a squeal before adding, "I'm also pregnant."

Thank you for reading!

If anything about Josie's story has resonated with you, please consider leaving a review on Amazon, Goodreads, StoryGraph, social media, and/or any other places where you purchase, borrow, or talk about books. It's people like you who can help spread awareness and get this story into people's hands and hearts, hopefully helping some of them to connect and to feel less alone. Thank you for your support!

Acknowledgments

Thank you to anyone and everyone willing to give this story an early read, including but not limited to: Coral Rivera, my fabulous editor; Shelynn Kelly, the most thorough and enthusiastic beta reader I could have imagined; and the handful of agents who gave constructive feedback and urged me forward in search of a market they feared might be too niche.

This book would not exist if it were not for the patience and support of my beautiful wife, Rachael—my forever partner in this wonderful, adventurous life. Thank you for assuming the endless hours of parenting duties while I poured my soul into this process. And to our baby boys, who could never be invisible because your lights shine brighter than all of the sunny days of our lifetimes combined. Mama loves you more than you can ever know.

Finally, thank you to my biggest cheerleader—my mom. From day one, you showed me to go after what I want and to never settle for less. So here I am, going after it!

To my dad, who was my best friend: This one is for you.

Under The Weeping Willow Tree

"A coming of age story"

Under The Weeping Willow Tree
Loosely based on the life of Rose L. Hammond and written by Rose L. Hammond

ISBN: 979-8-218-34486-3
LCCN: 2024901124

Book cover design: Rose L. Hammond

For information contact: Run With It, LLC, P.O. Box 1419, Grand Rapids, MI 49501-1419 or rdarlene22@hotmail.com